THE SHAPE OF NIGHT

www.penguin.co.uk

BY TESS GERRITSEN

Rizzoli & Isles Novels

The Surgeon
The Apprentice
The Sinner
Body Double
Vanish
The Mephisto Club
Keeping the Dead
The Killing Place
The Silent Girl
Last to Die
Die Again
I Know a Secret

Other Novels

Girl Missing
Harvest
Life Support
The Bone Garden
Playing with Fire
The Shape of Night

THE SHAPE
OF NIGHT

Tess Gerritsen

BANTAM PRESS

TRANSWORLD PUBLISHERS
61–63 Uxbridge Road, London w5 5sa
www.penguin.co.uk

Transworld is part of the Penguin Random House group of companies
whose addresses can be found at global.penguinrandomhouse.com

 Penguin
Random House
UK

First published in Great Britain in 2019 by Bantam Press
an imprint of Transworld Publishers

A CIP catalogue record for this book
is available from the British Library.

ISBNs
9781787631649 (hb)
9781787631656 (tpb)

Printed and bound in Great Britain by Clays Ltd, Elcograf S.p.A.

Penguin Random House is committed to a sustainable future
for our business, our readers and our planet. This book is made
from Forest Stewardship Council® certified paper.

1 3 5 7 9 10 8 6 4 2

TO CLARA

THE SHAPE
OF NIGHT

Prologue

Even now I still dream about Brodie's Watch, and the nightmare is always the same. I am standing in the gravel driveway and the house looms before me like a ghost ship adrift in the fog. Around my feet mist curls and slithers and it coats my skin in icy rime. I hear waves rolling in from the sea and crashing against the cliffs, and overhead, seagulls scream a warning to stay far, far away. I know that Death waits behind that front door, yet I do not retreat because the house is calling to me. Perhaps it will always call to me, its siren song compelling me to once again climb the steps to the porch, where the swing creaks back and forth.

I open the door.

Inside, everything is wrong, all wrong. This is no longer the magnificent house I once lived in and loved. The massive carved banister is strangled by vines that twist like green serpents around the railing. The floor is carpeted by dead leaves which have blown in through shattered windows. I hear the slow tap, tap of rainwater dripping relentlessly from the ceiling, and I look up to see one solitary crystal pendant dangling from the skeletal chandelier. The walls, once painted cream and adorned with handsome crown molding, are now streaked with tentacles of mold. Long before Brodie's Watch was here, before the men who built it hauled up wood and stone, hammered beams to posts, this hill where it stands was a place of moss and forest. Now the forest is reclaiming its territory. Brodie's Watch is in retreat and the smell of decay hangs in the air.

I hear the humming of flies somewhere above me, and as I start up the staircase the ominous sound grows louder. The once-sturdy steps I climbed every night sag and groan with my weight. The banister, once polished to satiny smoothness, bristles with thorns and vines. I reach the second-floor landing and a fly appears, buzzing as it circles and dive-bombs my head. Another fly moves in, and another, as I start down the hallway toward the master bedroom. Through the closed door I can hear the flies' greedy hum in the room beyond, where something has drawn them to feast.

I open the door and the hum instantly becomes a roar. They attack me in a cloud so thick I am choking. I wave and flail at them but they swarm my hair, my eyes, my mouth. Only then do I realize what has drawn the flies to this room. To this house.

Me. They are feasting on me.

One

I had felt no such apprehension on that day in early August when I turned onto North Point Way and drove toward Brodie's Watch for the first time. I knew only that the road needed maintenance and the pavement was rippled by the roots of encroaching trees. The property manager had explained to me on the phone that the house was over a hundred fifty years old and currently still under renovation. For the first few weeks, I would have to put up with a pair of carpenters swinging hammers up in the turret, but that was the reason why a house with such a commanding ocean view could be rented for a song.

"The tenant who was renting it had to leave town a few weeks ago, months before her lease was up. So you called me at just the right time," she said. "The owner doesn't want his house to stand vacant all summer and he's anxious to find someone who'll take good care of it. He's hoping to find another female tenant. He thinks women are much more responsible."

The lucky new female tenant just happens to be me.

In the backseat my cat, Hannibal, yowls, demanding to be released from the pet carrier he's been trapped in since we left Boston six hours ago. I glance back and see him glaring at me through the grate, a hulking coon cat with pissed-off green eyes. "We're almost there," I promise, although I'm beginning to worry that I've taken a wrong turn. Roots and frost heaves have cracked the pavement and the trees seem to crowd in ever closer. My old Subaru, already weighed down with luggage and kitchenware, scrapes the road as we bounce along an ever-narrowing tunnel through pines and spruce. There is no room here to turn around; my only choice is to continue up this road, wherever it may lead. Hannibal yowls again, this time more urgently as if to warn: *Stop now, before it's too late.*

Through the overhanging branches I catch glimpses of gray sky, and the woods suddenly give way to a broad slope of granite mottled with lichen. The weathered sign confirms that I've arrived at the driveway for Brodie's Watch, but the road climbs into fog so thick that I can't see the house yet. I continue up the unpaved driveway, my tires sputtering and spitting gravel. Mist veils my view of windswept scrub brush and granite barrens but I can hear seagulls circling overhead, wailing like a legion of ghosts.

Suddenly there is the house, looming in front of me.

I shut off the motor and just sit for a moment, staring up at Brodie's Watch. No wonder it had been invisible from the bottom of the hill. Its gray clapboards blend in perfectly with the fog and only faintly can I make out a turret, which soars into low-hanging clouds. Surely there's been a mistake; I'd been told it was a large house, but I was not expecting this hilltop mansion.

I step out of the car and stare up at clapboards weathered to a silvery gray. On the porch a swing rocks back and forth, squeaking, as if nudged by an unseen hand. No doubt the house is drafty and the heating system is archaic and I imagine damp rooms and air that smells of mold. No, this is not what I had in mind as a summer refuge. I'd hoped for a serene place to write, a place to hide.

A place to heal.

Instead this house feels like enemy territory, its windows glaring at me like hostile eyes. The seagulls scream louder, urging me to run while I still can. I back away and I'm about to retreat to my car when I hear tires crunch up the gravel road. A silver Lexus pulls to a stop behind my Subaru and a blond woman climbs out, waving as she walks toward me. She's about my age, trim and attractive, and everything about her radiates chipper confidence, from her Brooks Brothers blazer to her *I'm your best friend* smile.

"You're Ava, right?" she says, extending her hand. "Sorry I'm a bit late. I hope you haven't been waiting too long. I'm Donna Branca, the property manager."

As we shake hands, I'm already hunting for an excuse to back out of the rental agreement. *This house is too big for me. Too isolated. Too creepy.*

"Gorgeous spot, isn't it?" Donna gushes, gesturing toward the granite barrens. "It's a shame you can't see anything right now with this weather, but when the fog lifts, the ocean view will knock your socks off."

"I'm sorry, but this house isn't exactly what—"

She's already climbing the porch steps, the house keys dangling in her hand. "You're lucky you called about it when you did. Right after you and I spoke, there were two other inquiries about this house. Summer's been a madhouse in Tucker Cove, with all the tourists scrambling for rentals. It seems like no one wants to spend the summer in Europe this year. They'd rather be closer to home."

"I'm glad to hear there are other people interested in the place. Because I think it might be too much house for—"

"Voilà. Home sweet home!"

The front door swings open, revealing a gleaming oak floor and a staircase with an elaborately carved banister. Whatever excuses I had on the tip of my tongue suddenly evaporate and an inexorable force seems to pull me over the threshold. In the entryway, I stare up at a crystal chandelier and a ceiling with intricate plasterwork. I had imagined the house to be cold and damp, to smell of dust and mold, but what I smell now is fresh paint and wood polish. And the sea.

"The renovations are almost finished," says Donna. "The carpenters still have a bit more to do up in the turret and on the widow's walk, but they'll try to stay out of your hair. And they only work on weekdays, so you'll be left alone on weekends. The owner was willing to lower the rent for the summer because he knows the carpenters are an inconvenience, but they'll only be here for a few weeks. Then you'll have this fabulous house all to yourself for the rest of the summer." She sees me gazing up in wonder at the crown molding. "They've done a nice job restoring it, haven't they? Ned, our carpenter, is a master craftsman. He knows every nook and cranny of this house better than anyone alive. Come on, let me show you the rest of the place. Since you'll probably be testing recipes, I'm guessing you'll want to check out the *fabulous* kitchen."

"Did I tell you about my work? I don't remember talking about it."

She gives a sheepish laugh. "You said on the phone you were a food writer, and I couldn't help googling you. I've already ordered your book about olive oils. I hope you'll autograph it for me."

"I'd be happy to."

"I think you'll find this the *perfect* house to write in." She leads me into the kitchen, a bright and airy space with black and white floor tiles set in a geometric pattern. "There's a six-burner stove and an extra-large oven. I'm afraid the kitchenware's rather basic, just a few pots and pans, but you did say you were bringing your own cookware."

"Yes. I have a long list of recipes I need to test, and I never go anywhere without my knives and sauté pans."

"So what's your new book about?"

"Traditional New England cooking. I'm exploring the cuisine of seafaring families."

She laughs. "That would be salt cod and more salt cod."

"It's also about their way of life. The long winters and cold nights and all the risks that fishermen took just to haul in the catch. It wasn't easy, living off the sea."

"No, it certainly wasn't. And the proof of that is in the next room."

"What do you mean?"

"I'll show you."

We move into an intimate front parlor, where the fireplace has already been laid with wood and kindling, ready to be lit. Above the mantelpiece is an oil painting of a ship heeling on a turbulent sea, its bow cutting through wind-tossed foam.

"That painting's just a reproduction," says Donna. "The original painting's on display in the historical society, down in the village, where they also have a portrait of Jeremiah Brodie. He cut quite a figure. Tall, with jet black hair."

"Brodie? Is that why this house is called Brodie's Watch?"

"Yes. Captain Brodie made his fortune as a ship's master sailing between here and Shanghai. He built this house in 1861." She looks at the painting of the ship plowing through waves and she shudders. "I get seasick just looking at that picture. You couldn't pay me to set foot on one of those things. Do you sail?"

"I did as a child, but I haven't been on a boat in years."

"This coastline is supposed to be one of the best places in the world for sailing, if that's your thing. It's certainly not mine." She crosses to a set of double doors and swings them open. "And here's my favorite room in the whole house."

I step through the doorway and my gaze is instantly riveted to the view beyond the windows. I see rolling drifts of fog, and through the curtain of mist I catch glimpses of what lies beyond: the sea.

"When the sun comes out, this view will take your breath away," says Donna. "You can't see the ocean now, but just wait till tomorrow. This fog should clear up by then."

I want to linger by that window but already she's moving on, hurrying me through the tour, into a formal dining room furnished with a heavy oak table and eight chairs. On the wall hangs another ship's painting, this one by a far less skillful artist. The vessel's name is mounted on the frame.

The Minotaur.

"That was his ship," says Donna.

"Captain Brodie's?"

"It's the one he went down on. His first mate painted this picture and gave it to Brodie as a gift, the year before they were both lost at sea."

I stare at the painting of *The Minotaur* and the hairs on the back of my neck suddenly rise, as if a chill wind has swept into the room. I actually turn to see if a window is open, but all of them are shut tight. Donna seems to feel it too, and she hugs herself.

"It's not a very good painting, but Mr. Sherbrooke says it belongs with the house. Since the first mate himself painted it, I assume the ship's details are accurate."

"But it's a little unsettling, having it hanging here," I murmur, "knowing that this was the ship he went down on."

"That's exactly what Charlotte said."

"Charlotte?"

"The woman who was renting this house just before you. She was so curious about its history, she was planning to talk to the owner about it." Donna turns away. "Let me show you the bedrooms."

I follow her up the winding staircase, my hand skimming the polished banister. It is made of masterfully crafted oak and feels solid and permanent. This house was built to last for centuries, to be a home for generations to come, yet here it stands empty, waiting to host one lone woman and her cat.

"Did Captain Brodie have any children?" I ask.

"No, he never married. After he died at sea, the house passed down to one of his nephews, then it changed hands a few times. Arthur Sherbrooke owns it now."

"Why doesn't Mr. Sherbrooke live here?"

"He has a home down in Cape Elizabeth, near Portland. He inherited this house from his aunt years ago. It was in pretty bad shape when it came to him and he's already spent a fortune restoring it. He's hoping a buyer will take it off his hands." She pauses and glances back at me. "In case you're interested."

"I could never afford to keep up a house like this."

"Oh, well. I just thought I'd mention it. But you're right, the upkeep on these historic houses is a nightmare."

As we walk along the second-floor hallway, she points through doorways into two sparsely furnished bedrooms and continues to a door at the end of the hall. "This," she says, "was Captain Brodie's bedroom."

As I step inside, I once again inhale a strong whiff of the sea. I had noticed the scent downstairs, but this time it's overwhelming, as if I'm standing before a crashing surf, the spray washing across my face. Then suddenly, the scent vanishes, as if someone has just closed a window.

"You'll *love* waking up to this view," says Donna, gesturing to the window, although at the moment there's nothing to see beyond the glass but fog. "In the summer, the sun rises right there, over the water, so you can watch the dawn."

I frown at the bare windows. "No curtains?"

"Well, privacy's not an issue because there's no one out there to see you. The property extends all the way to the high-tide line." She turns and nods toward the fireplace. "You know how to light a fire, right? Always open the flue first?"

"I used to visit my grandmother's farmhouse in New Hampshire, so I've had plenty of experience with fireplaces."

"Mr. Sherbrooke just wants to be sure you're careful. These old houses can go up in flames pretty fast." She pulls the key ring from her pocket. "I think that's about it for the tour."

"You said there's a turret upstairs?"

"Oh, you don't want to go up there. It's a mess right now, what with all the power tools and lumber. And definitely don't step out on the widow's walk until the carpenters replace the deck. It's not safe."

I have not yet taken the keys that she's holding out to me. I think about my first glimpse of the house, its windows staring at me like dead, glassy eyes. Brodie's Watch had promised no comfort, no sanctuary, and my first impulse had been to walk away. But now that I've stepped inside, breathed the air and touched the wood, everything seems different.

This house has accepted me.

I take the keys.

"If you have any questions, I'm in the office Wednesday through Sunday, and I'm always on my cellphone for emergencies," Donna says as we walk out of the house. "There's a handy list of local numbers that Charlotte posted in the kitchen. The plumber, doctor, electrician."

"And where do I pick up my mail?"

"There's a roadside mailbox at the bottom of the driveway. Or you can rent a PO box in town. That's what Charlotte did." She pauses beside my car, staring at the cat carrier in the backseat. "Wow. That's quite a kitty you have."

"He's fully housebroken," I assure her.

"He's enormous."

"I know. I need to put him on a diet." I reach into the backseat to haul out the pet carrier, and Hannibal hisses at me through the grate. "He's not happy about being cooped up in the car all this time."

Donna crouches down for a closer look at Hannibal. "Do I see extra toes? Maine coon cat, right?"

"All twenty-six pounds of him."

"Is he a good hunter?"

"Whenever he gets the chance."

She smiles at Hannibal. "Then he is going to love it here."

Two

I haul the pet carrier into the house and release the kraken. Hannibal emerges from the cage, glares at me, and lumbers off toward the kitchen. Of course that's the first room he'd head for; even in this unfamiliar house, Hannibal knows exactly where his dinner will be served.

It takes me a dozen trips to the car to unload my suitcase, the cardboard boxes filled with books and bedding and kitchenware, and the two bags of groceries I purchased in the village of Tucker Cove, enough to last me for the first few days. From my Boston apartment, I've brought everything I need to sustain me through the next three months. Here are the novels that have been gathering dust on my shelves, books that I've always intended to read and will finally crack open. Here are my jars of precious herbs and spices that I feared I wouldn't be able to find in a small Maine grocery store. I have packed bathing suits and sundresses as well as sweaters and a puffy down jacket, because even in summer, you can't predict the weather in DownEast Maine. Or so I've heard.

By the time I've carried everything into the house, it's well past seven and I'm thoroughly chilled by the mist. All I want now is to sip a drink by a crackling fire, so I unpack the three bottles of wine I've brought with me from Boston. When I open the kitchen cabinet to look for a glass, I discover that the previous tenant must have had similar cravings. On the shelf, beside a copy of *Joy of Cooking*, are two bottles of single-malt Scotch whiskey, one of them almost empty.

I put away the wine and take out the nearly empty bottle of whiskey instead.

It's my first night in this grand old house, so why not? I'm home for the night, I've had an exhausting day, and on this damp and chilly evening, whiskey is perfectly appropriate. I feed Hannibal and pour two fingers' worth of Scotch into a cut-crystal glass I find in the cabinet. Right there, standing at the kitchen counter, I reward myself with the first sip and sigh with pleasure. As I drink the rest of the glass, I idly flip through *Joy of Cooking*. The book is stained and grease-spattered, clearly much used and well-loved. On the title page is a handwritten inscription.

Happy birthday, Charlotte! Now that you're on your own, you'll be needing this.

Love, Nana

I wonder if Charlotte has realized she left behind her book. As I turn the pages, I see the many notes she's written in the margins of recipes. *Needs more curry powder . . . Too much work . . . Harry loved this one!* I know how upset I'd be if I misplaced any of my beloved cookbooks, especially one given to me by my grandmother. Charlotte will certainly want this back. I'll have to mention it to Donna.

The whiskey is performing its magic. As its heat flushes my face, my shoulders relax and my tension melts away. At last here I am in Maine, just me and my cat, alone in a house by the sea. I refuse to think about what has brought me to this place, nor will I think about who and what I have left behind. Instead I busy myself doing what invariably comforts me: cooking. Tonight I will make risotto because it is simple and filling and its preparation requires only two pots and patience. I sip whiskey as I sauté mushrooms and shallots and uncooked rice, stirring until the grains begin to crackle. When I add white wine to the pot, I also splash some into my now-empty whiskey glass. It's not exactly the proper sequence for beverages, but who's around to raise an eyebrow? I ladle hot broth into the pot and stir. Sip wine. Stir some more. Another ladle of hot broth, another sip. Keep stirring. While other cooks may lament the boredom of watching over risotto, that is exactly what I love about cooking it. You cannot rush it; you cannot be impatient.

And so I stand watch at the stove, stirring with a wooden spoon, content to focus on nothing more than what simmers on the burner. Into the pot I sprinkle fresh peas and parsley and grated Parmesan and the fragrance makes my mouth water.

By the time I finally set my meal on the dining room table, night has fallen. In Boston, nights are always polluted by city lights but here I see nothing beyond the windows, no passing ships, no pulsing beams from a lighthouse, just the black, black sea. I light candles, open a bottle of Chianti, and pour it into a glass. A proper wineglass, this time. My table setting is perfect: candlelight, a linen napkin, silverware flanking a parsley-dusted bowl of risotto.

My cellphone rings.

Even before I look at the name on the screen, I know who is calling me. Of course she is calling me. I picture Lucy in her apartment on Commonwealth Avenue, phone pressed to her ear, waiting for me to answer. I can see the desk where she's sitting: the framed wedding photo, the china bowl filled with paper clips, the rosewood clock I gave her for her medical school graduation. As my phone rings again and again, I sit with fists clenched, nausea coiling in my stomach. When it finally stops, the silence is a blessed relief.

I take one bite of risotto. Although I've cooked the recipe a dozen times before, this spoonful is as tasteless as wallpaper paste, and my first sip of Chianti is bitter. I should have opened the bottle of prosecco instead, but it was not yet chilled and sparkling wine must always be thoroughly chilled, the bottle preferably submerged deep in ice.

The way I served champagne last New Year's Eve.

Once again I can hear the clink of ice cubes and jazz playing on the stereo and the chatter of friends and family and colleagues crowded into my Boston apartment. I had pulled out all the stops for my party and had splurged on Damariscotta oysters and a whole leg of Jamón Ibérico de Bellota. I remember looking around at my laughing guests, noting which men I'd already slept with, and wondering who I might be sleeping with that night. It was, after all, New Year's Eve, and one can't celebrate alone.

Stop, Ava. Don't think about that night.

But I can't help poking at that wound, unroofing the scab so it bleeds again. I refill my wineglass and cycle back through the memories. The laughter, the clatter of oyster shells, the happy fizz of champagne on my tongue. I remember my editor Simon tipping a glistening oyster into his mouth. I remember Lucy, on call that night for the hospital, virtuously sipping only sparkling water.

And I remember Nick skillfully popping the cork on a bottle. I remember thinking how jaunty he looked that night, with his tie askew and his sleeves rolled up to his elbows. Whenever I think of that night it always, always comes back to Nick.

The candle on my dining table sputters out. I look down and to my surprise I find the bottle of Chianti is now empty.

When I rise to my feet the house seems to sway, as though I'm standing on the rolling deck of a ship. I haven't opened any windows, but the smell of the sea once again sweeps through the room and I can even taste salt on my lips. Either I'm hallucinating or I'm more tipsy than I thought.

I'm too tired to clear the dishes so I leave my barely touched risotto on the table and make my way to the stairs, turning off lights as I go. Hannibal darts past and I stumble over him, banging my shin against the second-floor landing. Already the damn cat knows this house better than I do. By the time I make it to the bedroom he's already claimed his spot on the comforter. I don't have the energy to move him; I just turn off the lamp and sprawl onto the bed beside him.

I fall asleep, with the scent of the sea in my nostrils.

In the night, I feel the mattress shift and I reach out, seeking the warmth of Hannibal's body, but he is not there. I open my eyes and for a moment I don't remember where I am. Then it comes back to me: Tucker Cove. The sea captain's house. The empty bottle of Chianti. Why did I think running away would change anything? Wherever you go, you drag along your own misery like a rotting carcass, and I have dragged mine up the coast to this lonely house in Maine.

A house where I am clearly not alone.

I lie awake, listening to the scritch-scratch of tiny claws moving through the walls. It sounds like dozens, maybe hundreds of mice are using the wall behind my bed as a superhighway. Hannibal is awake too, meowing and pacing the room, driven mad by his killer feline instincts.

I climb out of bed and open the bedroom door to let him out, but he won't leave the room. He just paces back and forth, meowing. The mice are noisy enough; how can I sleep through Hannibal's yowls? I am wide awake now anyway, so I settle into the rocking chair and gaze out the window. The fog has lifted and the sky is breathtakingly clear. The sea stretches out to the horizon, every ripple silvered by moonlight. I think of the full bottle of whiskey in the kitchen cabinet, and wonder if another drink might help me sleep through the rest of the night, but now I'm too comfortable sitting in this chair and I don't want to get up. And the view is so beautiful, the sea stretching out like battered silver. A breeze wafts against my cheek, brushing across my skin like a cool kiss, and I smell it again: the scent of the sea.

Instantly the house goes quiet. Even the mice in the walls fall still, as if something, someone, has alarmed them. Hannibal gives a loud hiss and every hair on my arms stands up.

Someone else is in this room.

I scramble to my feet, my heart hammering. The chair keeps rocking back and forth as I retreat toward the bed and scan the darkness. All I see are the silhouettes of furniture and Hannibal's glowing eyes, reflecting the moonlight as he stares at something in the corner. Something I cannot see. He gives a feral growl and slinks away into the shadows.

For an eternity I stand watching, listening. Moonlight floods the window and slants across the floor and in its silvery glow, nothing moves. The chair has stopped rocking. The smell of the sea has vanished.

There is no one else in the room. Just me and my cowardly cat.

I scramble back into bed and pull the covers up to my chin, but even under the duvet I am chilled and shaking. Only when Hannibal at last emerges from under the bed and lies down beside me do I stop shivering. There is something about a warm and purring cat pressed against you that sets the world right, and with a sigh, I bury my fingers in his fur.

The mice are once again skittering inside the wall.

"Tomorrow," I murmur, "we need to find another place to rent."

Three

Three dead mice are lying beside my slippers.

Still groggy and hungover, I stare down at the gruesome gifts that Hannibal has delivered during the night. He sits beside his offerings, chest puffed out in pride, and I remember the property manager's remark yesterday when I told her my cat liked to hunt.

He is going to love it here.

At least one of us loves it here.

I pull on jeans and a T-shirt and head downstairs to collect paper towels for the cleanup. Even through multiple layers of paper, the mouse corpses feel sickeningly squishy as I pick them up. Hannibal gives me a glare of *what the hell are you doing with my gift?* as I bundle up the mice, and he trails after me when I carry them downstairs and out the front door.

It is a glorious morning. The sun is shining, the air is crisp, and a nearby thicket of roses is in full bloom. I consider tossing the dead mice in a patch of shrubbery, but Hannibal lurks nearby, no doubt waiting to reclaim his prize, so I circle around to the back of the house, to toss them into the ocean instead.

My first glimpse of the sea dazzles me. Blinking in the sunlight, I stand at the cliff's edge and gaze down at waves rolling in, at glistening tendrils of seaweed clinging to the rocks far below. Gulls swoop overhead, and in the distance a lobster boat glides across the water. I am so mesmerized by the view I almost forget why I've come outside. I unwrap the dead mice and throw them over the cliff's edge. They drop onto the rocks and are swept away by an outgoing wave.

Hannibal slinks off, no doubt to hunt for fresh game.

Curious about where he'll go next, I leave the crumpled paper towels anchored under a rock and follow him. He looks like a cat on a mission as he prowls along the cliff's edge, moving down a trail that's little more than a pin-scratch through moss and scraggly grass. The soil is poor here, the ground mostly granite caked with lichen. Gradually it descends, toward a tiny crescent of a beach flanked by boulders. Hannibal continues to lead the way, his tail pointing to the sky like a furry standard, pausing only once to glance back and confirm I'm following him. I catch the scent of roses and spot a few hardy rugosa bushes, which are somehow thriving despite the wind and salt air, their blossoms a vivid pink against the granite. I scramble past them, scratching my bare ankles on the thorns, and drop from the rocks onto the beach. There is no sand here, just small pebbles that clatter back and forth in the lapping waves. At both sides of the little cove, tall boulders jut into the water, screening the beach from view.

It could be my own private hideaway.

Already, I'm planning a picnic. I'll bring a blanket and a lunch and of course a bottle of wine. If the day heats up, maybe I'll even brave a dip in that frigid water. With the sunshine warming my face and the scent of roses in the air, I feel calmer, happier than I have in months. Maybe this really *is* the place for me. Maybe this is exactly where I need to be, where I'll be able to work. Where I will finally make peace with myself again.

Suddenly I'm famished. I can't remember the last time I've felt this hungry, and over the past few months I've lost so much weight that what I used to call my skinny jeans now hang loose on my hips. I climb back up the path, thinking of scrambled eggs and toast and gallons of hot coffee with cream and sugar. My stomach growls and I can already taste the homemade blackberry jam I brought with me from Boston. Hannibal trots ahead of me, leading the way. Either he's forgiven me for tossing away his mice, or he's thinking of his breakfast, too.

I clamber up the cliff and follow the path toward the point. There, where the land juts out like a ship's prow, the house stands alone. I imagine the doomed Captain Brodie gazing out to sea from the rooftop widow's walk, keeping watch through fair weather and foul. Yes, this is exactly where a sea captain would choose to build his home, on that wind-lashed outcropping of . . .

I freeze, staring up at the widow's walk. Did I imagine it, or did I just glimpse someone standing there? I see no one now. Perhaps it's one of the carpenters, but Donna told me they worked only on weekdays, and today is Sunday.

I hurry along the path and around the house to the front porch, but I find no other vehicles parked in the driveway, only my Subaru. If it *was* one of the carpenters, how did he arrive at the house?

I thump up the steps into the house and call out: "Hello? I'm the new tenant!" No one answers. As I climb the stairs and head down the second-floor hallway, I listen for the sound of workmen in the turret, but I hear no hammering or sawing, not even the creak of footsteps. The door to the turret staircase gives a loud squeak as I open it to reveal a dark and narrow staircase.

"Hello?" I shout up the stairs. Again no one answers.

I have not yet been up to the turret. Peering up into the gloom,

I spy faint cracks of light through the closed door at the top of the stairs. If someone is working up there, he's strangely silent, and for a moment I consider the unsettling possibility that the intruder is *not* one of the carpenters. That someone else has slipped into the house through the unlocked front door and now lurks upstairs, waiting for me. But this isn't Boston; this is a small Maine town where people leave their doors unlocked and the keys in their cars. Or so I've been told.

The first step gives an ominous creak when I place my weight on it. I pause, listening. There is still no sound above.

Hannibal's loud meow makes me jump. I glance back and see him at my heel, not looking the least bit alarmed. He slithers past me, trots up to the closed door at the top of the staircase, and waits for me in the gloom. My cat is braver than I am.

I tiptoe up the stairs, my pulse quickening with each step. By the time I reach the top, my hands are sweating and the doorknob feels slippery. Slowly I turn it and nudge the door open.

Sunlight floods my eyes.

Blinded, I squint against the glare, and the turret room comes into focus. I see windows streaked with salt. Silky cobwebs dangle from the ceiling, swaying in the newly disturbed air. Hannibal sits beside a stack of wooden planks, calmly licking his paw. Everywhere is woodworking equipment—a band saw, floor sanders, sawhorses. But no one is here.

A door leads outside to the widow's walk, the rooftop deck that overlooks the sea. I open the door and step out into a bracing wind. Gazing down, I see the cliff path where I'd been walking only moments earlier. The sound of the waves seems so close, I might be standing on the bow of a ship—a very old ship. The balcony railing looks rickety, the paint long ago scoured away by the elements. I take another step and the wood suddenly sags beneath me. Instantly I retreat and look down at rotted planks. Donna had warned me to stay off the widow's walk, and if I'd walked out much farther, the deck might well have collapsed under my weight. Yet only moments ago, I thought I'd spotted someone standing on this balcony, where the wood looks as insubstantial as cardboard.

I retreat back inside the turret and close the door against the wind. With its east-facing windows, the room is already warm from the morning sun. I stand bathed in that golden light, trying to make sense of what I saw from the cliff, but I can summon no answers. A reflection, perhaps. Some odd distortion caused by the antique glass in the windows. Yes, that must be what I saw. When I look through the window, the view is warped by ripples, as though I'm peering through water.

At the periphery of my vision, something shimmers.

I spin around to look, but see only a swirl of floating dust, glittering like a million galaxies in the sunlight.

Four

Donna is talking on the phone when I walk into the office of Branca Property Sales and Management. She gives me a welcoming wave and gestures to the waiting area. I sit down near a sunny window and as she continues her conversation, I flip through a book of properties listed for rent. I can't find any listing for Brodie's Watch, but there are other enticing options, from shingled beachside cottages to in-town apartments to a stately mansion on Elm Street that comes at an equally stately price. As I flip through pages of beautifully photographed homes, I think about the view from my bedroom in Brodie's Watch and my morning walk along the cliff with its perfume of roses. How many homes in this book came with their own private beach?

"Hello, Ava. How are you settling in at the house?"

I look up at Donna, who's finally finished her phone call. "I have, um, a few little problems I need to talk to you about."

"Oh dear. What problems?"

"Well to begin with, mice."

"Ah." She sighs. "Yes, it's an issue with some of our older houses around here. Since you have a cat, I don't recommend putting out poison, but I can supply you with some mousetraps."

"I don't think a few mousetraps are going to take care of the problem. It sounds like there's an army of them living in the walls."

"I can ask Ned and Billy—they're the carpenters—to close up any obvious entry points so more mice can't get in. But it is an old house, and up here, most of us just learn to live with them."

I hold up the book of rental properties. "So even if I moved to a different place, I'd run into the same problem?"

"Right now there isn't anything available for rent in the area. It's the height of summer and everything's booked, except for maybe a week here and a week there. And you wanted a longer term rental, right?"

"Yes, through October. To give me time to finish the book."

She shakes her head. "I'm afraid you won't find anything that can match the views and privacy of Brodie's Watch. The only reason your rent's so reasonable is because the house is under renovation."

"That's my second question. About the renovation."

"Yes?"

"You said the carpenters would only be working on weekdays."

"That's right."

"This morning, when I was out on the cliff path, I thought I saw someone up on the widow's walk."

"On a Sunday? But they don't have a key to the house. How did they get in?"

"I left the front door unlocked when I went out for my walk."

"Was it Billy or Ned? Ned's in his late fifties. Billy's just twenty-something."

"I didn't actually *speak* to anyone. When I got back, no one was in the house." I pause. "I suppose it *could* have been just a trick of the light. Maybe I didn't see anyone after all."

For a moment she's silent, and I wonder what's going through her head. *My tenant is a loon?* She manages a smile. "I'll give Ned a call and remind him not to disturb you on weekends. Or you can tell him yourself when you see him. They should both be up at your house tomorrow morning. Now, about the mouse problem, I can bring you some traps tomorrow, if you'd like."

"No, I'll pick some up right now. Where do they sell them in town?"

"Sullivan's Hardware is right down the street. Turn left and you can't miss it."

I'm almost at the door when I suddenly remember one more thing I need to ask. I turn back. "Charlotte left a cookbook in the house. I'll be happy to send it to her if you let me know where she wants it mailed."

"A cookbook?" Donna shrugs. "Maybe she didn't want it anymore."

"It was a gift from her grandmother and it has Charlotte's handwritten notes all over it. I'm sure she does want it back."

Donna's attention is already shifting away from me and back to her desk. "I'll shoot her an email and let her know."

The sunshine has brought out all the tourists and as I walk down Elm Street, I dodge baby strollers and give a wide berth to children clutching drippy ice cream cones. As Donna said, it really is the height of summer and everywhere in town, cash registers are merrily ringing, restaurants are crowded, and scores of unlucky lobsters are meeting their steamy fates. I continue past the Tucker Cove Historical Society, past half a dozen shops all selling the same T-shirts and saltwater taffy, and finally spot the sign for Sullivan's Hardware.

When I step inside, a bell tinkles on the door and the sound brings back a memory from my childhood, when my grandfather would bring me and my older sister, Lucy, into a hardware store just like this one. I pause and inhale the familiar scents of dust and freshly sawn wood and remember how Grandpa would lovingly peruse the hammers and screws, hoses and washers. A place where men of his generation knew their purpose and happily embraced it.

I don't see anyone, but I can hear two men somewhere at the rear of the store discussing the merits of brass versus stainless steel faucets.

I head down an aisle, searching for mousetraps but find only gardening implements. Trowels and spades, gloves and shovels. I turn down the next aisle, which is stocked with nails and screws and spools of wire chain in every possible link size. Everything you need to build a torture chamber. I'm about to start down a third aisle when a head suddenly pops up from behind a pegboard of screwdrivers. The man's white hair stands up like dandelion fluff and he peers at me through drooping spectacles.

"Help you find something, miss?"

"Yes. Mousetraps."

"Got yourself a little rodent problem, eh?" He chuckles as he rounds the end of the aisle and approaches me. Although he's wearing work boots and a tool belt, he looks far too old to still be swinging a hammer. "I keep the mousetraps down this way, with the kitchen utensils."

Mousetraps as kitchen utensils. Not an appetizing thought. I follow him to a back corner of the store, where I see an array of spatulas and cheap aluminum pots and pans, all of them covered with dust. He snatches up a package and hands it to me. In dismay, I eye the spring-loaded Victor snap traps, six to a packet. The same brand of traps my grandparents would set out in their New Hampshire farmhouse.

"Do you have something a little more, uh, humane?" I ask.

"Humane?"

"Traps that don't kill them. Like a Havahart?"

"And what do you plan to do with 'em after you catch 'em?"

"Let them go. Outside somewhere."

"They'll just come right back in again. Unless you're planning on taking 'em for a long drive." He gives a loud guffaw at the idea.

I look at the snap traps. "These just seem so cruel."

"Dab on a little peanut butter. They sniff it, step on the spring, and *whap!*" He grins when I jump at the sound. "They won't feel a thing, I promise ya."

"I really don't think I want to—"

"Got an expert here in the store who can reassure you." He yells across the store: "Hey, Doc! Come tell this young lady she's got nothin' to be squeamish about!"

I hear approaching footsteps and turn to see a man around my age. He's wearing blue jeans and a plaid shirt, and with his clean-cut good looks, he might have just stepped off the pages of an L.L.Bean catalogue. I almost expect to see a golden retriever trotting at his heels. He's carrying a brass faucet set, the apparent winner of the stainless steel-or-brass debate I'd overheard earlier.

"How can I help, Emmett?" he says.

"Tell this nice lady here that the mice won't suffer."

"What mice?"

"The mice in my house," I explain. "I came in to buy traps, but these . . ." I look down at the package of snap traps and shudder.

"I keep tellin' her they'll do the trick, but she thinks they're cruel," says Emmett.

"Ah. Well." Mr. L.L.Bean gives an unhelpful shrug. "No killing device is going to be one hundred percent humane, but those old Victor traps have the advantage of being almost instantaneous. The bar snaps the backbone, which severs the spinal cord. That means no pain signals can be transmitted, minimizing the animal's suffering. And there are studies that show—"

"Excuse me, but why are you an expert on this?"

He gives a sheepish smile. I notice his eyes are a striking blue and he has enviably long lashes. "It's basic anatomy. If signals can't travel up the spinal cord to the brain, the animal won't feel a thing."

"Dr. Ben should know," says Emmett. "He's our town doctor."

"Actually, it's Dr. Gordon. Everyone just calls me Dr. Ben." He shifts the brass bathroom fixture under his left arm and reaches out to shake my hand. "And you are?"

"Ava."

"Ava with the mouse problem," he says, and we both laugh.

"If you don't want to use mousetraps," says Emmett, "maybe you just oughta get a cat."

"I have a cat."

"And he hasn't taken care of the problem?"

"We just moved into the house yesterday. He's already caught three mice, but I don't think even he can take care of the whole problem." I look at the mousetraps and sigh. "I suppose I'll have to get these. They're probably more humane than getting eaten by my cat."

"I'll throw in an extra pack of 'em, how 'bout it? On the house," says Emmett. He heads up front to the cash register, where he rings up my purchase. "Good luck, young lady," he says, handing me a plastic bag with my traps. "Just be careful when you set 'em, 'cause it ain't much fun having 'em snap down on your fingers."

"Use peanut butter," says Dr. Gordon.

"Yes, I just heard that advice. It's next on my shopping list. I guess this is just part of renting an old house."

"Which house would that be?" Emmett asks.

"The one up on the point. It's called Brodie's Watch."

The sudden silence speaks louder than anything either man could have said. I catch the look that flies between them and notice Emmett's eyebrows knit together, carving deep furrows in his face.

"So you're the gal who's renting Brodie's Watch," says Emmett. "You staying there long?"

"Through the end of October."

"You, uh, like it up there on the point?"

I look back and forth at the two men, wondering what isn't

being said. Knowing that something is being left out of the conversation, something important. "Except for the mice, yes."

Emmett covers up his consternation with a forced smile. "Well, you come on back if you need anything else."

"Thank you." I start to leave.

"Ava?" says Dr. Gordon.

"Yes?"

"Is anyone staying up there with you?"

His question takes me aback. Under other circumstances, a stranger asking if I live alone would put me on guard, make me wary of revealing my vulnerability, but I don't sense any threat from his question, only concern. Both men are watching me, and there's a strange tension in the air, as if both of them are holding their breaths, waiting for my answer.

"I've got the house all to myself. And my cat." I open the door and pause. Looking back, I add: "My very big, very *mean* cat."

That night, I bait six mousetraps with peanut butter, leave three in the kitchen, two in the dining room, and the sixth one in the upstairs hallway. I don't want Hannibal to trap his paw in any of them, so I bring him into my bedroom. Clever Hannibal is an escape artist who's learned how to turn doorknobs with his paws, so I slide the latch shut, locking him inside with me. He's not happy about this and he paces the room, yowling for a chance to go on another mouse hunt.

"Sorry, kiddo," I tell him. "Tonight you're my prisoner."

I turn off the lamp and in the moonlight I can see him continue to pace. It is another clear, still night, the sea as calm and flat as molten silver. In the darkness I sit by the window sipping a bedtime glass of whiskey and marveling at the view. What could be more romantic than a moonlit night in a house by the sea? I think of other nights when moonlight and a few drinks made me believe that *this* man might be the one who'd make me happy, the one who'd stand the test of time. But a few days, a few weeks later, the cracks would inevitably begin to show and I'd realize: No, he's not the man for me. Time to move on and keep looking. There's always someone else out there, someone better, isn't there? Never settle for Mr. Good Enough.

Now I sit alone, my skin flushed from my day in the sun and by the alcohol that now courses through my veins. I reach down yet again for the bottle, and when my arm brushes across my breast, it leaves my nipple tingling.

It has been months since any man has touched me there. Months since I've felt even the faintest hint of lust. Not since New Year's Eve. My body has been asleep, all desire frozen in a state of hibernation. But this morning, when I'd stood on the beach, I had felt something inside me flicker back to life.

I close my eyes and in an instant the memory of that night is back. My kitchen counter covered with used wineglasses and dirty plates and platters of empty oyster shells. The cold tiles under my naked back. His body on top of mine, thrusting into me again and again. But I won't think about *him*. I cannot bear to think of him. Instead I conjure up a faceless, guilt-free *someone,* a man who does not exist. A man for whom I feel only lust, not love. Not shame.

I refill my glass with whiskey, even though I know I have already had too much tonight. My shin still aches from banging it on the landing last night, and this afternoon I noticed a fresh bruise on my arm, but I can't remember when or where I got it. This drink will be my last for the night. I gulp it down and flop onto the bed, where moonlight, pale as cream, washes across my body. I peel open my nightdress and let the cool sea air whisper across my skin. I imagine a man's hands touching me here, and here, and here. A faceless, nameless man who knows my every desire, a perfect lover who exists only in my fantasies. My breaths quicken. I close my eyes and hear myself moan. For the first time in months my body is hungry again to feel a man inside me. I imagine him grasping both my wrists and pinning them above my head. I feel his calloused hands, his unshaven face against my skin. My back arches and my hips rise to meet his. A breeze blows in through the open window, flooding the room with the smell of the sea. I feel his hand cradling my breast, stroking my nipple.

"You are the one I've been waiting for."

The voice is so close, so *real,* I gasp and my eyes fly open. In terror I stare at the dark shape hovering above me. Not solid, but merely a swirl of shadow that slowly drifts away and dissipates like mist in the moonlight.

I bolt straight up in bed and flip on the lamp. Heart banging, I frantically scan the room for the intruder. All I see is Hannibal sitting in the corner, watching me.

I jump to my feet and scramble to check the door. It is still locked tight. I cross to the closet, yank it open, and rake aside my hanging clothes. I find no intruder lurking inside, but I spy an unfamiliar bundle of silk in the deepest corner of the closet. I unfurl a rose-colored silk scarf—not mine. Where did this come from?

There's only one more place in the room to look. Confronting every childhood nightmare about monsters hiding under the bed, I drop to my knees and peer under the box spring. Of course, no one is there. All I find is a stray flip-flop. Like the silk scarf, it was probably left behind by the woman who lived here before me.

Bewildered, I sink onto the bed and try to make sense of what I just experienced. Only a dream, surely, but one so vivid I am still shaking from it.

Through my nightdress, I feel my own breast and think of the hand on my skin. My nipple still tingles at the memory of what I felt. What I heard. What I smelled. I look down at the scarf I found in the closet. Only then do I notice the French fabric tag and I realize this is an Hermès scarf. How could Charlotte leave this behind? If it were mine, I'd make sure it was one of the first things that went into my suitcase. She must have been in a rush to pack if she'd left behind her well-loved cookbook and this expensive scarf. I think of what I just experienced. The hand caressing my breast, the shape swirling in the shadows. And the voice. A man's voice.

Did you hear him too, Charlotte?

Five

Two men have invaded my house. Not fantasy men but real men named Ned Haskell and Billy Conway. I hear them hammering and sawing up on the roof, where they're now replacing the rotted deck of the widow's walk. As they hammer upstairs, downstairs in the kitchen, I cream together butter and sugar, chop walnuts and blend it together into a batter. I left my Cuisinart at home in Boston, so I must now cook the old-fashioned way, using my muscles and bare hands. The physical labor is comforting, even though I know I will have sore arms tomorrow. Today I am testing a toffee cake recipe I found in an 1880 memoir by a sea captain's wife, and it's a joy to work in this bright and spacious kitchen, which was designed with a large domestic staff in mind. Judging by the grand scale of the rooms, Captain Brodie was a wealthy man and he would have employed a cook and housekeeper and several kitchen maids. In his day, there would have been a wood-burning stove, and instead of the refrigerator, a zinc-lined cold closet chilled by ice that would be regularly replenished by the local iceman. As my toffee cake bakes, perfusing the kitchen with the scent of cinnamon, I imagine the household staff laboring in this room, chopping vegetables, plucking chickens. And in the dining room, the table would be set with fine china and candles. Sea captains brought home souvenirs from around the world, and I wonder where all Captain Brodie's treasures are now. Handed down to his heirs or lost to antique shops and landfills? This week I will pay a visit to the local historical society and see if they have any of the captain's possessions in their collection. My editor, Simon, was intrigued by my description of the house and in his email this morning, he asked me to hunt down more information about Captain Jeremiah Brodie. *Tell us what sort of man he was. Tall or short? Handsome or ugly?*

How did he die?

The oven timer dings.

I take the cake out of the oven, inhaling the rich scent of molasses and spices, the same aromas that once might have filled this kitchen and wafted throughout the house. Did the captain enjoy cakes just like this one, topped with sweet churned cream and served on a dainty china plate? Or did his tastes lean toward roasted meat and potatoes? I'd prefer to think of him as a man with an adventurous palate. After all, he was daring enough to challenge the perils of the sea.

I cut a slice of cake and savor the first bite. Yes, this is definitely a recipe worth including in my book, along with the story of how I discovered it, handwritten in the margins of the crumbling journal I'd bought at an estate sale. But as delicious as it is, I certainly can't eat the whole thing myself. I cut it into squares and carry my offering upstairs to the two men who by now must have worked up a healthy appetite.

The turret is cluttered with stacked wood, sawhorses, toolboxes, and a band saw. I pick my way through the obstacle course and open the door to the widow's walk, where the carpenters are hammering a plank into place. Yesterday they removed the rotted railing and from their now-unprotected perch, it's a dizzying drop to the ground.

I don't dare set even one foot out the door, but call to them: "If you want cake, I've just taken one out of the oven."

"Now *this* is a good time for a break," says Billy, the younger man, and they both set down their tools.

There are no chairs in the turret, so both men grab squares of cake and we stand in a circle while they eat in focused silence. Although Ned is three decades older than Billy, the two men look so much alike they could be father and son. They're both deeply tanned and muscular, their T-shirts powdery with sawdust, their jeans sagging with the weight of their tool belts.

Billy grins at me with a mouth full of cake. "Thank you, ma'am! First time any client's baked a treat for us!"

"Actually, this is my job," I tell him. "I've collected a long list of recipes I need to test, and I certainly can't eat everything I cook."

"Are you a baker by trade?" asks Ned. Silver-haired and serious, he strikes me as a man who considers every word before he speaks. Everywhere I look in this house, I see the evidence of his meticulous craftsmanship.

"I'm a food writer. I'm working on a book about the traditional foods of New England, and I need to test every recipe before I include it in the book."

Billy raises his arm. "Private Billy Conway reporting for duty. I volunteer to be your guinea pig. You cook and I'll eat," he says, and we all laugh.

"How much longer until the deck's finished?" I ask, pointing to the widow's walk.

"It should take us another week or so to replace the boards and put up the new railing," says Ned. "Then we need to get back to work in here. That'll take us another week."

"I thought you were all done with this turret."

"We thought so, too. Until Billy swung a plank and accidentally punched into that plaster." He points to a gouge in the wall. "It's hollow back there. There's a space behind it."

"How big a space, do you think?"

"I looked in with a flashlight and I can't see the opposite wall. Arthur told us to open it up and find out what's back there."

"Arthur?"

"The owner, Arthur Sherbrooke. I've been keeping him up to date on our progress, and this has got him real curious. He had no idea there was anything behind that wall."

"Maybe it's a secret stash of gold," Billy says.

"Just as long as it isn't a dead body," grunts Ned, clapping crumbs from his hands. "Well, we'd better get back to work. Thanks for the cake, ma'am."

"Please, call me Ava."

Ned politely tips his head. "Ava."

They're both heading back to the widow's walk when I call out: "Did either of you happen to come by the house Sunday morning?"

Ned shakes his head. "We don't work here on weekends."

"I was walking on the cliff path when I looked up and saw someone on the widow's walk."

"Yeah, Donna mentioned you'd seen someone, but we can't get into the house if you're not here. Unless you'd like to leave us a key like the last tenant did."

I stare out at the widow's walk. "It's so strange. I can swear he was standing right *there*." I point to the edge of the deck.

"That'd be mighty foolhardy of him," says Ned. "The deck's just about rotted through. Wouldn't support anyone." He grabs a crowbar, ventures out on the new boards they've nailed into place, and pokes the crowbar into one of the old planks. The metal sinks in, punching straight through rotted wood. "If anyone stepped out here, the boards would've collapsed right under him. Truth is, it's a lawsuit waiting to happen. The owner should've had this deck repaired years ago. He's just lucky there hasn't been another accident."

I have been staring down at the disintegrating wood, and his words take a minute to sink in. I look up at him. "Another accident?"

"I didn't know about any accident," says Billy.

"'Cause you would've been in diapers. It happened twenty-something years ago."

"What happened?"

"The house was already in rough shape when Miss Sherbrooke died. I used to do odd jobs for her, but the last few years she was alive, she didn't like folks coming around to fix things, so everything sorta fell apart. After she died, the house sat empty for years and became a magnet for the local kids, especially on Halloween. Kind of a rite of passage to spend a night in the haunted house, drinking and making out."

My hands suddenly feel cold. "Haunted?" I ask.

Ned snorts. "Empty old houses like this, people always think they're haunted. Every Halloween, kids'd break in and get themselves plastered. That year, one fool girl climbed over the railing, got onto the roof. Those tiles are slate, so they're wicked slippery when they're wet, and it was drizzling." He points to the ground far below. "Her body would've landed down there, on the granite. You can see no one would survive the fall."

"Jesus, Ned. I never heard that story," says Billy.

"No one likes to talk about it. Jessie was a pretty little thing too, and only fifteen years old. What a shame she was hanging out with a bad crowd. The police called it an accident, so that was the end of it."

I stare out at the widow's walk and imagine a misty Halloween night and a booze-fueled teenager named Jessie, clambering over the railing and dangling there, high on the thrill. Was she startled by something she saw, something that made her lose her grip? Was that how it happened? I think of what I experienced last night in my bedroom. And I think of Charlotte, packing in haste, fleeing this house.

"They're sure the girl's death was just an accident?" I ask Ned.

"That's what everyone said, but I wondered about it at the time. I still wonder about it." He pulls his hammer from his tool belt and turns his attention back to his job. "But no one cares what I think."

Six

Hannibal has vanished.

Only as I finish eating supper do I realize I haven't seen my cat since Ned and Billy packed up and left for the day. Now it's dark outside, and if there's anything reliable about Hannibal, it's the fact he will always be sitting by his bowl at dinnertime.

I pull on a sweater and step outside, where an evening chill has swept in from the sea. Calling his name, I circle the house toward the cliff's edge. On the granite ledge I pause, thinking about the girl whose body would have landed here. In the light that shines from the window, I can almost see the girl's blood still spattered across the rock, but of course it's just dark patches of lichen on the stone. I glance up at the widow's walk, where the girl had dangled from the railing, and I imagine her plummeting through the darkness to land on this unforgiving granite. I don't want to think about what such a fall does to a human body, but I can't shut out the image of a shattered spine and a skull cracking open like an egg. Suddenly the sea is so loud it sounds like a wave is roaring straight toward me and I retreat from the cliff's edge, my heart pounding. It's too dark to search any further; Hannibal will have to fend for himself. Isn't that what tomcats do, prowl around all night on the hunt? At twenty-six pounds, he can afford to skip a meal or two.

I really should get him neutered.

I walk back into the house and am just locking the door when I hear a faint meow. It comes from upstairs.

So he's been inside the house all this time. Has he gotten himself shut into a room somewhere? I climb to the second floor and open the doors to the unused bedrooms. No Hannibal.

I hear another meow, still from above. He's up in the turret.

I open the door to the turret staircase and flip on the wall switch. I'm halfway up the stairs when the lone lightbulb suddenly gives a *pop* and goes out, plunging me into darkness. I should not have drunk that fourth glass of wine; now I have to steady myself on the railing as I climb. I feel as if the darkness is liquid and I'm dragging the weight of my body through water, struggling to surface. When at last I reach the turret, I grope along the wall for the light switch and flip it on.

"There you are, you bad boy."

A smug-looking Hannibal sits among the jumble of carpenter's tools with a freshly killed mouse at his feet.

"Well, come on. If you want dinner."

He appears utterly disinterested in following me downstairs; in fact, he's not looking at me at all, but is staring steadily at the window that faces the widow's walk. Why isn't he hungry? Is he actually *eating* the mice he catches? I shudder at the thought of him hopping into bed with me, his belly full of rodents.

"Come *on*," I plead. "I've got tuna for you."

He merely glances at me, then his gaze returns to the window.

"That's it. It's time to go." I reach down to pick him up and am shocked when he gives a ferocious hiss and lashes out with his claws. I jerk away, my arm stinging. I've owned Hannibal since he was a kitten and he's never attacked me before. Does he think I'm trying to steal his mouse? But he's not even looking at me; his gaze is still fixed on the window, staring at something I cannot see.

I look down at the claw marks he raked across my skin, where parallel tracks of blood are now oozing. "That's it. No dinner for *you*." I turn off the light switch and am about to feel my way back down the dark staircase when I hear his feral growl. The sound makes every hair on the back of my neck suddenly stand up.

In the darkness I see the unearthly glow of Hannibal's eyes.

But I also see something else: a shadow that thickens and congeals near the window. I cannot move, cannot make a sound; fear roots me in place as the shadow slowly assumes a form that is so solid I can no longer see through it to the window beyond. The smell of the sea floods my nostrils, a scent so powerful it's as if a wave has just washed over me.

A man looms in the window, his shoulders framed by moonlight. He stares out to sea, his back turned to me as if he's not even aware I am in the room. He stands straight and tall, his hair a mass of thick black waves, his long dark coat molded to broad shoulders and a narrow waist. Surely this is a trick of the moonlight; men do not suddenly materialize. He cannot be standing here. But Hannibal's eyes are aglow as he too stares at this figment of my imagination. If there is nothing there, what is my cat looking at?

Frantically I reach for the light switch, but I feel only bare wall. Where is it, where is it?

The figure turns from the window.

I freeze, my hand pressed to the wall, my heart banging. For a moment he stands with his face silhouetted in profile and I see a sharp nose, a jutting chin. Then he faces me, and even though his eyes are only a faint shimmer, I know he is looking straight at me. The voice I hear seems to come from nowhere and everywhere at once.

"Do not be afraid," he says.

Slowly I lower my hand to my side. No longer am I frantic to find the light switch; I am focused only on him, on a man who cannot possibly be standing before me. He approaches so silently that all I can hear is the whoosh of my own blood through my ears. Even as he draws closer I cannot move. My limbs have gone numb; I feel as if I am floating, my own body dissolving into shadow. As if I am the phantom, adrift in a world not my own.

"Under my roof, no harm will come to you."

The touch of his hand on my face is as warm as my own flesh, and just as alive. I take in a shuddering breath and inhale the briny scent of the ocean. *It is his scent.*

But even as I savor his touch, I feel his hand dissolving. The faint glimmer of moonlight shines through him. He gives me one last lingering look and he turns and walks away. Already he's faded to barely a wisp of shadow, as insubstantial as dust. At the closed door to the widow's walk he doesn't pause but passes straight through wood and glass to the balcony outside, onto the edge of the deck where there are no boards, where there is now only a gaping hole. He doesn't stumble, doesn't plummet, but strides across empty air. Across time.

I blink, and he is gone.

So is the smell of the ocean.

With a gasp I reach out to the wall and this time I find the switch. In the sudden glare I see the power saw and carpenter's tools and the stack of planks. Hannibal is sitting right where he'd been, and he's serenely licking his paws. The dead mouse is gone.

I cross to the window and stare out at the balcony.

No one is there.

Seven

Donna is sitting at her computer, fingers clacking away with quick efficiency. She doesn't look up at me until I'm standing right in front of her desk, and even then it's just a quick glance, an automatic smile as she continues to type.

"Be with you in just a sec. I have to finish this email," she says. "One of our properties just had a plumbing catastrophe and I need to find backup lodging for some very unhappy renters . . ."

As she keeps typing, I wander over to the *For Sale* listings displayed on the wall. If I moved to Maine, I could afford so much more house than I can in Boston. For the price of my two-bedroom apartment, I could own a house in the country with six acres of land, or a four-bedroom fixer-upper in the village, or a farm up in Aroostook County. I'm a food writer and I can live anywhere in the world; all I need is my laptop, an Internet connection, and a functioning kitchen for testing recipes. Like so many other vacationers who visit Maine in the summertime, I can't help but entertain the fantasy of pulling up roots and starting a new life here. I imagine myself planting peas in the spring, harvesting heirloom tomatoes in the summer, picking apples in the fall. And during the long dark winters, as snow swirls outside, I would bake bread while a pot of stew simmers on the stove. I would be a brand-new Ava, alert and happy and productive, not drinking myself into a stupor every night, desperate for sleep.

"Sorry to keep you waiting, Ava, but this morning has been crazy."

I turn to Donna. "I have another question. About the house."

"Is it about the mice again? Because if they really do bother you, I might be able to find you an apartment rental in another town. It's in a new building and it doesn't have a view, but—"

"No, I can deal with the mice. In fact, I've already caught half a dozen of them in the last week. My question is about the turret."

"Oh." She sighs, already assuming what my complaint is. "Billy and Ned told me the repairs will take longer than they expected. They need to open up that hidden space behind the wall. If that's not acceptable for you, I can ask them to delay the work until October, after you're gone."

"No, I'm perfectly fine having them work in the house. They're nice to have around."

"I'm glad you think so. Ned's gone through some tough times in the last few years. He was really happy when Mr. Sherbrooke gave him the job."

"I'd think a good carpenter would have more than enough work around here."

"Yes, well . . ." She looks down at her desk. "*I've* always found him reliable. And I'm sure that turret's going to be gorgeous when he's done with it."

"Speaking of the turret . . ."

"Yes?"

"Did the previous tenant mention anything, um, odd about it?"

"What do you mean by 'odd'?"

"Funny creaks. Noises. Odors." *Like the smell of the ocean.*

"Charlotte never mentioned anything to me."

"What about any of the tenants before her?"

"Charlotte's the only other tenant I've rented that house to. Before her, Brodie's Watch sat empty for years. This is the first season it's been available to rent." She searches my face, trying to glean what I'm really asking. "I'm sorry, Ava, but I'm not entirely clear about what problems you're experiencing. Every old house has creaks and noises. Is there something in particular I can address?"

I consider telling her the truth: that I believe Brodie's Watch is haunted. But I'm afraid of what this no-nonsense businesswoman will think of me. In her place, I know what *I* would think of me.

"It's not a problem, actually," I finally say. "You're right, it's just an old house, so I guess it comes with the odd creak now and then."

"Then you don't want me to find an apartment for you? Somewhere in a different town?"

"No, I'll stay through October as I planned. That should give me time to finish a big chunk of my book."

"You'll be glad you stayed. And October really *is* the nicest time of year."

I'm already at the door when I think of one more question. "The owner's name is Arthur Sherbrooke?"

"Yes. He inherited the house from his aunt."

"Do you think he'd mind if I contacted him about the history of Brodie's Watch? It would be interesting background for my book."

"He comes up to Tucker Cove every so often to check on Ned's progress. I'll find out when he'll be in town again, but I'm not sure how willing he is to talk about the house."

"Why not?"

"He's having a hard enough time selling the place. The last thing he needs is someone writing about the mouse problem."

I walk out of Donna's office, into the heat of a summer's day. The village is bustling, every table taken in the Lobster Trap Restaurant, and a long line of tourists snakes out of Village Cone Ice Cream. But no one seems interested in the white clapboard building that houses the Tucker Cove Historical Society. When I step inside, I don't see a single soul, and except for the ticking of a grandfather clock, it is silent. Tourists come to Maine to sail its waters and hike its forests, not to poke around inside gloomy old houses filled with dusty artifacts. I examine a glass display case containing antique dinner plates and wine goblets and silverware. It is a setting for a sit-down supper, circa 1880. Beside the place setting is an old cookbook, open to a recipe for salt mackerel baked in new milk and butter. It's just the sort of dish that one would have been served in a coastal village like Tucker Cove. Simple fare, made with ingredients pulled from the sea.

Hanging above the glass case is an oil painting of a familiar three-masted ship in full sail, plowing through turbulent green waves. It is identical to the painting that now hangs in Brodie's Watch. I lean in close and am so focused on the artist's brushstrokes that I don't realize someone has approached me from behind until the floorboard gives a squeak. With a start, I turn and see a woman watching me, her eyes enormous through the thick lenses in her glasses. Age has bowed her spine and she is only as tall as my shoulder, but her gaze is steady and alert, and she stands without the aid of a cane, her feet squarely planted in ugly but sensible shoes. Her docent name tag reads: MRS. DICKENS, which seems to match her almost too perfectly for it to be true.

"It's a very fine painting, isn't it?" she says.

Still surprised by her unexpected arrival, I merely nod.

"That's the *Mercy Annabelle*. She used to sail out of Wiscasset." She smiles, laugh lines creasing a face like worn leather. "Welcome to our little museum. Is this your first time in Tucker Cove?"

"Yes."

"Staying for a while?"

"Through the summer."

"Ah, good for you. Too many tourists just zoom up the coast, rushing through town after town, and everything blends together for them. It takes time to feel the pulse of a place and get to know its character." Her heavy glasses slide down her nose. Pushing them back up, she gives me a closer look. "Is there something in particular I can help you find? Some aspect of our history you'd like to know?"

"I'm staying up at Brodie's Watch. I'm curious about its history."

"Ah. You're the food writer."

"How did you know?"

"I ran into Billy Conway at the post office. He says he's never been so happy to go to work every morning. Your blueberry muffins are getting quite the reputation in town. Ned and Billy are hoping you'll settle down here and open up a bake shop."

I laugh. "I'll think about it."

"Do you like living up on the hill?"

"It's beautiful up there. Exactly the place you'd expect a sea captain to build his house."

"You'll be interested in this." She points to a different display case. "These items belonged to Captain Brodie. He brought them back from his voyages."

I lean in to examine the two dozen seashells which gleam under glass like colorful jewels. "He collected seashells? I never would have guessed that."

"We had a biologist from Boston look at these specimens. She told us these shells come from all around the world. The Caribbean, the Indian Ocean, the South China Sea. Rather a sweet hobby for a big burly sea captain, don't you think?"

I notice the journal lying open in the case, its yellowed pages covered with meticulous handwriting.

"That's his logbook from the earlier ship he was master of, *The Raven*. He seemed to be a man of few words. Most of his entries are strictly about the weather and sailing conditions, so it's hard to tell much about the man himself. Clearly, the sea was his first love."

And it was ultimately his doom, I think, as I study the handwriting of a man long dead. *Fair winds, following seas* he had written that day of the voyage. But the weather is always changing and the sea is a treacherous mistress. I wonder about his final words in *The Minotaur* logbook, just before his ship went down. Did he catch the scent of death in the wind, hear its scream in the rigging? Did he realize that he would never again set foot in the house where I now sleep?

"Do you have anything else in your collection that belonged to Captain Brodie?" I ask.

"There are a few more items upstairs." The doorbell tinkles and she turns as a family with young children enters. "Why don't you wander around and take a look? All the rooms are open to visitors."

As she greets the new arrivals, I walk through a doorway into the parlor, where chairs upholstered in red velvet are arranged around a tea table, as though for a ladies' gathering. On the wall are twin portraits of the gray-haired man and woman who once owned this building. The man looks stiff and uncomfortable in his high-collared shirt, and his wife stares from her portrait with steely eyes, as if to demand what I am doing in her parlor.

In the other room, I hear a child scampering about and the mother pleads: "No no, sweetheart! Put that vase down!"

I escape the noisy family and head into the kitchen, where a wax cake, artificial fruit, and a giant plastic turkey represent the makings of a holiday meal. I consider what it was like to cook such a meal on the cast-iron wood-burning stove, the backbreaking labor of hauling in water, feeding wood to the flames, plucking the bird. No, thank you; a modern kitchen for me.

"Mo*mmeee*! Let me *go*!" The child's shrieks move closer.

I flee up a back staircase and ascend narrow steps that servants must once have climbed. Displayed in the second-floor hallway are portraits of distinguished residents of Tucker Cove from a century ago, and I recognize names which are now displayed on storefronts in the village. Laite. Gordon. Tucker.

I do not see the name Brodie.

The first bedroom has a four-poster bed and in the next bedroom is an antique crib and a child's rocking horse. The last room, at the end of the hall, is dominated by a massive sleigh bed and an armoire, the door open to show a lace wedding gown hanging inside. But I pay no attention to the furniture; instead my attention is riveted on what hangs over the fireplace.

It is a painting of a striking man with wavy black hair and a prominent brow. He stands posed before a window, and over his left shoulder is a view of a ship in the harbor, its sails aloft. His dark coat is simple and unadorned but perfectly tailored to his broad shoulders, and in his right hand he holds a gleaming brass sextant. I do not need to look at the label affixed to the painting; I already know who this man is because I have seen him by moonlight. I have felt his hand caress my cheek and heard his voice whisper to me in the darkness.

Under my roof, no harm will come to you.

"Ah. I see you've found him," says the docent.

As she joins me in front of the fireplace, my gaze remains fixed on the portrait. "It's Jeremiah Brodie."

"He was a fine-looking fellow, don't you think?"

"Yes," I whisper.

"I imagine the ladies in town must have swooned whenever he came striding down the gangplank. What a shame he left no heirs."

For a moment we stand side by side, both of us spellbound by the image of a man who has been dead for nearly a century and a half. A man whose eyes seem to gaze directly at me. Only at me.

"It was a terrible tragedy for this village when his ship went down," says Mrs. Dickens. "He was so young, only thirty-nine, but he knew the sea as well as anyone could. He grew up on the water. Spent more of his life at sea than he did on land."

"Yet he built that beautiful house. Now that I've been living in Brodie's Watch for a while, I'm starting to appreciate just how special it really is."

"So you like it there."

I hesitate. "Yes," I finally say, and it's true; I *do* like it there. Mice and ghost and all.

"Some people have quite the opposite reaction to that house."

"What do you mean?"

"Every old house comes with a past. Sometimes people can sense if it's a dark past."

Her gaze makes me uncomfortable; I turn away from her and once again lock eyes with the painting. "I admit, when I first saw the house, I wasn't sure I wanted to stay."

"What did you feel?"

"As if—as if the house didn't want me there."

"Yet you moved in anyway."

"Because that feeling changed the moment I stepped inside. Suddenly I didn't feel unwelcome anymore. I felt as if it accepted me."

I realize I've said too much, and her gaze makes me uncomfortable. To my relief, the wayward child suddenly thumps along the hallway and the docent turns just as a three-year-old boy darts into the room. He makes a beeline for the fireplace tools, of course, and in a flash he's pulled out the poker.

"Travis? Travis, where are you?" his mother calls from another room.

The docent snatches the poker out of the boy's hands and places it out of reach on the mantelpiece. Through gritted teeth she says: "Young man, I'm sure your mommy can find a *much* better place for you to play." She grabs the boy's hand and half-leads him, half-drags him out of the room. "Let's go find her, shall we?"

I take that opportunity to quietly slip out of the room and make my way back down the staircase to the exit. I don't want to talk to her, to anyone, about what happened to me in Brodie's Watch. Not yet. Not when I myself am not certain of what I actually *saw*.

Or didn't see.

I walk toward my car, joining the throngs of tourists on the street. The world of living, breathing people who do not drift through walls, who do not appear and disappear like wisps of shadow. Does there exist a parallel world that I cannot see, a world inhabited by those who came before us, who even now are walking this same path I walk? Squinting against the glare of sunlight, I can almost see Tucker Cove as it once was, horses clopping across cobblestones, ladies swishing by in long skirts. Then I blink and that world is gone. I am back in my own time.

And Jeremiah Brodie has been dead for a hundred and fifty years.

Grief suddenly overwhelms me, a sense of loss so profound that my steps falter. I come to a stop right there on the crowded sidewalk as people stream past me. I don't understand why I'm crying. I don't understand why the passing of Captain Brodie should fill me with such sorrow. I drop down onto a bench and rock forward, my body shaking with sobs. I know that I am not really weeping for Jeremiah Brodie. I weep for myself, for the mistake I've made and for what I have lost because of it. Just as I cannot bring back Captain Brodie, I cannot bring back Nick. They are gone, both of them ghosts, and my only escape from the pain is the blessed bottle that waits in my kitchen cabinet. How easily one drink becomes two, then three, then four.

That is how it all went wrong in the first place. A few too many glasses of champagne on a snowy New Year's Eve. I can still hear the happy clink of glassware, feel bubbles fizz on my tongue. If only I could go back to that night and warn New Year's Ava: *Stop. Stop now while you still can.*

A hand touches my shoulder. I snap straight up on the bench and turn to see a familiar face frowning at me. It's that doctor I met in the hardware store. I don't remember his name. I certainly don't want to talk to him, but he sits down beside me and asks quietly:

"Are you all right, Ava?"

I wipe away tears. "I'm fine. I just got a little dizzy. It must be the heat."

"Is that all it is?"

"I'm *perfectly* okay, thank you."

"I don't mean to be nosy. I was just on my way to get coffee and you looked like you needed help."

"What, are you the town psychiatrist?"

Unruffled by my retort, he asks gently, "Do you think you need one?"

I'm afraid to admit the truth, even to myself: Maybe I do. Maybe what I've experienced in Brodie's Watch are the first signs of my sanity unraveling, the threads spooling away.

"May I ask, have you eaten anything today?" he says.

"No. Um, yes."

"You're not sure?"

"A cup of coffee."

"Well then, maybe that's the problem. I prescribe food."

"I'm not hungry."

"How about just a cookie? The coffee shop's right around the corner. I won't force-feed you or anything. I just don't want to have to stitch you up when you faint and hit your head." He holds out his hand, an act of kindness that takes me by surprise and it seems rude to turn him down.

I take his hand.

He leads me around the corner and down a narrow side street to the No Frills Café, which turns out to be a disappointingly accurate description. Under fluorescent lights, I see a linoleum floor and a glass case with an unappetizing array of baked goods. It's not a café I'd ever choose to step into, but it's clearly a gathering place for locals. I spot the butcher from the grocery store biting into a cheese Danish and a mailman standing in line to pay for his cup of to-go coffee.

"Have a seat," the doctor says. I still can't remember his name and I'm too embarrassed to admit it. I sit down at a nearby table, hoping someone will call him by name, but the girl behind the counter greets him with only a cheery "Hey, Doc, what'll it be?"

The door swings open and yet another person I recognize steps into the café. Donna Branca has shed her blazer and the humidity has fluffed up her usually tidy helmet of blond hair. It makes her look younger, and I can see the girl she once must have been, sun-kissed and pretty, before adulthood forced her to don a business-woman's uniform. Spotting the doctor, she lights up and says, "Ben, I was hoping to run into you. Jen Oswald's son is applying to medical school and you'd be the perfect man to give him advice."

Ben. Now I remember. His name is Ben Gordon.

"I'd be happy to give him a call," he says. "Thanks for letting me know." As he heads toward my table, Donna stares after him. Then she stares at me, as if something is not right with this pic-ture. As if I have no business sharing a table with Dr. Gordon.

"Here you go. That should get your blood sugar up," he says and places a cookie in front of me. It's the size of a saucer, thickly studded with chocolate chips.

I have absolutely no interest in eating this cookie, but to be polite I take a bite. It is irredeemably sweet, as boringly one-note as spun sugar. Even as a child, I knew that in every good recipe, sweet must be balanced with sour, salt with bitter. I think of the first batch of oatmeal raisin cookies I ever made by myself, and how eagerly Lucy and I had sampled the results after they came out of the oven. Lucy, always generous with praise, pronounced them the *best ever* but I knew better. Like life itself, cooking is about balance, and I knew that next time I must add more salt to the batter.

If only every mistake in life could be so easily corrected.

"How is it?" he asks.

"It's fine. I'm just not hungry."

"Not up to your high standards? I'm told you make killer blueberry muffins." At my raised eyebrow, he laughs. "I heard it from the lady at the post office, who heard it from Billy."

"There really are no secrets in this town."

"And how's your mouse problem these days? Emmett at the hardware store predicted you'd be back within a week for more traps."

I sigh. "I was planning to pick up some today. Then I got distracted at the historical society, and . . ." I fall silent as I notice that Donna, sitting alone a few tables away, is looking at us. Her eyes lock with mine, and her gaze unsettles me. As if she has caught me trespassing.

The door suddenly bangs open, and we all turn as a man wearing fishermen's overalls lurches into the café. "Doc?" he calls out to Ben. "They need you down at the harbor."

"Right now?"

"Right now. Pete Crouse just tied up at the landing. You need to see what he dragged outta the bay."

"What is it?"

"A body."

Almost everyone in the café follows Ben and the fisherman out the door. Curiosity is infectious. It forces us to look at what we do not really want to see, and like the others, I'm pulled along with the grim parade as it heads down the cobblestoned street toward the harbor. Clearly the news about a dead body has already spread and a small crowd stands gathered around the pier where a lobster boat has tied up. A Tucker Cove policeman spots Ben and waves.

"Hey, Doc. It's on deck, under the tarp."

"I found it near Scully's Rocks, tangled up in seaweed," says the lobsterman. "Didn't want to believe what I was seeing at first, but as soon as I snagged it with the boat hook, I knew it was real. Afraid I might've caused some, um, damage when I hauled it aboard. But I couldn't leave it just drifting out there, and I was afraid it might sink. Then we'd never find it again."

Ben climbs onto the lobster boat and approaches the blue plastic tarp, which covers a vaguely human shape. Although I can't see what he's looking at, I can read his appalled expression as he lifts up one corner of the tarp and stares at what lies beneath. For a long time he simply crouches there, confronting the horrors of what the sea can do to a human body. On the landing, the crowd has gone silent, respectful of this solemn moment. Abruptly Ben drops the tarp and looks up at the police officer. "You called the ME?"

"Yes, sir. He's on his way." The officer looks at the tarp and shakes his head. "I'm guessing it's been in the water for some time."

"A few weeks at least. And based on the size and what's left of the clothing, it's most likely a woman." Grimacing, Ben rises to his feet and clambers off the lobster boat. "You have any current missing persons reports?"

"Nothing reported in the last few months."

"This time of year, there's a lot of boats out on the bay. She could've fallen overboard and drowned."

"But if she's been in the water for weeks, you'd think someone would've called it in by now."

Ben shrugs. "Maybe she was sailing solo. No one's realized she's missing yet."

The cop turns and stares over the water. "Or someone didn't want her to be found."

As I drive back to Brodie's Watch, I am still shaken by what I witnessed on the dock. While I did not glimpse the body itself, I saw the unmistakably human shape beneath the blue tarp, and my imagination fills in all the gruesome details that Ben was forced to confront. I think of Captain Brodie, whose body was consigned to the same inexorable forces of the ocean. I think of what it's like to drown, limbs flailing as salt water floods into your lungs. I think of fish and crabs feasting on flesh, of skin and muscle dragged by currents across razor-sharp coral. After a century and a half underwater, what remains of the strapping man who stared back at me from the portrait?

I turn into my driveway and groan at the sight of Ned's truck parked in front of the house. I've started leaving a house key for the carpenters, and of course they're here working, but I'm in no mood to sit through another afternoon of hammering. I slip into the house just long enough to pack a picnic basket with bread and cheese and olives. A bottle of red wine, already opened, calls to me from the countertop and I add it to my basket.

Loaded down with lunch and a blanket, I scrabble across lichen-flecked rocks like a mountain goat, following the path to the beach. Glancing back, I can see Billy and Ned at work up on the widow's walk. They're busy installing the new railing and they don't notice me. Down the path I go, past the blooming roses, and I jump down onto the pebbly beach that I'd discovered that first morning. A beach where no one can see me. I spread my blanket and unpack my lunch. I may be losing my mind, but I still know how to lay out a proper meal. Although it's a simple outdoor picnic, I don't stint on ceremony. I lay out a cloth napkin, a fork and knife, a glass tumbler. The first sip of wine floods my body with warmth. Sighing, I lean back against a boulder and stare out to sea. The water is eerily flat, the surface as still as a mirror. This is exactly what I need to do today: absolutely nothing. I will soak up the sun like a tortoise and let this wine do its magic. Forget the dead woman pulled from the sea. Forget Captain Brodie, whose bones lie scattered beneath the waves. Today is about healing.

And forgetting. Most of all, forgetting.

The salt air makes me hungry and I tear off a piece of bread, smear it with Brie, and eat it in two bites. Devour a few olives and wash it all down with another glass of wine. By the time I finish my meal, the bottle of Rioja is empty and I'm so drowsy I can barely keep my eyes open.

I stretch out on the blanket, cover my face with a sun hat, and tumble into a deep and dreamless sleep.

It's the cold water lapping at my feet that awakens me.

Nudging aside my hat, I look up and see the sky has darkened to violet, and the sun is dipping behind the boulder. How long have I slept? The rising tide has already brought the water halfway up my little beach, and the bottom edge of my blanket is soaked. Hungover and groggy, I clumsily gather up the remains of the picnic, stuff everything into the basket, and stumble away from the water. My skin feels hot and flushed, and I desperately crave a glass of sparkling water. And perhaps a splash of rosé.

I scramble up the path to the top of the cliff. There I pause to catch my breath and I look up at the widow's walk. What I see makes me freeze. Although I cannot make out the man's face, I know who is standing there.

I begin to run toward the house, the empty wine bottle clattering and rolling around in my picnic basket. Somewhere along the path I lose my hat, but I don't turn back to retrieve it; I just keep running. I bound up the porch steps and burst through the front door. The carpenters have left, so there should be no one in the house but me. In the foyer, I drop the picnic basket and it lands with a clunk but I hear no other sound, only the beating of my own heart. That drumbeat accelerates as I climb to the second floor and move down the hall to the turret staircase. At the bottom of those steps I pause to listen.

Silence upstairs.

I think of the man in the painting, the eyes that looked straight at me, only at me, and I long to see his face again. I want— I *need*—to know that he is real. Up the steps I climb, setting off a series of familiar creaks, the glow of twilight lighting my way. I step into the turret room, and the scent of the ocean sweeps over me. I recognize it for what it is: *his* scent. He loved the ocean and it was the ocean that took him. In its embrace, he found his eternal resting place, but in this house, a trace of him still lingers.

I cross the tool-littered room and step out onto the widow's walk. All the rotted boards have been replaced, and for the first time I'm able to walk out onto the deck. No one is here. No carpenters, no Captain Brodie. I can still smell the sea, but this time it's the wind itself that carries the scent, blowing it in from the water.

"Captain Brodie?" I call out. I don't really expect an answer, but I hope to hear one anyway. "I'm not afraid of you. I want to see you. *Please* let me see you."

The wind ruffles my hair. Not a cold wind, but the gentle breath of summer, and it carries the scent of roses and warm soil. The smell of land. For a long time I gaze at the sea, as once he must have done, and wait to hear his voice, but no one speaks to me. No one appears.

He is gone.

Eight

I lie in the darkness of my bedroom, listening once again to mice scurrying in the walls. For months, alcohol has been my anesthetic and only by drinking myself into a stupor have I been able to fall asleep, but tonight, even after two glasses of whiskey, I'm not the least bit drowsy. I know, somehow I know, that this is the night he will appear to me.

Hannibal, who has been slumbering beside me, suddenly stirs and sits up. In the walls the mice fall silent. The world has gone quiet and even the sea has ceased its rhythmic murmur.

A familiar scent wafts into the room. The smell of the ocean.

He is here.

I sit up in bed, my pulse throbbing in my neck, my hands ice cold. I scan the room, but all I see is the green glow of Hannibal's eyes watching me. No movement, no sound. The smell of the ocean grows stronger, as if the tide has just swept through the room.

Then, near the window, there is a swirl of darkness. Not yet a figure, just the faintest hint of a silhouette taking shape in the night.

"I'm not afraid of you," I announce.

The shadow drifts away like smoke, and I almost lose sight of it. "Please come back, Captain Brodie!" I call out. "You *are* Captain Brodie, aren't you? I want to see you. I want to know that you're real!"

"The question is, are *you* real?"

The voice is startlingly clear, the words spoken *right beside me.* With a gasp, I turn and stare straight into the eyes of Jeremiah Brodie. This is not merely a shadow; no, this is a flesh-and-blood man with thick black hair silvered by moonlight. His deep-set eyes focus on me so fiercely that I can almost feel the heat of that gaze. This is the face I saw in the painting, the same rugged jaw, the same hawkish nose. He has been dead for a century and a half, yet I am looking at him now, and he is solid enough, real enough, to make the mattress sag as he sits down on the bed beside me.

"You are in my house," he says.

"I live here now. I know this is your house, but—"

"Too many people forget that fact."

"I won't forget, ever. This *is* your house."

He eyes me up and down and his gaze lingers for a tantalizing moment on the bodice of my nightgown. Then he focuses once again on my face. When he touches my cheek, his fingers feel startlingly warm against my skin. "Ava."

"You know my name."

"I know far more about you than just your name. I sense your pain. I hear you weep in your sleep."

"You watch me?"

"Someone must watch over you. Have you no one else?"

His question brings tears to my eyes. He caresses my face and it is not the cold hand of a corpse I feel. Jeremiah Brodie is alive and his touch makes me tremble.

"Here in my house, what you seek is what you will find," he says.

I close my eyes and shiver as he gently nudges aside my night-gown and kisses my shoulder. His unshaven face is rough against my skin and I sigh as my head lolls back. The nightgown slips off my other shoulder and moonlight spills across my breasts. I am shaking and utterly exposed to his gaze, yet I don't feel afraid. His mouth meets mine and his kiss tastes of salt and rum. I gasp in a breath and smell damp wool and seawater. The scent of a man who has lived too long on a ship, a man who is hungry for the taste of a woman.

As hungry as I am for the taste of a man.

"I know what you desire," he says.

What I desire is *him*. I need him to make me forget everything but what it feels like to be embraced by a man. I topple onto my back and at once he is on top of me, his weight pinning me to the mattress. He grasps both my wrists and traps them over my head. I cannot resist him. I don't want to resist him.

"I know what you need."

I suck in a startled breath as his hand closes around my breast. This is not a gentle embrace but a claiming, and I flinch as if he has just burned his brand into my skin.

"And I know what you deserve."

My eyes fly open. I stare up at no one, at nothing. Wildly I look around the room, see the shapes of furniture, the glow of moon-light on the floor. And I see Hannibal's eyes, green and ever watch-ful, staring at me.

"Jeremiah?" I whisper. No one answers.

The whine of an electric saw awakens me and I open my eyes to dazzling sunlight. The sheets are twisted around my legs, and be-neath my thighs, the linen is damp. Even now, I am still wet and aching for him.

Was he really here?

Heavy footsteps creak upstairs in the turret and a hammer pounds. Billy and Ned are back at work, and here I lie in the room just beneath them, my legs splayed apart, my skin flushed with desire. Suddenly I feel exposed and embarrassed. I climb out of bed and pull on the same clothes I wore yesterday. They're still lying on the floor; I don't even remember taking them off. Hannibal is already pawing at the closed door and he gives an impatient meow, demanding to be let out. As soon as I open the door, he darts out and heads downstairs to the kitchen. To breakfast, of course.

I don't follow him, but make my way up to the turret room, where I'm startled to see a large hole in the wall. Billy and Ned have broken through the plaster, and they stand peering into the newly exposed cavity.

"What on earth is back there?" I ask.

Ned turns and frowns at my unkempt hair. "Oh, gosh. I hope we didn't wake you up."

"Um, yeah. You did." I rub my eyes. "What time is it?"

"Nine-thirty. We knocked on the front door but I guess you didn't hear us. We figured you went out for a walk or something."

"What happened to you?" asks Billy, pointing at my arm.

I glance down at the claw marks. "Oh, that's nothing. Hannibal scratched me the other day."

"I mean your other arm."

"What?" I stare down at a bruise encircling my forearm like an ugly blue bracelet. I don't remember how I got it, just as I don't remember how I bruised my knee the other night. I think of the captain and how he had pinned my arms to the bed. I remember the weight of his body, the taste of his mouth. But that was merely a dream, and dreams do not leave bruises. Did I stumble in the dark on my way to the bathroom? Or did it happen yesterday afternoon on the beach? Numb with wine, if I'd banged my arm against a rock, I might not have felt any pain.

My throat is so dry I can barely answer Billy's question. "Maybe I got it in the kitchen. Sometimes I get so busy cooking, I don't even notice when I hurt myself." Anxious to escape, I turn to leave. "I really need coffee. I'll get the pot going, if you want some."

"First come take a look at what we found behind this wall," says Ned. He pulls off another chunk of drywall, opening up a wider view of the cavity behind it.

I peer through the opening and see the glint of a brass sconce and walls painted a mint green. "It's a little alcove. How strange."

"The floor back there's still in good shape. And take a look at that crown molding. It's original to the house. This space is like a time capsule, preserved all these years."

"Why on earth would anyone wall off an alcove?"

"Arthur and I talked about it, and neither of us has any idea. We're thinking it was done before his aunt's time."

"Maybe it was a bootlegger's space, to hide liquor," Billy suggests. "Or to hide a treasure."

"There's no door anywhere in or out, so how would you get to it?" Ned shakes his head. "No, this space was closed off, like a tomb. Like someone was trying to erase the fact it was ever here."

I can't help shivering as I peer into a room that has been frozen in time for at least a generation. What scandalous history could have led someone to close up this space and plaster over any trace of its existence? What secret were they trying to conceal?

"Arthur wants us to open it up, paint the walls to match the rest of the turret," says Ned. "And we'll need to sand and varnish the floor, so that'll take us another week or two. We've been working on this house for months, and I'm starting to think we'll never get finished."

"Crazy old house," says Billy and he picks up a sledgehammer. "I wonder what else it's hiding."

Billy and Ned sit at my kitchen table, both wearing grins as I set down two steaming bowls, fragrant with the scent of beef and bay leaves.

"Smelled this cooking all morning," says Billy, whose bottomless appetite never fails to amaze me. Eagerly he picks up a spoon. "We wondered what you were whipping up down here."

"Lobscouse," I answer.

"Looks like beef stew to me." He shovels a spoonful into his mouth and sighs, his eyes closed in utter contentment. "Whatever it is, I think I've died and gone to heaven."

"It's known as sailor's beef stew," I explain as both men tuck into their lunch. "The recipe originated with the Vikings, but they used fish. As the recipe traveled with sailors around the world, the fish was replaced with beef instead."

"Yay, beef," Billy mumbles.

"And beer," I add. "There's lots and lots of beer in this dish."

Billy raises a fist. "Yay, beer!"

"Come on, Billy, you can't just inhale it. You have to tell me what you *think* about it."

"I'd eat it again." Of course he would. When it comes to food, Billy is the least discriminating person I have ever met. He'd eat roasted shoe leather if I placed it in front of him.

But Ned takes his time as he spoons chunks of potato and beef into his mouth and he thinks as he chews. "I'm guessing this is a lot tastier than what those old-time sailors ate," he concludes. "This definitely needs to go in the book, Ava."

"I think so, too. I'm glad to have the Ned Haskell seal of approval."

"What're you cooking for us next week?" Billy asks.

Ned gives him a punch on the shoulder. "She's not cooking for *us*. This is research for her book."

A book for which I've already compiled dozens of worthy recipes, from a generations-old French Canadian recipe for tourtière pork pie, luscious and dripping with silky fat, to a saddle of venison with juniper berries, to an endless array of dishes involving salt cod. Now I can test them all on real Mainers, men with appetites.

Billy gobbles down his stew first and heads back upstairs to work, but Ned lingers at the table, savoring the final spoonfuls.

"Gonna be real sorry to finish up in your turret," he says.

"And I'll be sorry to lose my taste testers."

"I'm sure you'll have no end of eager volunteers, Ava."

My cellphone rings and I see the name of my editor pop up on the screen. I have been avoiding his calls but there's no way to put him off forever. If I don't pick up now, he'll just keep calling.

"Hello, Simon," I answer.

"So you haven't been eaten by a bear after all."

"I'm sorry I haven't called back. I'll send you a few more chapters tomorrow."

"Scott thinks we should drive up there and drag you home."

"I don't want to be dragged home. I want to keep writing. I just needed to get away."

"Get away from what?"

I pause, not knowing what to say. I glance at Ned, who discreetly rises from the table and carries his empty bowl to the sink.

"I've got a lot on my mind, that's all," I say.

"Oh? What's his name?"

"Now you are *really* barking up the wrong tree. I'll call you next week." I hang up and look at Ned, who is meticulously washing the dishes. At fifty-eight years old, he still has the lean, athletic build of a man who works with his muscles, but there's more to him than mere brawn; there's a depth to his silence. This is a man who watches and listens, who takes in far more than others might realize. I wonder what he thinks of me. If he considers it odd that I have isolated myself in this lonely house with a badly behaved cat as my only companion.

"You don't have to do the dishes," I tell him.

"It's okay. Don't like to leave a mess." He rinses his bowl and picks up a dishcloth. "I'm particular that way."

"You said you've been working on this house for months?"

"Going on six months now."

"And you knew the tenant who lived here before me? I think her name is Charlotte."

"Nice lady. She teaches elementary school in Boston. Seemed to like it up here well enough, so I was surprised when she packed up and left town."

"She didn't tell you why?"

"Not a word. We came to work one day, and she was gone." He finishes drying the bowl and sets it in the cabinet, right where it belongs. "Billy had something of a crush on her, so he was real hurt she never even said goodbye."

"Did she ever mention anything, um, odd about the house?"

"Odd?"

"Like sounds or smells she couldn't explain. Or other things."

"What other things?"

"A feeling that someone was . . . watching her."

He turns to look at me. I'm grateful that at least he takes the time to actually consider my question. "Well, she *did* ask us about curtains," he finally says.

"What curtains?"

"She wanted us to hang curtains in her bedroom, to keep anyone from looking in the window. I pointed out that her bedroom faces the sea, and there's no one out there to see her, but she insisted I talk to the owner about it. A week later, she left town. We never did hang those curtains."

I feel a chill ripple across my skin. So Charlotte felt it too, the sensation that she was not alone in this house, that she was being watched. But curtains cannot shut out the gaze of someone who's already dead.

After Ned heads upstairs to the turret, I collapse into a chair at the kitchen table and sit rubbing my head, trying to massage away the memory of last night. When considered in the light of day, it could only have been a dream. Of course it was a dream, because the alternative is impossible: that a long-dead man tried to make love to me.

No, I can't call it that. What happened last night was not love but a taking, a claiming. Even though it frightened me, I ache for more. *I know what you deserve,* he'd said. Somehow he knows my secret, the source of my shame. He knows because he watches me.

Is he watching me even now?

I sit up straight and nervously scan the kitchen. Of course there's no one else here. Just as there was no one in my bedroom last night except for the phantom I've conjured from my own loneliness. A ghost, after all, is every woman's perfect lover. I don't need to charm or amuse him, or worry that I'm too old or too fat or too plain. He won't crowd my bed at night or leave his shoes and socks strewn around the room. He materializes when I need to be loved, the way I *want* to be loved, and in the morning he conveniently vanishes into thin air. I never need to cook him breakfast.

My laughter has the shrill note of insanity. Either I'm going crazy or my house really is haunted.

I don't know whom to talk to or confide in. In desperation I open my laptop computer. The last document I typed is still on the screen, a list of ingredients for the next recipe: Whole cream, knobs of butter, shucked oysters combined in a rich stew that would have simmered on cast-iron stoves all along the New England coast. I close the file, open a search engine. What the hell should I search for? Local psychiatrists?

Instead I type: *Is my house haunted?*

To my surprise, the screen fills with a list of websites. I click on the first link.

Many people believe their house is haunted, but in the vast majority of cases, there are logical explanations for what they are experiencing. Some of the phenomena people describe include:

Pets behaving oddly.

Strange noises (footsteps, creaks) when no one else is in the house.

Objects vanishing and reappearing in a different place.

A feeling of being watched . . .

I stop and glance around the kitchen again, thinking of what he'd said last night. *Someone must watch over you.* As for pets behaving oddly, Hannibal is so focused on scarfing down his lunch, he doesn't once look up from his bowl. Perfectly usual behavior for Mr. Fatty.

I scroll down to the next page on the website.

The appearance of vaguely human forms or moving shadows.

Feeling of being touched.

Muffled voices.

Unexplained smells that come and go.

I stare at those last four signs of haunting. Dear god, I've experienced all of these. Not merely touches or muffled voices. I have felt his weight on top of me. I can still feel his mouth on mine. I take a deep breath to calm myself. There are multiple websites devoted to this, so I am not the only one with this problem. How many others have frantically searched the Internet for answers? How many of them wondered if they were going insane?

I focus once again on my laptop screen.

What to do if you think your house is haunted.

Observe and document every unusual occurrence. Record the time and location of the phenomena.

Record video of any physical or auditory occurrences. Keep a cellphone nearby at all times.

Call an expert for advice.

An expert. Where the hell do I find one of those? "Who ya gonna call?" I say aloud and my laughter sounds unhinged.

I return to the search engine and type: *Maine ghost investigations.*

A fresh page with website links appears. Most of the sites are devoted to tales of haunted houses, and it seems Maine has generated scores of such stories, some of which made it onto television shows. Ghosts in inns, ghosts on highways, ghosts in movie theaters. I scroll down the list, my skepticism growing. Rather than true hauntings, these look like mere myths, meant to be told around campfires. The hitchhiking woman in white. The man in the stovepipe hat. I scroll down the page and am almost ready to close it when the link at the bottom catches my eye.

Help for the Haunted. Professional Ghost Investigations, Maine.

I click on the link. The website is sparse, only a brief statement of purpose:

We investigate and document paranormal activity in the state of Maine. We also serve as an informational clearinghouse and we provide emotional and logistical support to those who are dealing with paranormal phenomena.

There is a contact form, but no phone number.

I type in my name and phone number. In the space for *Reason for contacting us* I type: *I believe my house is haunted. I don't know what to do about it,* and hit send.

It flits off into the ether and almost immediately I feel ridiculous. Did I really just contact a ghost hunter? I think of what my ever-logical sister, Lucy, would say about this. Lucy, whose medical career is rooted in science. I need her advice now more than ever, but I don't dare call her. I'm afraid of what she'll say to me, and even more afraid of what I'll say to *her.* I won't call my longtime friend and editor Simon either, because he'll certainly laugh at me and tell me I've gone round the bend. And then remind me how late my manuscript is.

Desperate to distract myself, I scrape the remaining beef stew into a bowl and carry it to the refrigerator. I yank open the door and focus on the bottle of sauvignon blanc gleaming inside. It's so tempting I can already taste its cold, crisp bite of alcohol. The bottle calls to me so seductively I almost miss the chime of the email landing in my in-box.

I turn to the laptop. The email is from an unfamiliar account, but I open it anyway.

FROM: MAEVE CERRIDWYN
RE: YOUR HAUNTING.
WHEN WOULD YOU LIKE TO MEET?

Nine

It's a two-hour drive from Tucker Cove to the town of Tranquility, where the ghost hunter lives. According to the map it's only fifty-five miles as the crow flies, but that old Maine saying *You can't get there from here* has never seemed so apt as I navigate from back road to back road, slowly making my way inland from the coast. I drive past abandoned farmhouses with collapsing barns, past long-fallow fields invaded by saplings, into woodlands where trees crowd out all sunlight. My GPS directs me down roads that seem to lead nowhere, but I obey the annoying voice issuing from the speaker because I have no idea where I am. It has been miles since I've seen another car, and I begin to wonder if I've been going in circles; everywhere I look I see only trees and every bend in the road looks identical.

Then I spot the roadside mailbox with a pale blue butterfly painted on the side: #41. I've arrived at the right place.

I bounce up the dirt driveway, and the woods part to reveal Maeve Cerridwyn's home. I had imagined a ghost hunter's house to be dark and ominous, but this cottage in the woods looks like a home where you'd find seven charming dwarves. When I step out of my car, I hear tinkling wind chimes. Behind the house is a stand of birch trees, their white trunks like ghostly sentinels of the forest. In the sunny patch of front yard, an herb garden blooms with sage and catmint.

I follow the fieldstone path through the garden, where I recognize my usual culinary friends: thyme and rosemary, parsley and tarragon, sage and oregano. But there are other herbs here that I do not recognize, and in this magical woodland spot I can't help wondering what mysterious uses they might have. For love potions, perhaps, or the warding off of demons? I bend down to examine a vine with blackberries and tiny purple flowers.

When I rise to my feet, I'm startled to see a woman watching me from her porch. How long has she been there?

"I'm glad you made it, Ava," she says. "It's easy to get lost along the way."

Maeve Cerridwyn is not what I expected a ghost hunter to look like. Neither mysterious nor scary, she is a petite woman with a plain, sweet face. The sun has freckled her skin and etched deep laugh lines around her brown eyes, and her dark hair is half silver. I can't imagine this woman facing down ghosts or battling demons; she looks like she'd bake them cookies instead.

"I'm sorry you had to come all this way to see me. Normally I drive out to the client's house, but my car's still in the shop."

"That's all right. I felt like I needed to get away for the day." I look at her garden. "This is beautiful. I write about food, and I'm always on the hunt for new culinary herbs I haven't tried yet."

"Well, you wouldn't want to cook with that one," she says, pointing to the vine I was just admiring. "That's belladonna. Deadly nightshade. A few berries could kill you."

"Why on earth do you grow it?"

"Every plant has its uses, even the poisonous ones. A tincture of belladonna can be used as an anesthetic and to help wounds heal." She smiles. "Come on in. I promise I won't put anything in your tea except honey."

I step into the house, where I pause for a moment, looking around in wonder at the mirrors that hang on almost every wall. Some are mere chips of glass, others extend from floor to ceiling. Some are mounted in lavishly decorated frames. Everywhere I look I glimpse movement—my own, as I turn from reflection to reflection.

"As you can see, I have an obsession with mirrors," she admits. "Some people collect porcelain frogs. I collect mirrors from around the world." She points to each one as we move down the hall. "That's from Guatemala. That one is from India. Malaysia. Slovenia. No matter where you go in the world, most people want to look at themselves. Even guinea fowl will sit and stare at their own reflections."

I stop before one particularly striking example. Encircling the mirrored glass is a tin frame decorated with grotesque and frightening faces. *Demons.* "Interesting hobby you have," I murmur.

"It's more than a hobby. It's also for protection."

I frown at her. "Protection from what?"

"Some cultures believe that mirrors are dangerous. That they serve as portals to another world, a way for spirits to move back and forth and cause mischief. But the Chinese believe mirrors are a defense, and they hang them outside their homes to scare away evil spirits. When a demon sees its own reflection, it's frightened away and it won't disturb you." She points to the mirror hanging above the doorway to the kitchen, its frame painted bright green and gold. "That's a Ba Gua mirror. Notice how it's concave? That's so it absorbs negative energies, preventing them from going into my kitchen." She sees my dubious expression. "You think this is all hokum, don't you?"

"I've always been skeptical about the supernatural."

She smiles. "Yet here you are."

We sit in her kitchen, where crystals dangle in the window, casting little rainbows on the walls. In this room there are no mirrors; perhaps she considers the kitchen safe from invasion, protected by that obstacle course of demon-repelling mirrors in the hallway. I'm relieved that I can't catch glimpses of myself in this room. Like those demons, I'm afraid of my own reflection, afraid to look myself in the eye.

Maeve sets two steaming cups of chamomile tea on the table and sits across from me. "Now tell me about your ghost problem."

I can't help a sheepish laugh. "I'm sorry, but this feels ridiculous."

"Of course it does. Since you don't believe in spirits."

"I really don't. I never have. I've always thought that people who saw ghosts were either delusional or prone to fantasies, but I don't know how else to explain what's happening in my house."

"You believe these events are paranormal?"

"I don't know. All I know is, I *didn't* imagine them."

"I'm sure you didn't. But old houses come with creaky floors. The wood expands and contracts. Faucets drip."

"None of those things can explain what I saw. Or what I felt when he touched me."

Her eyebrow lifts. "Something actually *touched* you?"

"Yes."

"Where?"

"My face. He touched my face." I won't tell her where else he touched me. Or how he pinned my body to the bed with his.

"You said on the phone you also smell things. Unusual odors."

"It's almost always the first thing I notice, just before he appears."

"Odors are often described as sentinels of a supernatural presence. Is it an unpleasant odor?"

"No. It's like—like a wind from the ocean. The smell of the sea."

"What else do you notice? You said your cat sometimes behaves oddly."

"I think he's aware. I think he sees him."

Maeve nods and takes a sip of tea. Nothing I've said appears to surprise her, and her placidity about what seems like an outlandish tale somehow calms me. It makes me feel my story is not so ridiculous after all. "What do *you* see, Ava? Describe it."

"I see a man. He's my age, tall, with thick black hair."

"A full-body apparition."

"Yes, head to toe." *And more.* "He wears a dark coat. It's plain, unadorned. Like the coat Captain Brodie wears in his portrait."

"Captain Brodie is the man who built your house?"

I nod. "His portrait hangs in the Tucker Cove Historical Society. They say he died at sea, which explains why I smell the ocean whenever he appears. And when he spoke to me, he said: 'You are in my house.' He believes it's *still* his house. I don't know if he's even aware he's passed on . . ." I am so anxious for her to believe me that when I look down, I see my hands are knotted on the table. "It's Captain Brodie. I'm sure it is."

"Do you feel welcome in that house?"

"I do now."

"You didn't earlier?"

"When I first saw it from the outside, the house seemed unfriendly, as if it didn't want me there. Then I stepped inside and smelled the sea. And suddenly I felt welcome. I felt the house had accepted me."

"You don't feel even a little bit afraid, then?"

"I did at first, but not now. Not any longer. Should I?"

"It depends on what you're actually dealing with. If it's *just* a ghost."

"What would it be, if not a ghost?"

She hesitates, and for the first time I sense her uneasiness, as if she doesn't want to tell me what she's thinking. "Ghosts are spirits of the deceased who haven't managed to fully escape our world," she explains. "They linger among us because of unfinished business. Or they're trapped because they haven't realized they're dead."

"Like Captain Brodie."

"Possibly. Let's hope that's all this is. A benign ghost."

"Are there ghosts who aren't benign?"

"It depends on what sort of person he was in real life. Friendly people make friendly ghosts. Since your entity doesn't seem to frighten you, perhaps that's all you have. A ghost who's accepted you into his house. Who may even try to protect you against harm."

"Then I have nothing to worry about."

She reaches for her cup of tea and takes a sip. "Probably not."

I don't like the sound of that word: *probably*. I don't like the possibilities it conjures up. "Is there something I *should* be worried about?"

"There are other entities that can attach themselves to a house. Sometimes they're attracted by negative energy. Poltergeists, for instance, seem to show up in households where adolescent children live. Or where families are in emotional turmoil."

"I live alone."

"Are you dealing with any personal crises at the moment?"

Where do I begin? I could tell her I've spent the last eight months paralyzed by guilt. I could tell her that I fled Boston because I cannot bear to face up to the past. But I tell her none of this and say simply: "I'm trying to finish writing a book. It's almost a year overdue and my editor keeps bugging me about it. So yes, I'm under some stress right now." She studies me, her gaze so intent that I'm compelled to look away as I ask, "If it *is* a poltergeist, how would I know?"

"Their presentation can be quite physical. Objects move or levitate. Dishes fly, doors slam shut. There can even be violence."

My head lifts. "Violence?"

"But you haven't experienced that. Have you?"

I hesitate. "No."

Does she believe me? Her silence implies doubt, but after a moment, she simply moves on. "I'll do some background research on your house, see if there's any relevant history that will explain a haunting. Then we can decide if an amelioration is in order."

"Amelioration? You mean—get rid of it?"

"There are ways to make the phenomena cease. Are these events happening every day?"

"No."

"When was the last time?"

I look down at my teacup. "It's been three nights." Three nights of lying awake, waiting for the captain to reappear. Wondering if I merely imagined him.

Worrying that I will never see him again.

"I don't want to drive him away," I tell her. "I just wanted reassurance that what I've experienced is *real*."

"So you're willing to tolerate his presence?"

"What else can I do?"

"You can ask him to leave."

"It's that simple?"

"Sometimes that's all it takes. I've had clients who demanded their ghost vacate the house and move on. And that's it, problem solved. If that's what you want to do, I can help you."

I say nothing for a moment, thinking about how it would feel to never again glimpse him in the shadows. To never again sense his presence watching over me. Protecting me. *Under my roof, no harm will come to you.*

"Are you willing to live with this entity?" she asks.

I nod. "Strangely enough, I feel safer knowing he's there."

"Then doing nothing is a reasonable choice. In the meantime, I'll search for any information about Brodie's Watch. The Maine State Library in Augusta has newspaper archives going back hundreds of years, and I have a friend who works there."

"What will you be searching for?"

"Any tragic events that occurred in the house. Deaths, suicides, murders. Reports of any paranormal activity."

"I already know of one tragedy that happened in the house. My carpenter told me about it. He said it happened twenty or so years ago, on a Halloween night. Some teenagers broke into the house, got drunk and rowdy. One of the girls fell from the widow's walk and died."

"So there *has* been a death."

"But it was just an accident. It's the only tragedy I know of."

Her gaze drifts to the kitchen window, where multicolored crystals dangle. Quietly she says, "If there were others, that would make me wonder."

"About what?"

She looks at me. "If your problem is actually a ghost."

It is already late afternoon when I start my drive back to Tucker Cove. Along the way I stop at a diner to eat dinner and to mull over what Maeve told me: *I can help you. There are ways to make the phenomena cease.* Ways to make Captain Brodie vanish forever. But that's not what I want; I knew that even before I spoke with her. What I wanted was simply to be believed. I wanted to know that what I saw and felt in Brodie's Watch was real. No, I'm not afraid of Captain Brodie's ghost.

What terrifies me is the possibility that he doesn't exist and I'm going insane.

As I wait for my order of fried chicken, I scroll through the messages on my phone. I had muted it during my meeting with Maeve and now I see several new voice mails. The first is from my editor, Simon, who's called again about the status of my overdue manuscript. *The chapters you've sent me are terrific! When can I see more? Also, we need to talk about a new release date.*

I'll email him tomorrow. At least I can report this much: the book is still going well. (And my carpenters are gaining weight.) I scroll through the next two voicemails, both from spam callers, and come to a familiar number.

At 1:23 P.M., Lucy called.

I don't listen to her message; I can't bring myself to hear her voice.

Instead I focus on my meal, which has just arrived. The fried chicken is dry and stringy and the mashed potatoes taste like they came out of a box. Even though I missed lunch I have no appetite, but I force myself to eat. I won't think about Lucy or Simon or the book I need to finish. No, I'll think instead about the ghost, which has become a welcome distraction. Maeve assures me that other people, sane people, see ghosts. I can certainly use a ghost's company and the house is more than big enough for us to share. What lonely woman *wouldn't* want to share her bed with a strapping sea captain?

Where have you been, Captain Brodie? Will I see you tonight?

I pay for my barely eaten meal and get back on the road.

By the time I arrive home, night has fallen. It's so dark I have to feel my way up the porch steps, and when I reach the front door I halt, every nerve humming. Even in the gloom, I can see the door is ajar.

Today is Friday so Billy and Ned would have been working in the house, but they would never leave the door unlocked. I think of everyone else who might have a key to the front door: Donna Branca. Arthur Sherbrooke. The tenant who lived here just before me. Did Charlotte forget to return her key when she left? Has someone else gotten hold of it?

A loud meow issues from inside the house and Hannibal pushes his head out to greet me. My clever coon cat has been known to twist knobs and push open doors and he looks utterly unperturbed. Since he's not alarmed, surely everything must be fine inside.

I give the door a gentle push and it gives an alarmingly loud squeal as it swings open. I flip on the light switch and I see nothing amiss in the foyer. Hannibal sits at my feet, tail twitching, meowing for his dinner. Maybe Ned did forget to lock the door. Maybe Hannibal managed to open it.

Maybe the ghost did it.

I follow Hannibal into the kitchen and flip on the light. He crosses straight to the cabinet where he knows the cat food is stored, but I'm no longer looking at him. I'm focused instead on a clump of dirt on the floor.

And the shoeprint.

I spot another print, and another, and I follow the trail backward to its origin: the kitchen window, gaping open.

Ten

The police search every room, every closet of my house. By *the police*, I mean Officer Quinn and Officer Tarr. The Hare and the Tortoise is what first came to mind when I watched them step out of their patrol car, the younger Quinn springing out of the passenger seat like a rabbit while fiftyish Officer Tarr slowly oozed his way out of the driver's seat. With indolent Tarr at the wheel, no wonder they had taken forty-five minutes to respond to my 911 call.

But respond they finally did, and they approach this break-in with all the gravity of a murder investigation. They accompany me upstairs to the bedrooms, Officer Quinn taking the steps at a quick hop while Tarr lumbers behind him, and I confirm that nothing seems to be missing or out of place. While Tarr painstakingly writes in his notebook, Quinn searches the closets, then dashes up to the turret to confirm the intruder is not lurking upstairs.

Back downstairs in the kitchen, they take a closer look at the shoeprints, which are too large to be mine. Then Tarr turns his attention to the open window, the obvious point of entry.

"Was this window open like this when you left the house?" he asks me.

"I'm not sure. I know I had it open this morning, while I was cooking breakfast." I pause, unable to remember whether I'd closed it without latching it. Lately I've been so distracted, by the book, by the ghost, that details I *should* remember have been slipping past me. *Like where I got those bruises.*

"Have you seen anyone hanging around here lately? Anyone suspicious?"

"No. I mean, there are two carpenters who've been working on the house, but I wouldn't call them suspicious."

He turns to a fresh page in his notebook. "Their names?"

"Ned and Billy." Their last names have slipped my mind and Tarr glances up at me.

"Ned? Ned Haskell?"

"Right, that's his name."

There's a silence as he mulls over this information, a silence that makes me uneasy. "They already have access to the house," I point out. "I leave a key for them. They could just walk in the front door, so they'd have no need to climb in through the window."

Tarr's gaze slowly pans the kitchen and comes to a stop at my laptop computer, which sits undisturbed on the kitchen table, still powered on and plugged in. His gaze travels, sloth-like, to the countertop where a handful of spare change sits in a bowl, untouched. While Officer Tarr may be slow-moving, he is not stupid, and he's reading the clues, which lead to a baffling conclusion.

"The intruder pops off the window screen, tosses it in the bushes," he says, thinking aloud. "Climbs through the open window and proceeds to track dirt across this floor." His tortoise-like head dips down as he follows the shoeprints, which fade away halfway across the kitchen. "He's in your house yet he doesn't take a single valuable item. Leaves the laptop sitting there. Doesn't even scoop up the spare change."

"So this wasn't a robbery?" says Quinn.

"I'm not ready to say that yet."

"Why didn't he take anything?"

"Maybe because he never got the chance." Tarr lumbers out of the kitchen into the foyer. Grunting, he slowly drops to a crouch. Only then do I notice what he's looking at: a clump of dirt just inside the threshold of the front door, which I'd missed earlier.

"Cast off from his shoes," says Tarr. "Funny, isn't it? He didn't track dirt anywhere else in the house. Just in the kitchen and here, on his way out the front door. Which makes me think . . ."

"What?" I ask.

"Why did he leave so quickly? He didn't take anything. Didn't go upstairs. Just climbed in the window, walked across the kitchen, and then left the house in such a hurry he didn't even bother to close the door." Tarr grunts as he rises back to his feet. The effort leaves his face flushed a bright red. "That's the puzzle, isn't it?"

The three of us stand silent for a moment, considering the explanation for the intruder's odd behavior. Hannibal slinks past me and sprawls at the feet of Officer Tarr, whose torpor seems to match his own.

"Obviously something scared him off," offers Quinn. "Maybe he saw her headlights coming up the driveway and ran."

"But I didn't see anyone," I tell him. "And there was no car in the driveway when I got home."

"If it was a kid, he might not have come in a car," says Quinn. "Could've walked here using the cliff path. The trailhead starts at the public beach only a mile from here. Yeah, I bet that's what we're dealing with. Some kid who thought he was breaking into a vacant house. It's happened here before."

"So I've heard," I say, remembering what Ned had told me about the Halloween break-in and the unfortunate girl who fell to her death from the widow's walk.

"We'll just give you the same advice we gave her. Keep the doors and windows locked. And let us know if—"

"Her?" I look back and forth at the two officers. "Who are you talking about?"

"The lady who was renting the house before you. The school-teacher."

"Charlotte had a break-in, too?"

"She was in bed when she heard a noise downstairs. Came down to find a window open. By then he was gone, and nothing was taken."

I look down at the clump of dirt, cast off from the shoe of the intruder who violated my home tonight. An intruder who might still have been here in my house as my car came up the driveway. Suddenly I am shivering and I hug myself. "What if it wasn't just some kid who did this?" I ask quietly.

"Tucker Cove is a very safe town, ma'am," says Officer Quinn. "There's the occasional shoplifter, sure, but we haven't had a major incident in—"

"It's always smart to take precautions," interjects Tarr. "Keep your doors and windows locked. And maybe think about getting a dog." He looks at Hannibal, who's contentedly purring against his boot. "I don't think your cat here's scary enough to chase off a burglar."

But I know someone who is. *The ghost.*

I bolt the front door and walk through the first floor of the house, closing and latching all the windows. The police have checked every room, every closet, but I am still jittery and certainly not ready to go to bed.

So I go into the kitchen and pour myself a glass of whiskey. And then another.

The second bottle is nearly empty. When I moved into Brodie's Watch, this bottle was full; have I really gone through all the whiskey that quickly? I know I should limit myself to one drink, but after this truly disturbing day, I need a comforting sip. I carry my glass and the bottle with its last few inches of whiskey and head upstairs.

In my bedroom, I cannot help but scan the room as I unbutton my blouse and slide off my blue jeans. Standing in only my underwear, I feel exposed, although there is no one else here. No one, at least, that I can see. The ocean is restless tonight, and through the open window I hear the swoosh of waves rolling ashore. Black as oil, the sea stretches out to a starlit horizon. Although my room looks out over deserted cliffs and water, I understand why Charlotte wanted curtains over this window. The night itself seems to have eyes that can see me, standing here framed in the light.

I turn off the lamp and let darkness cloak me. No longer do I feel exposed as I stand at the window, letting the cool air wash over my skin. I will miss this when I return to Boston, these nights of falling asleep to the sound of the waves, the salt air on my skin. What if I never go home to the city? Lately this possibility has been on my mind more and more. After all, I can work anywhere, write anywhere; I have burned my bridges in Boston, carelessly torched my old life like a drunken arsonist. Why not stay here in Tucker Cove, in this house?

I pull on my nightgown, and as it slips over my head, I glimpse a flicker of light beyond my window. It flares for just an instant, then vanishes.

I stare out at the night. I know there is nothing out there but the cliff and the sea—where did that light come from? I'm invisible in my dark bedroom, but only moments ago, anyone watching this window would have seen me standing here undressed, and the thought makes me back away, deeper into the gloom. Then I see more flashes of light, bobbing like a cinder adrift in the wind. It floats past the window and winks away into the night.

A firefly.

I sip my whiskey and think of other warm summer nights when Lucy and I would chase fireflies on our grandparents' farm. Running through a meadow that glittered with a thousand stars, we'd swing our nets and trap entire galaxies in Mason jars. Back to the farmhouse we'd go, like twin fairies carrying our firefly lanterns. The memory is so vivid I can feel the grass tickling my feet, and once again I hear the creak of the screen door as we stepped back into the house. I remember how we stayed awake half the night, marveling at the lights whirling inside our jars, one on her nightstand, the other on mine. A matched pair, like Lucy and me.

The way we used to be.

I empty the last of the whiskey into my glass, gulp it down, and stretch out on the bed.

It's now the fourth night since Captain Brodie last appeared. I've lain awake for far too many hours, plagued by doubts that he exists. Wondering if my sanity has finally cracked. Today, when I visited the ghost hunter, what I'd wanted most was her reassurance that I'm not delusional, that what I've experienced is real. Now my doubts are back.

God, I need to sleep. What I would give for just one good night's sleep. I'm tempted to go down to the kitchen and open a new bottle of wine. Another glass or two might quiet this electric hum in my brain.

Hannibal, lying beside me on the bed, suddenly lifts his head. His tufted ears are pricked up and alert as he stares toward the open window. I see nothing unusual there, no telltale swirl of mist, no thickening shadow.

I climb out of bed and gaze out at the sea. "Come back to me," I plead. "Please come back."

A touch grazes my arm, but surely it's just my imagination. Has my desperate longing for company conjured up a ghostly caress from the mere whisper of a breeze? But now I feel the warm weight of a hand resting on my shoulder. I turn and *there he is,* standing face-to-face with me. As real as any man can be.

I blink away tears. "I thought I would never see you again."

"You have missed me."

"Yes."

"How much, Ava?"

I sigh and close my eyes as his fingers stroke down my cheek. "God, so much. You're all I think about. All I . . ."

"Desire?"

The question, asked so softly, sends a sudden thrill through me. I open my eyes and look at a face obscured by shadow. In the starlight I see only the sharp cliff of his nose, the jutting cheekbones. What more does the darkness hide?

"Do you desire me?" he asks.

"Yes."

He strokes my face, and although his fingers are gentle, my skin feels scorched by his touch. "And you will submit?"

I swallow hard. I don't know what he wants, but I am ready to say yes. To anything.

"What would you have me do?" I ask.

"As much as you are willing."

"Tell me."

"You are no virgin. You have known men."

"Yes, I have."

"Men with whom you have sinned."

My answer is barely a whisper. "Yes."

"Sins for which you have not yet atoned." His hand, which had so gently cupped my face, suddenly tightens on my jaw. I stare straight into his eyes. He knows. Somehow he has looked into my soul and has seen my guilt. My shame.

"I know what torments you, Ava. And I know what you desire. Will you submit?"

"I don't understand."

"Say it." He leans closer. "Say you will submit."

My voice is barely audible. "I will submit."

"And you know who I am."

"Jeremiah Brodie."

"I am the ship's master. I command. You obey."

"What if I choose not to?"

"Then I will bide my time and wait for a woman more suited to my attentions. And you will depart this house." Already I feel his touch melting away, see his face dissolving into shadow.

"Please," I call out. "Don't leave me!"

"You must agree."

"I do."

"To submit?"

"Yes."

"To obey?"

"Yes."

"Even if there is pain?"

At this I go silent. "How much pain?" I whisper.

"Enough to make your pleasure all the sweeter."

He strokes my breast and his caress is warm and gentle. I sigh and my head rolls back. I crave more, so much more. He traps my nipple and my knees go weak as the unexpected pain blooms into pleasure.

"When you are ready," he whispers, "I will be here."

I open my eyes, and he is gone.

I stand alone in my room, shaking, my legs unsteady. My breast tingles, the nipple still tender from his assault. I am wet, so wet with desire that I feel moisture trickle down my thigh. My body aches to be filled, to be claimed, but he has abandoned me.

Or was he ever really here?

Eleven

The next morning, I awaken with a fever.

The sun has already burned away the mist and birds are chirping outside, but the soft sea air that wafts in through the open window feels like an arctic blast. Chilled and shivering, I stumble out of bed to close the window and then crawl back under the bedcovers. I don't want to get up. I don't want to eat. I just want to stop shaking. I curl up into a ball and sink into a deep, exhausted sleep.

All day I stay in bed, rising only to use the toilet or take sips of water. My head pounds and sunlight hurts my eyes so I pull the covers over my head.

I barely hear the voice calling my name. A woman's voice.

When I peel back the comforter, I see that daylight has faded and the room is deep in shadow. I lie half awake, wondering if someone really was calling to me, or if I'd merely dreamt it. And how is it possible I've slept all day? Why didn't Hannibal claw me awake, demanding his breakfast?

Through aching eyes, I scan the room, but my cat is nowhere to be seen, and the bedroom door is wide open.

Someone pounds on the door downstairs, and again I hear my name. So it wasn't a dream after all.

I don't really want to drag myself out of bed, but whoever's knocking on the door sounds like she is not giving up. I pull on a robe and wobble out of the room to the stairs. Twilight has darkened the house and I feel my way down the steps, holding on to the banister as I descend. When I reach the foyer, I'm startled to see that the front door is open and my visitor stands silhouetted in the doorway, backlit by car headlights.

I fumble for the wall switch and when I flip it on, the foyer lights are so bright they hurt my eyes. Still dazed, I need a moment to retrieve her name from my memory, even though it was only yesterday when I spoke to her, yesterday when I visited her house.

"Maeve?" I finally manage to say.

"I tried calling you. When you didn't answer the phone, I thought I'd drive up here anyway, just to take a look at the house. I found your front door wide open." She frowns at me. "Are you all right?"

A wave of dizziness sends me reeling and I grab the banister. The room sways and Maeve's face goes out of focus. Suddenly the floor falls away and I'm tumbling, tumbling into the abyss.

I hear Maeve cry out: "Ava!"

And then I don't hear anything at all.

I don't know how I ended up on the parlor sofa, but that's where I now find myself lying. Someone has lit a fire and flames dance in the hearth, a cheery illusion of warmth which has not yet penetrated the blankets now shrouding me.

"Your blood pressure is up to ninety over sixty. That's much better now. I think you were just dehydrated and that's why you blacked out."

Dr. Ben Gordon removes the cuff and the Velcro gives a loud crackle as it peels away from my arm. It's a rare doctor who makes house calls these days, but maybe that's how life still is in small towns like Tucker Cove. It took only a phone call from Maeve, and twenty minutes later, Ben Gordon walked into my house with his black bag and a look of concern.

"She was already conscious by the time I called you," Maeve says. "And she absolutely refused to go anywhere by ambulance."

"Because I fainted, that's all it was," I tell him. "I've been lying in bed all day and I haven't had anything to eat."

Dr. Gordon turns to Maeve. "Could you bring her another glass of orange juice? Let's fill up her tank."

"Coming right up," says Maeve and she heads to the kitchen.

"Such a lot of fuss." I sigh. "I'm feeling much better now."

"You didn't look very good when I arrived. I was ready to send you to the ER."

"For what, the flu?"

"It could be the flu. Or it could be something else." He peels back the blankets to examine me and immediately focuses on my right arm. "What happened here? How did you get these?"

I look at the series of tiny blisters that track across my skin. "That's nothing. It was just a scratch."

"I noticed your cat. A really big cat. He was sitting on the porch."

"Yes. His name's Hannibal."

"Named after Hannibal who crossed the Alps?"

"No, Hannibal Lecter, the serial killer. If you knew my cat, you'd understand how he got the name."

"And when did your serial killer cat scratch you?"

"About a week ago, I think. It doesn't hurt. It's just a little itchy."

He extends my arm and leans in to examine me, his fingers probing my armpit. There is something deeply intimate about the way his head is bent so close to mine. He smells like laundry soap and wood smoke and I notice strands of silver mingled in his brown hair. He has gentle hands, warm hands, and all at once I'm painfully aware that under my nightgown, I'm wearing nothing at all.

"Your axillary lymph nodes are enlarged," he says, frowning.

"What does that mean?"

"Let me examine the other side." As he reaches out to examine my other armpit, he brushes across my breast and my nipple tingles, tightens. I'm forced to look away so he can't see that my face is flushed.

"I don't feel any enlarged nodes on this side, which is good," he says. "I'm pretty sure I know what the problem—"

A loud crash startles us. We both stare at the shattered remains of a vase lying on the floor. A vase that a moment earlier was perched on the mantelpiece.

"I swear I didn't touch it!" says Maeve, who's just returned to the parlor with a glass of orange juice. She frowns at the shards of glass. "How on earth did that fall off?"

"Things don't just fly off shelves on their own," says Dr. Gordon.

"No." Maeve looks at me with a strange expression and says quietly: "They don't."

"It must have been right on the edge," he offers, an explanation that sounds perfectly logical. "Some vibration finally tipped it over."

I can't help glancing around the room, searching for an invisible culprit. I know that Maeve is thinking the same thing I am: *The ghost did it.* But I would never say that to Dr. Gordon, man of science. Already he's resumed examining me. He palpates my neck, listens to my heart, and probes my belly.

"Your spleen feels perfectly normal." He covers me with the blanket and sits up straight. "I think I know what the problem is. This is a classic case of Bartonellosis. A bacterial infection."

"Oh my god, that sounds serious," says Maeve. "Can we catch it, too?"

"Only if you own a cat." He looks at me. "It's also called cat scratch disease. It's usually not serious, but it can lead to fevers and swollen lymph nodes. And in rare cases, encephalopathy."

"It can affect the brain?" I ask.

"Yes, but you seem alert and oriented. And certainly not delusional." He smiles. "I'll go out on a limb here and pronounce you sane."

Something he might not say if he knew what I experienced last night. I feel Maeve studying me. Does she wonder, as I'm wondering now, if my visions of Captain Brodie were nothing more than the product of a fevered mind?

Dr. Gordon reaches into his black bag. "The drug companies always leave me plenty of free samples and I think I have some azithromycin in here." He digs out a blister pack of pills. "You're not allergic to any medicines are you?"

"No."

"Then this antibiotic should do the trick. Follow the instructions on the packet until all the pills are gone. Come into my office next week, so I can recheck those lymph nodes. I'll have my receptionist call you and book the appointment." He snaps his black bag shut and looks me up and down. "Eat something, Ava. I think that's also why you're feeling weak. Plus, you could use a few extra pounds."

As he walks out of the house, Maeve and I are silent. We hear the front door close and then Hannibal struts into the room, looking completely innocent as he sits by the fireplace, calmly licking his paw. The cat who started all this trouble.

"Wish my doctor looked like *him*," says Maeve.

"How did you happen to call Dr. Gordon?"

"His name was on the list by the kitchen phone. Numbers for the plumber, doctor, and electrician. I just assumed he was your doctor."

"Oh, that list. It was left by the previous tenant." Dr. Gordon, it seems, is a popular choice in town.

Maeve settles into the armchair across from me and the firelight glows like a halo in her hair, highlighting the silver streaks. "It's lucky I happened to come by your house tonight. I hate to think of you falling down the stairs, with no one around to find you."

"I feel much better now, thank you. But I don't think I'm up to showing you around the house tonight. If you'd like to come back another time, I can walk you through the place then. Show you where I've seen the ghost."

Maeve looks up at the ceiling, at the play of firelight and shadow. "I really just wanted to get a sense of this house."

"And do you? Sense something?"

"I thought I did, just a while ago. When I came back into this room, with your juice. And that vase suddenly hit the floor." She glances at the spot where the broken vase had landed and she shivers. "I did feel *something*."

"Good? Bad?"

She looks at me. "Not entirely friendly."

Hannibal leaps onto the sofa and curls up at my feet. My twenty-six-pound furball, whom I have not seen all day. He does not look hungry, but seems perfectly content. What has he been eating lately? Suddenly I remember what Maeve had said earlier: *Your front door was wide open.* Hannibal must have gone outside and hunted down his own dinner.

"This is the second time my front door's been left open," I tell her. "Last night, when I got home after visiting you, I also found it hanging open. And I called the police."

"Don't you usually lock your door?"

"I *know* I locked it last night, before I went to bed. I don't understand how it ended up open again."

"And it was wide open, Ava. As if the house was asking me inside to check on you." She mulls over the evening's strange events.

"But when that vase shattered, everything felt different. That was definitely *not* a welcome. It was hostile." She looks at me. "Have you ever felt that in this house?"

"Hostility? No. Never."

"Then perhaps this entity has accepted you. Maybe it's even protecting you." She looks toward the front hall. "And it invited me into the house because it knew you needed my help. Thank god I didn't just leave the papers on your doorstep and drive away."

"What papers?" I ask.

"I told you I was going to check the newspaper archives about your house. Right after you left yesterday, I called my friend at the Maine State Library. She was able to dig up several documents this morning relating to a Captain Jeremiah Brodie of Tucker Cove. Let me get those papers for you. I left them in my car."

While I wait for her return, I can already feel my pulse kick up to a gallop. I've learned just the barest details about Captain Brodie and have seen only the one portrait of him in the historical society. All I really know about him is how he died, on a storm-tossed ocean, his ship battered by wind and waves.

That is why you carry the scent of the sea.

Maeve returns from her car and places a folder in my hands. "My friend made photocopies for you."

I open it to the first photocopy and see a page filled with ornately looping handwriting. It is a ship's register, dated September 4, 1862, and I instantly recognize the name: *The Minotaur.*

His ship.

"Those papers are just a start," says Maeve. "I expect my friend will turn up much more, and I'll check your local historical society. But for now, that will give you some idea of the man who may be haunting this house."

Twelve

By the next morning, my fever has broken and I wake up feeling famished but still weak. I wobble downstairs to the kitchen, where I find Hannibal finishing up the last nuggets of dry cat food in his bowl. Maeve must have filled it before she left last night. No wonder I wasn't rudely awakened this morning by a demanding claw to the chest. I fire up the coffeemaker, scramble three eggs with a dash of cream, and drop two slices of bread in the toaster. I devour it all, and by the time I finish my second cup of coffee, I'm feeling human again and ready to focus on the documents that Maeve left me.

I open the folder and find the ship's registry for *The Minotaur*. Last night, I'd had trouble reading the ornate handwriting, but now, in the bright morning light, I'm able to decipher the faded description of Captain Brodie's doomed ship. Launched September 4, 1862, *The Minotaur* was built by Goss, Sawyer & Packard in Bath, Maine. Wooden hulled and classified as a "Down Easter," she was a three-masted sailing ship, 250 feet long, 44 feet wide, and she weighed a little over two tons. She required a crew of thirty-five. Owned by the Charles Thayer syndicate of Portland, *The Minotaur* was a merchant vessel built for speed, but she was also rugged enough to survive the brutal passage around the Cape of Good Hope as she sailed between the Maine coast and the Far East.

I page through the next documents, which list the ship's voyages, the various ports she visited, and the cargoes she carried. Sailing to Shanghai, she carried animal hides and sugar, wool and something called case oil. On her return to America, she carried tea and silk, ivory and carpets. On her maiden voyage, she was under the command of Captain Jeremiah Brodie.

For twelve years, he was master of *The Minotaur* as she sailed to Shanghai and Macau, San Francisco and London. While these ship's documents do not tell me what he was paid for his services, it is clear from this house he built, with its grand proportions and fine woodwork, that his income from these voyages must have been handsome, but it was also hard-earned. After toiling so many months at sea, what joy he must have felt when he could finally return to this house and sleep in a bed that did not sway, and dine on fresh meat and greens pulled straight from the garden.

I flip past the registry pages and find a photocopied news clipping from the *Camden Herald,* January 1875.

Tragedy has befallen yet another Maine vessel in the turbulent waters off the Cape of Good Hope. The Down Easter *The Minotaur,* which sailed from Tucker Harbor six months ago, is now believed lost at sea. She last put in to port in Rio de Janeiro on the 8th of September and departed three days later, bound for Shanghai. Her route would have taken her round the fearsome cape, where heavy winds and monstrous waves regularly threaten the lives of the daring souls who brave the sea. It is in these waters that *The Minotaur* most likely met her terrible end. A portion of the mail bags she was carrying, as

well as splintered fragments of wood, have washed ashore at
Port Elizabeth near the southern tip of Africa. Among the
thirty-six souls presumed lost was Captain Jeremiah Brodie of
Tucker Harbor, an experienced ship's master under whose
command *The Minotaur* had safely made the same passage five
times previously. That a seasoned captain and crew on a sound
ship could meet their doom on a voyage so familiar to them is
a reminder that the sea is both perilous and unforgiving.

I open my laptop and google *the Cape of Good Hope*. It is a cru-
elly misleading name for the passage that was once called, by the
Portuguese, "the Cape of Storms." I study photos of terrifying
waves crashing on a rocky coastline. I imagine the howl of the
wind, the groan of ship's timbers, and the horror of watching your
men wash overboard as the rocks loom ever closer. So this was
where he died. The sea claims even the ablest sailor.

I turn the page, expecting to read more details of the tragedy.
Instead I find several photocopied pages of a handwritten letter,
dated a year before the sinking of *The Minotaur*. In the top corner
is a yellow Post-it on which either Maeve or her research librarian
friend has jotted an explanatory note:

Found this among papers from the estate of a Mrs. Ellen
Graham, died 1922. Note the reference to *The Minotaur*.

The letter itself appears written by a woman's hand, the words
neatly and elegantly formed.

Dearest Ellen,

*I send this latest news to you, along with the bolt of China silk which
you have so eagerly awaited all these months. The shipment arrived last
week aboard* The Minotaur, *a vast array of silks which were all so
tempting that Mama and I were quite unable to decide which ones to
purchase. We had to make our choices quickly, because all the young la-*

dies in town will soon be clamoring to snatch up what they can. Mama and I chose bolts of rose pink and canary yellow. For you, I chose the green, because I think it will suit your red hair quite nicely. How fortunate we were to have our pick of the treasures straight from the ship. By next week, the rest will be on their way to shops up and down the coast.

Our good fortune in this regard is courtesy of Mama's cordial relations with our seamstress, Mrs. Stephens, whose husband serves as Captain Brodie's first mate. She was kind enough to alert Mama about the bounty of silks that had just arrived, and we were invited to the warehouse to peruse the treasures on the very day they were unloaded.

Despite all the pretty silks and carpets, I admit I was quite distracted by another sight: the fine figure of Captain Brodie himself, who strode into the warehouse a short time after Mama and I arrived. I was crouching over a crate of silk when I heard him speaking to the warehouseman. I looked up and there he stood, framed by the light in the doorway, and I was so startled I must have looked like quite the codfish with my mouth agape. I do not think he noticed me at first, so I was quite at liberty to stare. When he last sailed from Tucker Harbor, I was but thirteen years old. Now it is three years later and I'm fully capable of appreciating a broad pair of shoulders and a fine square jaw. I must have stared for a good long minute before he noticed me and smiled.

And, dear Ellen, did I mention he is not married?

If he'd spoken to me, I do not think I could have managed to say a single word. But just then, Mama took my arm and said quietly: "We've made our purchases, Ionia. It's time for us to leave."

I did not want to leave. I could have stood in that cold warehouse for an eternity, staring at the captain and basking in the warmth of his smile. Mama was insistent that we hurry away, so I had only those few precious moments to admire him. I truly believed he returned my look with similar appreciation, but when I told Mama, she warned me not to entertain such thoughts.

"Keep your wits about you, for pity's sake," she told me. "You're just a girl. If you're not careful, a man will take advantage."

Is it wicked of me that I rather like that idea?

Next week, there will be a dinner party for the ship's officers at Brodie's Watch. I have been invited, but Mama has turned down the invitation! My friend Genevieve will be going, and Lydia too, but Mama insists I must stay home. Quietly knitting, I suppose, like the future spinster I will surely be. I am almost as old as the other girls, and I am certainly old enough to attend a dinner party with gentlemen, but Mama has forbidden it. It is so unfair! She says I am too innocent. She says I do not know the captain's sordid reputation. She has heard rumors about what goes on in his house late into the night. When I press her on this matter, her lips tighten like purse strings and she refuses to say more.

Oh, Ellen, it is sheer misery to know what I will be missing. I think of that grand house on the hill. I think of those other girls smiling at him (and even worse, of him smiling back at them*). I live in dread of some future wedding announcement. What if he chooses Genevieve or Lydia as his wife?*

It will all be Mama's fault.

I pause, my gaze returning to that sentence at the top of the page. *Mama says I do not know the captain's sordid reputation. She has heard rumors.*

What rumors might they be? What could have so scandalized Ionia's mother that she forbade her sixteen-year-old daughter from any contact with Brodie? There would be the age difference, as well. The year this letter was written, Jeremiah Brodie would have been thirty-eight years old, more than twice the girl's age, and based on her description of him, a strapping man in his masculine prime. I think of the portrait I saw hanging in the historical society, and can imagine how he must have set every young lady's heart aflutter. He was a man of the world, commander of a sailing vessel, and the master of this grand house on the hill. He was also unmarried; what young lady wouldn't want to catch his eye?

I imagine the dinner party at Brodie's Watch and picture the cooks and servants bustling about in this kitchen where I'm now sitting. And in the dining room would be ship's officers and flickering candles and young ladies dressed in those shimmering silks that *The Minotaur* had brought from China. There would be laughter and wine and more than a few amorous glances exchanged. And at the head of the table would be Jeremiah Brodie, whose notorious reputation made him off-limits for at least one innocent young lady.

Hungry to know more about his reputation, I turn to the next page of the letter. I'm disappointed to find only one final paragraph by Ionia.

Please, can you speak to your mama on my behalf? Ask her to speak to mine? The times have changed, and we are not the hothouse flowers they were at our age. If I cannot go to the party, I must find some other way to see him again. The Minotaur *is in need of repairs and remains in dock at least until May. Surely other opportunities will arise before my captain once again sets sail!*

As always, Ionia

I don't know Ionia's surname or what became of her, but I do know that three months after she wrote this letter, Captain Brodie would set sail on his doomed voyage.

I set down the pages, thinking of what she'd written: *She says I am too innocent. She has heard rumors about what goes on in his house late into the night.* I think of him standing in my bedroom. I think of his hand on my breast. And his words:

Do you submit?

My heart is pounding, my skin flushed. No, he is not a man suitable for the innocent Ionias of the world. He is a man who knows what he wants, and what he wants is a woman willing to take a bite of a dangerous apple. A woman willing to be led into a dark game where he holds all the power. Where the ultimate delights begin with complete surrender.

I am ready to play his game.

Thirteen

That night I sip wine as I take a long bath in the claw-foot tub. When I emerge I am flushed and rosy. I smooth lotion on my arms and legs and pull on a sheer nightgown as if preparing to meet a lover, even though I don't know if he'll appear tonight.

I don't even know if he's real.

In the darkness I lie in bed, waiting to catch the first whiff of the ocean. That is how I will know he's arrived, when I smell the sea that took him, and where his bones now rest. Hannibal lies curled up beside me, his purrs vibrating against my leg. Tonight there is no moon and only starlight glitters in the window. In the gloom, I can faintly make out the shapes of the dresser, the nightstand, the lamp.

Hannibal's head snaps up and the cold, bracing scent suddenly engulfs me, as if a wave has roared into the room. This time there is no premonitory swirl of shadow, no slowly forming silhouette. I look up and there he is, fully formed, standing over my bed. He is silent, but I can feel his gaze stripping away the darkness between us, leaving me utterly exposed.

He reaches down to take my hand. At his touch, I rise from the bed as though magically weightless and stand before him. Clad only in my nightgown, I am shivering from both anticipation and the damp sea air.

"Close your eyes," he commands.

I obey and wait for his next command. For something, anything to happen. *Yes, I am ready.*

His words are just a whisper: "Behold, Ava."

I open my eyes and gasp in wonder. Although we must still be standing in my bedroom, I do not recognize the green velvet drapes hanging at the windows nor the chinoiserie wallpaper nor the massive four-poster bed. In the hearth a fire crackles and the light from its flames dances on the walls, gilding everything in a golden glow.

"How can this be?" I murmur. "Is this a dream?"

He presses his fingers to my lips to silence me. "Do you wish to see more?"

"Yes. Yes!"

"Come." Still holding my hand, he leads me out of the bedroom. Looking down at our entwined hands, I see lace at my wrists. Only then do I realize my flimsy nightdress has vanished; in its place is a blue gown made of shimmering silk, like the bolts of fabric that once arrived aboard *The Minotaur.* Surely I *am* dreaming. At this moment, do I slumber in my bed while dream-Ava is led out of the bedroom?

In the hallway too, everything is different. The carpet is woven with a pattern of vines, and on the walls, candles burn in brass sconces, illuminating a series of portraits I do not recognize. In silence he leads me past the paintings and opens the door to the turret staircase.

The steps are in shadow, but a sliver of light shines under the closed door above. As I place my weight on the first step I expect to hear the familiar creak, but the board is silent; the creak is yet to come, in a century that has not yet dawned. All I hear is the whisper of silk against my legs, and the thud of his boots as he leads me up the stairs. Why are we going to the turret? What awaits me there? Even if I want to retreat, I cannot; his grasp has tightened and is now inescapable. I have made my choice and am now at his mercy.

We emerge into a room bathed in candlelight.

I stare, enchanted. Mirrors hang on every wall and I see reflection after reflection of myself, a multitude of blue-gowned Avas stretching into eternity. Many times have I stood in this same room and seen carpenters' tools and disrepair. Never had I imagined it as it is now, glittering with light, a room of mirrors and . . .

An alcove.

Red velvet curtains conceal the space that until last week was closed off by a wall. What lies behind those drapes?

"You are afraid," he observes.

"No." I swallow, and then admit the truth. "Yes."

"Yet you still submit?"

I stare up at him. Here is the man I saw in the painting: windswept black hair, face like rough-hewn granite. But now I see more than a mere painting could reveal. There is a hungry glitter in his eyes that warns of dangerous appetites. I can still retreat. I can flee from this room, from this house.

But I don't. I want to know what happens next.

"I submit," I answer.

His smile sends a shiver through me. He is in control now, and I feel as naïve as sixteen-year-old Ionia, a virgin in the hands of a man whose cravings will now be revealed. With the back of his hand he strokes my face, and his touch is so gentle I close my eyes and sigh. Nothing to fear. Everything to look forward to.

He leads me to the alcove and draws aside the curtain, revealing what lies beyond: a bed, draped in black silk. But the bed is not what rivets my attention; no, it's what dangles from each of the bed's four oaken posts.

Leather cuffs.

He grasps my shoulders and suddenly I am falling backward, onto the bed. My dress splays out across the sheets, silk against silk, blue on shimmering black. Without a word he wraps a leather cuff around my right wrist, drawing it so tight that I have no hope of slipping free. He circles the bed to secure my left wrist, moving with inexorable purpose. For the first time I am afraid, because when I look in to his eyes, I see a man who is in complete control. There is nothing I can do now to stop what is about to happen.

He moves to the foot of the bed, sweeps up the hem of my gown, and takes hold of my right foot so suddenly that I gasp. In seconds the leather cuff is looped around my ankle and pulled tight. Three of my limbs are now restrained. Even if I want to, I cannot free myself. I am pinned and helpless as he wraps the final strap around my left ankle and secures it to the bedpost. I lie spread-eagled, my heart battering my chest, waiting for whatever comes next.

For a moment he merely stands at the foot of the bed and admires the view. His arousal is obvious, yet he makes no move and simply savors my helplessness as his gaze devours my pinned body, my rumpled dress. Not a word passes his lips, and the silence alone is exquisite torment.

He reaches into his boot and pulls out a knife.

In fear I watch him hold up the blade to the candlelight and stare at the gleam reflected in the metal. Without warning he grasps the neckline of my dress and slashes the fabric, keeps slashing all the way down the skirt. He yanks open the ruined dress, exposing my flesh, and tosses aside the knife. He needs no blade to threaten me; he does so with his gaze alone, his eyes promising both pleasure and punishment. I flinch as he leans over to stroke my face, his fingers sliding down my neck, my breastbone, my belly. He smiles as he reaches between my legs. "Would you have me stop?"

"No. I don't *want* you to stop." I close my eyes and sigh. "I want more. I want *you*."

"Even if it makes you scream?"

I stare up at him. "Scream?"

"Is it not what you want? To be taken, to be punished?" In the flickering candlelight his smile suddenly looks cruel. Satanic. "I know what you crave, Ava. I know your darkest, most shameful desires. I know what you deserve."

Oh god, is this really happening? Is this real?

The man who now strips off his shirt and breeches is very real indeed, and all too imposing. It is the weight of a real man I feel on top of me, a real man who pins me to the bed. My hips automatically rise to welcome him, because as fearful as I am of his power, hunger has swept me past the point of no return. He gives me no chance to brace myself; with one savage thrust he's inside me, driving deep.

"Fight me," he commands.

I cry out, but there is no one to hear me. No one within miles of this windswept, lonely house.

"Fight me!" I stare up into eyes lit with a raging fire. *This* is the game he plays. A game of conquest and submission. He does not want me to surrender; he wants me to resist. To be conquered.

I twist beneath him, bucking left and right. My struggles only arouse him and he thrusts even more deeply.

"*This* is what you want, is it not?"

"Yes," I groan.

"To be taken. To be mastered."

"Yes . . ."

"To be blameless."

I can fight him no longer because I'm lost in his game. Lost in the fantasy of complete surrender. My head rolls back and his lips press against my neck, his beard scraping across my throat. I cry out, a half-sob, half-scream as delicious waves surge through me. He lets out a roar of victory and collapses on top of me, his body so heavy that I cannot move, can scarcely breathe.

At last he stirs and lifts his head. I look up into his eyes, which only a moment before had burned with lust, a look that had both frightened and aroused me. What I see now is a different man. A man who quietly releases the straps around my wrists and ankles. As I rub my bruised flesh, I cannot believe this is the same raging animal who attacked me. Now I see a different man. Calm, subdued. Even tender.

He grasps my hand and pulls me to my feet. We stand face-to-face, naked and exposed to each other's eyes, but when I look in to his, I can read nothing. I might as well be staring at a portrait on the wall.

"Now you know my secret," he says. "As I know yours."

"Your secret?"

"My needs. My cravings." I shudder as he traces a finger along my collarbone. "Did I frighten you?"

"Yes," I whisper.

"You need not be afraid. I never damage my possessions."

"Is that what I am to you?"

"And it excites you, does it not? To be taken the way I took you tonight? Ridden hard and given no choice about what I choose to do to you?"

I swallow and take an unsteady breath. "Yes."

"Then you will welcome my next visit. It will be different."

"How?"

He lifts my chin and stares into my eyes with a look that makes me shiver. "Tonight, dear Ava, was about pleasure. But when I return?" He smiles. "It will be about pain."

Fourteen

Dr. Ben Gordon's receptionist looks old enough to be his grandmother. When I glance up at the row of pictures hanging in the waiting room, I spot her much-younger face, wearing the identical cat's-eye glasses, smiling from a photo that was taken forty-two years ago, when this same building was the office of Dr. Edward Gordon. And there she is again in another photo two decades later, her hair now half silver, posing with Dr. Paul Gordon. Dr. Ben Gordon is third in a line of Dr. Gordons who've practiced in Tucker Cove, and Miss Viletta Hutchins has been the receptionist for them all.

"You're lucky he could squeeze you in today," she tells me as she hands me a clipboard with a blank patient information sheet. "Normally he doesn't see patients on his lunch hour, but he said you were an urgent follow-up. With all these summer folks in town, his schedule's been booked solid for weeks."

"And I'm very lucky he makes house calls," I say, handing her my insurance card. "I didn't think any doctors still did."

Miss Hutchins looks up at me with a frown. "He made a house call?"

"Last week. After I fainted."

"Did he, now?" is all she says before she discreetly looks down again at the appointment book. In this age of electronic medical charts, it's quaint to see patients' names handwritten in ink. "Please have a seat, Ms. Collette."

I settle into a chair to fill out the patient information sheet. Name, address, health history. When I come to the blank for *Emergency Contact,* I hesitate. For a moment I stare at the blank where I have always before written Lucy's name. Instead I write Simon's name and phone number. He's not a blood relation, but at least he's still my friend. That's one bridge I haven't burned. Yet.

"Ava?" Ben Gordon stands in the doorway, smiling at me. "Let's go back and take a look at that arm, shall we?"

I leave the clipboard with the receptionist and follow him down the hallway to the exam room, where all the equipment looks reassuringly modern, unlike the ancient Miss Hutchins. As I climb up onto the exam table, he goes to the sink and washes his hands, like any good medical professional.

"How's the fever?" he asks.

"It's gone."

"Finished the antibiotics?"

"Every pill. Just as you instructed."

"Appetite? Energy?"

"I'm feeling pretty good, actually."

"Ah, a medical miracle! Every so often, I *do* get it right."

"And I really want to thank you."

"For doing what I'm trained to do?"

"For going out of your way to help me. I got the feeling, talking to your receptionist, that house calls aren't something you usually do."

"Well, it's what my grandfather and my dad did all the time. Brodie's Watch isn't that far out of town, so it was easy enough for

me to pop by. I wanted to save you a very expensive trip to the ER."
He dries his hands and turns to face me. "Now let's take a look at
the arm."

I unbutton my shirtsleeve cuff. "It looks a lot better, I think."

"No more scratches from that ferocious cat?"

"He's really not as vicious as he seems. The day he scratched
me, he was just startled." Startled by something I will not tell Dr.
Gordon about, because it might make him question my sanity. I
roll the sleeve above my elbow. "You can hardly see the scratches
anymore."

He examines the healed claw marks. "The papules are definitely clearing up. No fatigue, no headache?"

"No."

He extends my arm and probes my elbow. "Let's see if those
lymph nodes have gotten any smaller." He pauses, frowning at the
bruise encircling my wrist. Although it has faded, it is still apparent.

I tug my arm away from him and yank down the sleeve. "I'm
fine. Really."

"How did you get that bruise?"

"I probably bumped into something. I don't even remember."

"Is there anything you want to talk about? Anything at all?"

His question is asked quietly, gently. What safer place to confess the truth than here, to this man whose job it is to hear his
patients' most embarrassing secrets? But I don't say a word as I
button the cuff of my shirt.

"Is someone hurting you, Ava?"

"No." I force myself to meet his gaze and answer calmly: "It really is nothing."

After a moment he nods. "It's my job to protect the well-being
of my patients. I know you live all alone up there, and I want to
make sure you feel safe. That you *are* safe."

"I am. I mean, aside from having an attack cat."

At that he laughs, and the sound defuses the tension between us. He must sense that I haven't told him everything, but for now he's not pressing me for the truth. And what would he say if I *did* tell him about what happened to me in the turret? Would he be shocked to hear that I'd actually enjoyed it? That ever since that night, I've waited eagerly for my phantom lover to return?

"I don't see any need for a follow-up visit, unless your fever returns," he says and closes the chart. "How much longer will you be staying in Tucker Cove?"

"I've arranged to rent the house through the end of October, but I'm starting to think I may stay even longer. It's turned out to be the perfect place for me to write."

"Ah yes," he says, as he walks me back to the reception area. "I've heard all about your book. Billy Conway told me you served him a beef stew that was to die for."

"Is there *anyone* you don't know in this town?"

"That's the charm of living in Tucker Cove. We know everything about everyone and yet we still talk to each other. Most of the time, anyway."

"What else have you heard about me?"

"Besides the fact you're a great cook? You're also very interested in our town's history."

"You heard that from Mrs. Dickens, right?"

He gives a sheepish laugh and nods. "Mrs. Dickens."

"It's unfair. You know all about me, but I don't know a thing about you."

"You could always learn more." He opens the door to reception and we both walk out into the waiting room. "Are you interested in art?"

"Why do you ask?"

"The Seaglass Gallery downtown has an opening reception tonight. It's to celebrate their new exhibition of local artists. Two of my paintings are in the show, if you'd like to drop by."

"I had no idea you're an artist."

"So now you know something about me. I'm not saying I'm Picasso or anything, but painting does keep me out of trouble."

"I just might stop in tonight and take a look."

"And while you're there, you can look at Ned's bird sculptures."

"You mean Ned, my carpenter?"

"He's more than just a carpenter. He's been working with wood all his life and his carvings are sold in galleries in Boston."

"He never once mentioned to me he's an artist."

"Lots of people in this town have hidden talents."

And secrets, too, I think as I walk out of his office. I wonder how he'd react if he learned my secrets. If he knew the reason why I left Boston. If he knew what happened to me in the turret room of Brodie's Watch. For nights I've been waiting, longing, for Captain Brodie's return. Perhaps this is part of the punishment he doles out, forcing me to wonder if he will ever reappear.

I walk down a street that's crowded with summer tourists, none of whom can possibly imagine the thoughts cycling in my head. The red velvet curtain. The leather cuffs. The hiss of my silk dress ripping open. Suddenly I halt, sweating in the heat, my pulse roaring in my ears. Is this what madness feels like, this wild caroming between shame and lust?

I think of the letter written a century and a half ago by a love-sick teenager named Ionia. She too had been obsessed with Jeremiah Brodie. What sordid rumors swirled around him, leading Ionia's mother to forbid any contact? While he was alive, how many women did he bring to his turret?

Surely I'm not the only one.

When I step into Branca Property Sales and Management, I find Donna at her desk and talking on the telephone as usual. She gives me an *I'll be right with you* wave and I sit down in the waiting area to peruse the photos of properties displayed on the wall. Farmhouses surrounded by verdant fields. Seaside cottages. A village Victorian with gingerbread trim. Did any of them come with resident ghosts or secret rooms furnished for scandalous pleasures?

"Everything okay up at the house, Ava?" Donna has hung up the phone and now sits with hands primly folded on her desk, the ever-polished businesswoman in a blue blazer.

"It's all going great," I answer.

"I just received Ned's final bill for the carpentry work. I guess he and Billy are finished with the repairs."

"They did a wonderful job. The turret looks beautiful."

"And now you have the house all to yourself."

Not exactly. For a moment I'm silent, trying to formulate a question that doesn't sound completely bizarre. "I, um, wanted to get in touch with the woman who lived in the house before me. You said her name was Charlotte? I don't know her last name."

"Charlotte Nielson. Why do you need to reach her?"

"The cookbook isn't the only thing she left behind in the house. I found a silk scarf in the bedroom closet. It's very expensive, Hermès, and I'm sure she'd want it back. I have a FedEx account and I'd be happy to send it to her, if you'll just give me her address. And her email, too."

"Of course, but I'm afraid Charlotte hasn't been answering her emails lately. I wrote her days ago about that cookbook, and she still hasn't responded." Donna swivels around to check her computer. "Here's her address in Boston: 4318 Commonwealth Ave, Apartment 314," she reads aloud and I jot it down on a scrap of paper. "It must be a pretty serious crisis."

I look up. "Excuse me?"

"After she left, she sent me a note that there was a family crisis, and she apologized for breaking the lease. She'd already paid the rent through the end of August, so the owner let it go. Still, it was abrupt. And a little strange."

"She didn't tell you what her crisis was?"

"No. All I got was the note in the mail. When I drove up to check on the house, she'd already packed up and left. Must have been in quite a hurry." Donna gives me her cheery Realtor smile. "But on the bright side, the house was available for you to rent."

I find this story of a tenant abruptly fleeing Brodie's Watch more than merely odd; I find it alarming, but I don't tell her this as I stand up to leave.

I'm at the door when Donna says: "I didn't realize you already had connections in town."

I turn back to her. "Connections?"

"You and Ben Gordon. You're friends, aren't you? I saw you together in the café."

"Oh, that." I shrug. "I got a little dizzy in the heat that day, and he was worried I'd faint. He seems like a nice man."

"He is. He's nice to everyone," she adds and the subtext is obvious: *Don't think you're special.* Judging by the chilly look she gives me, Dr. Ben Gordon is a subject best avoided between us in the future.

Once again she reaches for her phone; she's already dialing as I walk out the door.

I pull the silk scarf from my bedroom closet and once again admire the summery pattern of roses printed on silk. It's a scarf meant for a garden party, a scarf to flirt in, sip champagne in. It would be the perfect accessory to brighten up one of my boring black city dresses and I'm briefly tempted to keep it. After all, Charlotte hasn't asked about it, so how anxious can she be to have it returned? But this is her scarf, not mine, and if I hope to ask her about the ghost in the turret, this scarf could be the best way to open the conversation.

Downstairs, I fold the scarf in a layer of tissue paper and slip it, along with the cookbook, into a FedEx envelope. I include a note.

Charlotte, I'm the new tenant in Brodie's Watch. You left your cookbook and this gorgeous scarf in the house, and I'm sure you want them back.

I'm a writer and I'd love to chat with you about this house and your experience living here. It may be useful information for the new book I'm writing. Is there any way we can talk by phone? Please call me. Or I can call you.

I add my phone number and email address and seal the envelope. Off it will go tomorrow.

That afternoon I putter away cleaning the stove, feeding Hannibal (again), and writing a new chapter of the book, this one about fish pies. As the clock ticks toward evening, that package for Charlotte keeps distracting me. I think of the various items she left behind. The bottles of whiskey (which I've long since finished drinking, thank you very much). The scarf. The stray flip-flop. The copy of *Joy of Cooking* with her name inscribed in it. That last item I find most puzzling of all. The grease-spattered cookbook was clearly a faithful friend in the kitchen, and I can't imagine ever leaving behind one of my treasured cookbooks.

I close the laptop and realize I haven't spared a thought for dinner. Will this be yet another long night hoping that *he* will appear? I imagine myself ten, twenty years from now, still sitting alone in this house, hoping for a glimpse of the man whom only I have seen. How many nights, how many years, will I be waiting here with only a succession of cats to keep me company?

I glance up at the clock and see that it's already seven. At this moment in the Seaglass Gallery downtown, people are drinking wine and admiring art. They are talking not to the dead, but to the living.

I grab my purse and walk out of the house to join them.

Fifteen

Through the window of Seaglass Gallery, I see a well-dressed crowd sipping from champagne flutes and a woman with a long black skirt who sits plucking a harp. I don't know any of these people and I haven't dressed up for the occasion. I consider climbing back in the car and driving home, but then I spot Ned Haskell standing among the crowd. His name is on the list of featured artists posted in the gallery window, and although he's wearing blue jeans as usual, he's spiffed himself up for this event with a white button-down shirt. Seeing one familiar face is all it takes to draw me into the gallery.

I step inside, pluck up a champagne flute of liquid courage, and make my way across the room toward Ned. He stands next to a display of his bird carvings, which are perched on individual pedestals. How did I not know that my carpenter was also an artist, and an impressive one? Each of his birds has its own quirky personality. The emperor penguin stands with its head rolled back, its beak wide open as if roaring at the sky. The puffin has a fish tucked under each wing and a fierce *I dare you to take them from me* scowl. The carvings make me laugh and suddenly I see Ned in a different light. He's more than a skilled carpenter; he's also an artist with a delightful sense of whimsy. Surrounded by this elegant crowd, he looks ill at ease and intimidated by his own admirers.

"Only now do I find out about your secret talent," I tell him. "You've been working in my house for weeks, and you never once told me you were an artist."

He gives a modest shrug. "It's just one of my secrets."

"Any other secrets I should know?"

Even at fifty-eight, Ned can still blush, and I find it charming. I realize how little I actually know about him. Does he have children? He told me he's never married, and I wonder if there's ever been a woman in his life. He has shown me his skill as a woodworker, but beyond that, he has revealed nothing about himself.

In that way, we are more alike than he knows.

"I hear your carvings are sold down in Boston, too."

"Yeah, the gallery down there calls it 'rustic art' or some such nonsense. I haven't figured out if that's an insult."

I glance around at the champagne-sipping people. "This doesn't look like a rustic crowd."

"No, most of these folks are up from the city."

"I hear Dr. Gordon has a few paintings here tonight."

"In the other room. He's already sold one."

"I had no idea he was an artist, either. Yet another man with a secret talent."

Ned turns and stares across the room. "People are complicated, Ava," he says quietly. "What you see isn't always what you get."

I glance in the direction he's looking and notice that Donna Branca has just walked into the gallery. She's reaching for a glass of champagne when our gazes meet, and for an instant her hand freezes over the tray of drinks. Then she lifts a flute to her lips, takes a deliberate gulp, and walks away.

"Donna Branca and Ben Gordon—are they, um, involved?" I ask Ned.

"Involved?"

"I mean are they seeing each other?"

He frowns at me. "Why do you ask?"

"She seemed a little peeved when she saw me and Ben together the other day."

"Are *you* seeing him?"

"I'm just curious about him. He was kind enough to make a house call after I fainted last week."

For a long time Ned doesn't say anything, and I wonder if I, the outsider, have blundered into some forbidden topic. In a town as small as Tucker Cove, everyone knows each other so well that every romance must seem halfway incestuous.

"I thought you had a fellow down in Boston," he says.

"What fellow?"

"I heard you talking on the phone to someone named Simon. I assumed . . ."

I laugh. "He's my editor. And he's married, to a very nice man named Scott."

"Oh."

"So he's definitely not a prospect."

Ned eyes me curiously. "Are you looking for one?"

I survey the men in the gallery, some of them attractive, all of them very much alive. It's been months since I've felt any interest in the opposite sex, months during which all desire has been in hibernation.

"Maybe I am." I pick up a fresh flute of champagne and head into the next room, weaving past women in little black dresses. Like them, I too am a summer visitor, but in this crowd I feel like an outsider. Neither a Mainer nor an art collector, but in a category all my own: the cat lady who lives in the haunted house. I haven't eaten dinner, the champagne has gone straight to my head, and the room seems too noisy, too bright. Too full of art. I scan the walls, eyeing muddy abstracts and giant photos of old cars. I truly hope I don't hate Ben Gordon's paintings because I'm not a good enough liar to pull off a fake *love your work!* Then I spot a telltale red dot affixed to one of the frames, indicating it's been sold and I understand at a glance why someone would pay $2,500 for this piece. The painting captures the sea in all its liquid turmoil, the waves wind-tossed, the horizon an unsettling smear of storm clouds. The artist's signature, *B. Gordon,* is almost hidden in a swirl of green water.

Hanging beside it is another B. Gordon painting, still available for purchase. Unlike the ominous seascape, this image is of a beach with calm water lapping at the pebbles. The image seems so realistic it might be mistaken for a photograph, and I lean in closer to confirm the brushstrokes. Every detail, from the tree with its tortuously twisted trunk, to the seaweed-clad rocks, to the shoreline curving to a rocky exclamation point of an island, tells me this is a portrait of a real place. I wonder how many hours, how many days he sat painting on this beach as shadows grew and daylight faded.

"Do I dare ask for your opinion, or should I just slink away now?"

I've been so enchanted by the painting, I didn't notice that Ben is standing right beside me. Despite the press of people all around us, he is focused only on me, and his gaze is so intent I'm forced to turn away. I look instead at his painting.

"I'll be absolutely honest with you," I tell him.

"I guess I should brace myself."

"When you told me you were an artist, I didn't imagine your paintings would be *this* good. It seems so real I can feel the pebbles under my feet. It's almost a shame you became a doctor instead."

"Well, medicine wasn't my first choice."

"Then why did you go through all those years of training?"

"You've been in my office. You saw the photos of my dad and my grandfather. It seems like there's always been a Dr. Gordon in Tucker Cove, and who was I to break the tradition?" He gives a rueful laugh. "My father used to tell me I could always paint in my spare time. I wasn't brave enough to disappoint him." He stares at the seascape as if seeing his own life in those turbulent green waters.

"It's never too late to be a rebel."

For a moment we smile at each other as the crowd mills around us and harp music floats through the room. Someone taps him on the shoulder and he turns to face a trim brunette who's just ushered an older couple to meet him.

"Sorry to interrupt you, Ben, but this is Mr. and Mrs. Weber from Cambridge. They're very impressed by your piece *View from the Beach* and they wanted to meet the artist."

"Is this painting a real location?" Mrs. Weber asks. "Because it looks just too perfect."

"Yes, it's a real beach, but I cleaned it up a little. Left out the flotsam. I always choose real locations to paint."

As the Webers move in for a closer view and to pitch more questions, I retreat to let Ben close the sale. He snags my arm and murmurs, "Can you stay a bit, Ava? Maybe we can get a bite together later?"

I don't have time to think about it because the Webers and the brunette are both watching us. I just give a nod and move on.

Dinner with my doctor. Not what I was expecting tonight.

I wander the room, sipping champagne and mulling whether I've read more than I should into Ben's invitation. It's eight o'clock and the gallery is now so crowded I can't get close enough to view the most popular items in the collection. I don't count myself as an art expert but I do know what I like, and there are a few treasures to admire. A red sticker now adorns Ned's puffin carving, and he's been backed into a corner by a woman wearing a bright purple caftan. After too many nights spent alone in my house on the hill, I feel as if I've finally emerged from a coma. For this I have Ben Gordon to thank.

A group has coalesced around him, and he stands surrounded by the Webers, the brunette gallery owner, and half a dozen admirers. He casts an apologetic glance my way, and that's enough to keep me patiently waiting, even though I'm getting light-headed from hunger and champagne. Of all the women he could have asked to join him for dinner, why did he choose me? Because I'm the new gal in town? As an eligible bachelor in Tucker Cove, perhaps he's weary of being pursued, and I'm the one woman who isn't interested in him.

Or am I?

I wander the gallery, my gaze drifting past the art, while my attention is keenly focused on Ben. His voice, his laugh. I stop before an abstract bronze sculpture titled: *Passion.* It is all curved surfaces, bodies melded so completely that you can't see where one begins and the other ends. I think of the turret room, and Jeremiah Brodie. I think of leather cuffs around my wrists and our bodies sweating, colliding. My mouth goes dry. My face flushes. I close my eyes, my hand resting on the curve of the sculpture, and the bronze feels as hard and unforgiving as the muscles of his back. *Tonight. Please, come to me. I want you.*

"Ready to go, Ava?"

I open my eyes to see Ben smiling at me. The respectable Dr. Gordon is clearly interested, but am I interested in him? Could a real man satisfy me the way Jeremiah Brodie does?

We escape the gallery crowd and walk into the warm summer night. Everyone in Tucker Cove seems to be out this evening, strolling the village streets. The T-shirt shops are crowded and, as usual, a long line snakes out of the ice cream parlor.

"Doesn't look like we'll find an open table anywhere," I tell him as we walk past yet another packed restaurant.

"I know someplace where we don't need a table."

"Where?"

He grins. "Best meal in Tucker Cove. Trust me."

We turn away from the village center and head down a cobble-stoned street, toward the harbor. It is quieter on the landing, where only a few tourists are wandering about. We walk past wind-jammers creaking at their moorings, past a fisherman casting his line from the dock.

"Incoming tide. Mackerel's running," the fisherman calls out. I glance at his catch, and under the dim glow of the streetlight, I see silvery fish wriggling in his bucket.

Ben and I walk on, toward a small crowd of people gathered around a food cart, and I see steaming pots and catch their savory scent. Now I know why Ben has brought me down to the landing.

"No silverware, no linen, just lobsters," he says. "I hope that's okay with you."

It's more than okay; it's *exactly* what I'm craving.

We buy piping-hot steamed lobsters, corn on the cob and French fries, and carry our meals to the seawall. There we sit with our legs dangling over the rocks, our cardboard plates resting on our laps. All that's missing is a bottle of wine, but after drinking three glasses of champagne, I'm better off without any more booze tonight. Too hungry to make conversation, I tear straight into my meal, expertly extracting meat from the shell and popping it into my mouth.

"I see you don't need any lessons on how to take apart a lobster," he observes.

"I've had lots of practice in the kitchen. You should see how fast I shuck oysters." I wipe melted butter from my chin and grin at him. "This is what I'd call the perfect meal. No fussy waiters, no pretentious menu. Simplicity and freshness always wins the day."

"Says the food writer."

"Says the very enthusiastic eater." I take a bite of corn and it's just what I was hoping for, sweet and crisp. "I plan to devote an entire chapter in my book to lobsters."

"You know they used to be considered trash food? If you brought lobster in your lunch pail, everyone assumed you were poor."

"Yes, crazy, isn't it? That anyone ever thought that way about the food of the gods."

He laughs. "I don't know about food of the gods, but if you need any information at all about lobsters, I'll put you in touch with Captain Andy." He points to a boat bobbing in the harbor. "That one's his. The *Lazy Girl.* He can take you out on his boat and tell you more than you'll ever need to know about lobstering."

"I'd appreciate that. Thank you."

He surveys the dark harbor. "As a kid, I used to work on some of these boats. One summer, I was crew on the *Mary Ryan,* right over there." He points to a three-masted schooner tied up at the dock. "My dad wanted me to work in the hospital as a lab assistant, but I couldn't stand the thought of being cooped up inside all summer. I needed to be out there, on the water." He tosses an empty lobster shell into the harbor, where it lands with a soft splash. "Do you sail?"

"My sister and I grew up sailing on a lake in New Hampshire."

"So you have a sister. Is she older? Younger?"

"Two years older."

"And what does she do?"

"She's a doctor in Boston. An orthopedic surgeon." The subject of Lucy makes me uncomfortable and I quickly change the subject. "I've never sailed on the ocean, though. To be honest, the sea scares me a little. One mistake and it's all over. Which reminds me." I turn to him. "Whatever happened with that body the lobsterman pulled out of the water?"

He shrugs. "I haven't heard any follow-up. An accident, most likely. People go out on boats, drink too much. Get careless." He looks at me. "I don't get careless, not on the water. A good sailor gives the ocean the respect it's due."

I think of Captain Brodie, who surely knew the ocean as well as any man could. Yet even he was taken, and now his bones lie under the waves. I shiver, as though the wind has just whispered my name.

"I can help you get over your fear, Ava."

"How?"

"Come out sailing with me. I'll show you it's all about knowing what to expect, and being prepared for it."

"You have a boat?"

"A thirty-foot wooden sloop. She's old, but she's tried and true." He tosses another empty shell into the water. "Just to be perfectly clear, I'm not formally asking you out on a date."

"No?"

"Because doctors aren't supposed to date their patients."

"Then I guess we'll have to call this something else."

"So you will come out with me?"

For something that isn't a date, it's starting to sound suspiciously like one. I don't answer him right away, but take my time considering his offer as I tidy up the napkins and plastic utensils from our meal. I don't know why I'm hesitating; I've never been particularly cautious about men before, and on every practical level, Ben Gordon is a catch. I can almost hear the ever-logical voice of Lucy, who's spent all her life watching out for me. *He ticks all the right boxes, Ava! He's attractive, intelligent, and a doctor to boot. He's just the man you need after all the Mr. Wrongs you've been dating.* And Lucy has heard about them all, every drunken mistake I've made, every man I've ever slept with and regretted.

Except one.

I look at Ben. "Can I ask you a question?"

"Of course."

"Do you invite all your patients out for a sail?"

"No."

"Why me, then?"

"Why not?" He sees my questioning look and he sighs. "I'm sorry, I don't mean to sound flippant. It's just . . . I don't know what it is about you. I see a lot of summer people come through town. They stay for a few weeks, a few months, and then they're gone. I never saw the point of investing the emotional energy in a relationship with any of them. But you're different."

"How?"

"You intrigue me. There's something about you that makes me want to know more. As if, beneath the surface, there's a great deal to discover."

I laugh. "A lady with secrets."

"Is that who you are?"

We stare at each other and I'm afraid he'll try to kiss me, which is not what a doctor is supposed to do with his patient. To my relief he doesn't, but turns to look at the harbor again. "I'm sorry. That probably sounded really weird."

"It makes me sound like a puzzle-box you want to crack open."

"That's not what I meant at all."

"What did you mean?"

"I want to know *you*, Ava. All the things, big and small, that you'll let me learn about you."

I say nothing, thinking about what waits for me in the turret. How shocked Ben would be if he learned how eagerly I welcome both the pleasure and the pain. Only Captain Brodie knows my secret. He is the perfect partner in shame, because he will never tell.

My silence has stretched on too long and Ben gets the hint. "It's late. I should let you get home."

We both rise to our feet. "Thank you for inviting me. I enjoyed it."

"We should do it again. Maybe out on the water next time?"

"I'll think about it."

He smiles. "I'll make sure the weather's perfect. You won't have a thing to worry about."

When I arrive home, I find Hannibal sitting in the foyer, waiting for me. Watching me with his glowing cat's eyes. What else does he see? Does he sense the ghost's presence? I stand at the bottom of the stairs, sniffing the air, but all I smell is fresh paint and sawdust, the scent of renovation.

In my bedroom I undress and turn off the lights. In the darkness I stand naked, waiting, hoping. Why has he not returned? What must I do to lure him back? With every night that passes, every night that I do not see him, I grow more fearful that he never existed at all, that he was nothing more than a fantasy born of wine and loneliness. I press my hands to my temples, wondering if this is what insanity feels like. Or is it a complication of cat scratch fever, encephalitis, and brain damage, just the sort of logical explanation Lucy would accept. Microbes, after all, can be seen through a lens and grown in test tubes. No one doubts their existence, or the havoc they can wreak in a human brain.

Maybe this really is Hannibal's fault.

I climb into bed and pull the covers up to my chin. At least this much I know is real: The crispness of linen against my skin. The distant whoosh of the ocean and the rumble of Hannibal purring beside me.

Nothing takes shape in the darkness; no thickening shadow congeals into a man. Somehow I know he will not visit me tonight; perhaps he was never here at all. But there is a man who *could* be in my bed, if I wanted him. A real man.

It's time for me to choose.

Sixteen

The mainsail snaps taut and I cling to the starboard rail as *Callista* heels in the wind, her bow slicing through the swells.

"Nervous?" Ben calls out from the tiller.

"Um, a little!"

"There's nothing to worry about. Just sit back and enjoy the view. I've got everything under control."

And he does. From the moment I stepped aboard *Callista,* I knew I was in capable hands. Ben has thought of every detail to make this afternoon perfect. Sparkling water and wine are chilling in the cooler and the picnic hamper is packed with cheese and fruit and chicken sandwiches. I had offered to make lunch, but he'd assured me that everything was taken care of, and it has been. I glance around the pristine deck where all the ropes are neatly coiled, where every brass fitting gleams and the teak shines with fresh varnish.

"This boat doesn't look fifty years old," I say.

"She's wood so she's a lot of work to maintain, but she belonged to my dad. He'd roll over in his grave if I didn't take good care of her." He glances up at the mainsail and unties the jib sheet. "Okay, ready about!"

As he turns the bow through the wind, I scurry across to the port side. The boat heels, tilting me once again over the water. "How long ago did your dad pass away?" I ask.

"Five years. He was seventy years old and he still had a full-time medical practice. He collapsed while making rounds in the hospital. Which is not the way I want to go."

"How *do* you want to go?"

"Certainly not while at work. I'd rather be out on the water, like today. Having a good time with someone I like."

His answer seems casual enough, but I hear his emphasis on that last phrase, *someone I like.* I turn away and gaze toward the shoreline, where the forest tumbles down to the sea. There are no beaches here, only woods and granite cliffs where seagulls circle and swoop.

"Right around that point, there's a nice little cove," he says. "We can anchor there."

"What can I do to help?"

"Not a thing, Ava. I'm used to sailing solo, so I've got this."

With a few expert tacks he steers *Callista* around the point and into a secluded cove. I'm only a spectator as he lowers the sails and drops anchor, and he moves around the deck so efficiently that even if I did try to help, I'd probably slow him down. So I busy myself doing what I do best: uncorking the wine bottle and laying out our picnic. By the time he's secured the sails and coiled the lines, I'm ready to hand him a glass of wine. While *Callista* gently sways at anchor, we relax in the cockpit, sipping perfectly chilled rosé.

"I think I could learn to like this," I admit.

He gestures toward the cloudless sky. "A summer's day, a sturdy little boat. It doesn't get better than this." He looks at me. "Think I can talk you into staying beyond October?"

"Maybe. I do like it here in Tucker Cove."

"You'll have to stop being my patient."

"Why?"

"Because I'm hoping I can call you something else."

We both understand where this is going. Where *he* wants it to go, anyway. I haven't yet decided. The wine makes my head buzz and my face feels pleasantly flushed from the sun. And Ben Gordon has the most striking blue eyes, eyes that seem to see too much. I do not turn away as he leans toward me. As our lips meet.

He tastes like wine and salt and sunshine. This is the man I *should* be attracted to, the man who is everything a woman could want. This will happen if I let it, but is it really what I want? Is *he* what I want? He pulls me against him, but I feel an odd sense of detachment, as if I am standing outside my own body, watching two strangers kiss. Ben may be real, but his kiss fails to ignite any flame inside me. Instead, it makes me yearn even more for the lover I miss. A lover I am not even sure is real.

I'm almost relieved when his cellphone rings.

He sighs and pulls away. "I'm sorry, but that's a ringtone I need to answer."

"Of course."

He retrieves the phone from his boat bag. "This is Dr. Gordon."

I reach for the wine bottle and am refilling my glass when I hear the abrupt change in his voice.

"This is the final report? He's sure about this?"

I turn to look at him, but he doesn't see me watching him. His face has darkened and his lips have tightened into grim lines. He hangs up and says nothing for a moment, just stares at the phone as if it's betrayed him.

"Is something wrong?"

"That was the medical examiner's office. About the body they pulled out of the bay."

"Do they know who she is?"

"They haven't identified her yet. But they have the results of the toxicology screen, and there were no drugs or alcohol in her system."

"So she wasn't drunk when she drowned."

"She didn't drown." He looks at me. "They're calling it a homicide."

Seventeen

We are quiet as we motor back to the harbor, both of us silently processing the news, which will no doubt be all over Tucker Cove by this evening. For a town that relies on tourism, in a state whose motto is *The Way Life Should Be,* this news will not be welcome. We tie up at the dock and when I step out of the boat, I see the village of Tucker Cove with new eyes. On the surface it is still a pretty New England town with white clapboard buildings and cobblestoned streets, but now I see shadows everywhere. And secrets. A woman has been murdered, her body tossed into the sea, yet no one knows—or wants to reveal—her name.

At home that evening, I comfort myself the way I usually do; I cook. Tonight I roast a chicken and slice bread into cubes for croutons, a meal that's so familiar I can put it together in my sleep. Automatically I chop parsley and garlic and toss it with olive oil and bread cubes, but my mind is still on the murdered woman. I think back to the day her body was recovered. I remember the blue tarp glistening with seawater and the look of horror on Ben's face as he lifted that tarp and stared at what lay underneath.

I take the chicken out of the oven and pour myself a second glass of sauvignon blanc. Good for me, it's nine P.M. and I'm only at glass number two. After what I've seen today, this second glass is well deserved and I take a deep gulp. The alcohol flames its way through my blood like a kerosene fire, but even as my tension melts away, I'm still thinking about the dead woman. Was she young or old? Pretty or plain?

Why has no one reported her missing?

If I tumbled down the stairs and broke my neck tonight, how long would it take for anyone to miss *me*? Eventually Donna Branca would notice, of course, but only because she'd miss my monthly rent check. People always take notice when you don't pay your bills, but that could take weeks. By then my body would be well on its way to decay.

Or eaten by my cat, I think, as Hannibal hops up onto the dining table and stares at the slices of chicken on my plate.

Third glass of wine. I've been trying to cut down, but tonight I don't care whether I've had too much. Who's here to see me, scold me? Only Lucy ever really cared enough to get in my face about my drinking, but she's not here to protect me from myself, as she's always done.

I sit at the table and stare down at my meal, so perfectly presented: slices of chicken drizzled with gravy made from drippings and white wine. Roasted new potatoes. A salad tossed with fresh-baked croutons and Spanish olive oil.

Lucy's favorite dinner. The same dinner I cooked for her birthday.

I can see them again, both smiling at me across the table. Lucy and Nick, their wineglasses raised in a toast to the chef. "If ever I have to choose a final meal, I want it to be cooked by Ava," Lucy said. And then we went around the table, each of us talking about what we'd choose for our last meals. Lucy's would be "Ava's roast chicken." Mine would be a rustic *cacio e pepe* with a glass of crisp, chilled Frascati. Nick's choice was beef, of course. "A rib-eye steak, medium rare. No, make it beef Wellington! If it's my last meal, why not get a little fancy?" he'd said, and we'd all laughed because even though Nick had never eaten beef Wellington, he thought it sounded delicious.

If only I could go back to that birthday dinner, a night when we were all together and happy. Now I sit alone in this cavernous house. If I die here alone, I have only myself to blame.

I leave my scarcely touched dinner on the table, pick up the bottle, and carry it upstairs with me. The wine's no longer cold but I'm beyond caring how it tastes. I crave only the oblivion it offers. Up in my bedroom I finish off the bottle and flop onto the mattress. Dead woman in the water, drunk woman in the bedroom.

I turn off the light and stare at the darkness. The ocean is restless tonight and I hear waves pounding the rocks. A storm far off at sea has generated those waves, and here they come rolling in, crashing against the cliffs with wind-driven fury. The sound is so unnerving that I rise to close the window, but even then I still hear those waves. I can smell them too, a scent so powerful that I feel I'm drowning. That's when I suddenly realize: *He is here.*

I turn from the window. Jeremiah Brodie stands before me.

"You have been with a man today," he says.

"How do you . . ."

"You carry his scent."

"He's just a friend. I went out on his sailboat."

He moves closer and I shiver as he lifts a strand of my hair and lets it glide through his fingers. "You were close enough to touch."

"Yes, but—"

"Close enough to be tempted."

"It was just a kiss. It meant nothing."

"Yet I sense your guilt." He is so close now, I can feel the heat of his breath in my hair. "Your shame."

"Not about that. Not about today."

"You have cause to feel shame."

I stare into his eyes, which reflect the cold and pitiless gleam of starlight. His words have nothing to do with Ben Gordon and our innocent kiss. No, this is about what happened before I came to Maine. This is about New Year's Eve and the sin for which I will never forgive myself. What he smells on my skin is the permanent stench of guilt.

"You allowed him to touch you."

"Yes."

"Defile you."

I blink back tears. "Yes."

"You desired it. You desired him."

"I never meant it to happen. If I could go back to that night, if I could live it again—"

"But you cannot. That is why I'm here."

I stare into those diamond-bright eyes. I hear righteous judgment in his voice and the promise of what will come. My heart pounds and my hands shake. For days I've longed for his return, hungered for his touch. Now that he stands before me, I am afraid of what awaits me.

"To the turret," he commands.

My legs are unsteady as I walk out of the bedroom. Is it from drinking too much wine or is it fear that makes me stumble in the hallway? The floor feels like ice beneath my bare feet, and the damp air penetrates straight through my nightgown. I open the door to the staircase and halt, gazing up at the flickering candlelight above.

I stand at the threshold of his world. With each step I climb, I leave my own world farther and farther behind.

Up the stairs I go, the candlelight growing ever brighter. He is at my heels, his boot steps heavy and inexorable on the steps, preventing my retreat. There is only one direction I can go, and I ascend toward the room where I know both pleasure and punishment await.

At the top of the stairs, I swing the door wide open and step through, into the turret. Golden candlelight washes over me and I look down to see the skirt of coppery silk swishing at my ankles. No longer do I feel the night's chill; a fire burns in the hearth, its flames licking at birch logs. The light of a dozen candles flickers in wall sconces and in the sea windows I catch a glimpse of my own reflection. The gown molds itself to my hips and my ivory-white breasts swell above the low-cut bodice.

I am in his world. His time.

He crosses to the curtained alcove. Already I know what lies behind those drapes. I have lain spread-eagled on that bed, felt the pleasure of his brutal attentions. But when he slides open the curtain, this time he reveals more than a bed, and I shrink away.

He holds out his hand. "Come, Ava."

"What will you do to me?"

"What would you have me do?"

"You're going to hurt me."

"Is that not what you deserve?"

I do not have to answer him; he already knows that I can never punish myself enough for what has happened. He knows that guilt and shame are what have led me to this house, and to him. That I deserve whatever torment he chooses to deliver.

"I'm afraid," I whisper.

"But you are also tempted, are you not?" I flinch as he reaches out to stroke my cheek with the back of his hand. "Have I not taught you that pain is merely the other face of pleasure? That a cry of agony sounds no different from a cry of ecstasy? Tonight you will enjoy both, without guilt, without blame, because I am the one in command. Do you not feel yourself craving it, longing for it? Are you not already wet, your body preparing itself to accommodate what is to come?"

Even as he speaks, I feel heat building between my legs, the ache of a hollow crying out to be filled.

He reaches for my hand. Willingly I take it.

We cross the room and I step into the alcove and stare at the wrist shackles dangling from the beam overhead. But those shackles are not what frighten me. No, what scares me is what I see displayed on the wall. Leather whips. A riding crop. An array of billy clubs.

He tugs me toward the shackles and closes the manacle over my left wrist.

There is no going back now. I am at his mercy.

He grasps my right hand and efficiently snaps the second manacle around it. I stand with both my hands shackled over my head as he studies his prisoner, savoring my helplessness. Slowly he walks behind me and, with no warning, rips open the back of my gown, exposing my back. With the gentlest of touches, he strokes down my skin and I shudder.

I do not see him reach for the whip.

The first crack of leather against my back is so shocking, I jerk against the manacles. My skin throbs from the sting of the leather.

"Is this not what you deserve?"

"Stop. Please—"

"Tell the truth. Confess your shame." Again the whip cracks. Again I scream and writhe from its bite.

"Confess."

The third lash of the whip makes me sob. "I confess," I cry out. "I am guilty, but I never meant for it to happen. I never wanted—"

The next lash makes my knees buckle. I sag, my body suspended by those merciless manacles.

He leans in close and whispers into my ear, "But you did want it, Ava. Didn't you?"

I look up at him and his smile chills me. Slowly he strides a circle around me, comes to a stop at my back. I do not know what he will do next. I don't know if even now he's again raised his whip, and I brace for the next sting of his lash. Instead he unlatches both shackles. My legs give way and I kneel, quivering, waiting for whatever torment comes next.

I do not see what he reaches for, but I hear him slap it against his hand. I look up and see he is holding a billy club, its wood polished and gleaming. He sees my look of alarm. "No, I will not beat you. Never do I leave scars. This instrument is for a different purpose entirely." He strokes it against his palm, admiring its polish in the candlelight. "This one is meant only as an introduction. A training device, small enough for the tightest virgin." He looks at me. "But you are not a virgin."

"No," I murmur.

He turns to the wall and reaches for a different billy club. He holds it before me and I cannot look away, cannot stare at anything but the monstrous object looming before me.

"This one is meant for a harlot who's been well-ridden. One seasoned enough to accommodate any manner of man."

I swallow. "That's impossible."

"Is it?"

"No woman can take that . . . *thing*."

He slides the club across my cheek and the wood is smooth and terrifying. "Unless she is properly initiated. It's what whores do, Ava. You learn to please. Because you never know who will walk in the door and what he will demand. Some men just want to ride you. Others prefer to watch. And then there are those who want to see how much you can endure."

"This isn't what I want!"

"I am but a reflection of your own shame. I give you exactly what you desire. What you expect. Even if you do not know it." He tosses aside that monstrosity of a club and I flinch as it thuds to the floor. "You are your own cruelest judge, Ava, and you yourself hand down your punishment. I merely wield the instrument. I bend to your will, just as you bend to mine. Tonight, *this* is what you want. So *this* is what I deliver." He wrenches apart what remains of my dress. I do not resist as he grasps my hips and uses me like the whore I am. The whore I've proven myself to be. I am nothing but flesh, bought and paid for.

I give a scream of release and together we fall forward as he collapses on top of me.

For a long time we do not move. His arms curl around me and I feel the beating of his heart against my bare back. How can a dead man seem so alive? His skin is as warm as mine, his arms solid with muscle as they encircle me. No real man can match him.

No real man could understand my desires so completely.

He rolls off me. As we lie side by side on the floor, he gently traces a circle on my bare flank. "Did I frighten you?" he asks.

"Yes. You did."

"You need never be afraid."

"But fear is part of your game, isn't it?" I look at him. "The fear that you *might* hurt me. That you *might* actually use that thing on me." I glance at the billy club, lying a few feet away, and I shudder.

"Did it not excite you, just a little?" He smiles and I see the gleam of cruelty beneath the surface of those dark eyes.

"You wouldn't really use it on me, would you?"

"That is the mystery, is it not? How far will I go? Will I use the whip too savagely and tear your beautiful back? You do not know. You cannot predict what I will do next." He slides his fingers down my cheek. "Danger is intoxicating, Ava. So is pain. I give you only as much as you want. As much as you can bear."

"I don't know what I can bear."

"This we shall learn."

"Why?"

"Because it satisfies us both. Some have called me a monster because I enjoy the crack of the whip and the cry of the conquered. Because I am aroused by the screams and the struggle."

"Is that really what you enjoy?"

"As do you. You simply do not admit it."

"That's not true. It's not what I want."

"Then why do you allow me to do it?"

I look in to those diamond-cold eyes and see the truth staring back at me. I think of all the reasons I deserve every punishment he has doled out and more. For the sins I've committed, the pain I have caused, I deserve his whips, his clubs, his brutal assaults.

"I know you better than you know yourself, dearest Ava," he says. "It's why I chose you. Because I know you will come back for more, and for worse."

He caresses my face. His touch is unnervingly gentle, but I shiver. "How much worse?" I whisper.

He smiles. "Shall we find out?"

Eighteen

I jolt awake in the turret and blink against the sunshine that glares through the windows. My left hip is sore from lying on bare wood. My mouth feels like cotton and my head pounds from the hangover I fully deserve after the bottle of wine I drank last night. With a groan I cover my face with my arms, trying to block the light from my aching eyes. How did I end up sleeping here, on the floor? Why did I never make it back to bed?

Memories drift back. The climb up the staircase. The candles burning in the sconces.

And Captain Brodie.

With a start, I open my eyes again and wince as sunlight stabs my sockets. The fireplace is swept clean with no hint of ashes in the hearth. The alcove gapes empty, just bare walls and floor. No bed, no curtain, no manacles dangling from the ceiling. I am back in my time, in my world.

I look down at what I'm wearing. This is no dress of coppery silk, just the same thin nightgown that I wore to bed. I look at my wrists and see no scrapes or bruises from the manacles.

I stagger to my feet and grip the handrail as I slowly make my way down the turret staircase to my bedroom. There I pull off the nightgown and turn my back to the mirror. Last night, I'd writhed to the sting of his whip, had cried out as leather lashed my flesh, but in the glare of morning light, I see my back is unmarred by any bruises, any welts. I turn before the mirror, searching my naked body for any signs of the abuse I'd endured at his hands, but there are no telltale souvenirs of the punishment he meted out to me last night.

No, there is something.

I reach between my legs and feel the slick evidence of my arousal, so wet and copious that it might be his leavings that now trickle down the inside of my thigh. I stare at my glistening fingertips and wonder if this is the unholy mingling of our lust, the physical evidence that I have been violated by a man long dead. My cheeks flush in shame at the memory, but that shame also sets off a new tingle of desire.

My cellphone rings on the nightstand.

As I pick it up, my heart is still thudding, my hands unsteady. "Hello?"

"At last you pick up. I've left three voicemails for you."

"Hello, Simon." I sigh and sit down on the bed.

"You've been avoiding me."

"I didn't want to get distracted. I've been in the zone."

"What, the twilight zone?"

"Research. Writing."

"Yes, I read the chapters you sent me."

"What do you think?"

"They're good."

"Just good?"

"Okay, okay. They're fucking *great*. What you wrote about oysters made me so hungry I went out and gorged on two dozen, washed down with a martini."

"Then I did my job right."

"When do I get to read the rest of it?"

I look at the pile of clothes, which are still lying on the floor where I dropped them last night. The ghost has distracted me. How can I write when every moment I stop to sniff the air, hoping to catch his scent?

"The book *is* coming along," I assure him. "This house has been the perfect inspiration."

"Ah yes, Brodie's Watch. That's why I'm calling. I want to see it."

"Of course. I can send you some photos. I'm not the world's best photographer, but—"

"I want to see it in person. I was thinking this weekend."

"What?"

"It's ninety-two degrees here in the city and I need to get out of Boston before I melt. Look, Ava, you've been MIA for months now, and Theo insisted I check on your progress. He signed your advance check and now he wants reassurance that you're back on track to deliver. If I leave by noon Friday, I should be up there around five-ish. Or do you have a date with a hot lumberjack that evening?"

"I, um . . ." I have no excuse, none at all. All I can say is: "That would be fine."

"Good. I'll take you out to dinner, if you'd like."

"That's not necessary."

"Then I'll cook dinner. Or you cook. I'm just keen to lay eyes on this sea captain's house. Besides, it's time to think about marketing strategies. Based on the chapters you've sent me, this book is going to be about far more than food. You've given it a true sense of place, Ava, and now I want to see Brodie's Watch for myself."

"It's a long drive, just to see a house."

"I'm coming to see you, too. Everyone's been asking why you haven't been around lately. Why you've vanished."

If only I could vanish. If only I could melt away into these walls like Captain Brodie. Turn invisible so that no one can see what I've become. But I've known Simon for years, since long before he became my editor, and I know that once he's made up his mind, there's no changing it.

"If you're arriving that late in the afternoon, you'll probably want to spend the night here," I say.

"I was hoping you'd offer."

"Is Scott coming, too?"

"No, he's playing the dutiful son and he's off to see his mother. So it'll just be you and me. Like old times."

"All right, then. I'll see you on Friday."

"I'll bring the wine."

It's five P.M. on the dot Friday evening when my doorbell rings.

Simon stands on the porch looking as natty as ever in his striped oxford shirt and red bow tie. In all my years of working with him, I've never seen him without a bow tie, even while working in restaurant kitchens, and he'd look positively undressed without it.

"There's my gal!" He pulls me in for a hug. Thank god Simon's hugs aren't fraught with undercurrents of sexual tension; this is a brotherly embrace, from a man who's been happily married for a decade to his husband, Scott, and he has absolutely no interest in me as a woman. He steps into the house, sets down his leather weekender bag, and tilts up his nose, sniffing. "What's that I smell? Lobster?"

"I swear, you're like a bloodhound, Simon."

"I like to think I'm more like a truffle pig. Able to sniff out a fine Bordeaux from a mile away. So what's the preparation to-night? Boiled and boring, or something special?"

I laugh. "For you, something special, of course. I'm just on the first step of the recipe. If you'd like to freshen up, the guest room's at the top of the stairs."

"First I want to see what's cooking." He leaves his leather bag in the foyer and heads straight into the kitchen. Simon comes from a long line of cooks, no doubt dating back to some ancient ances-tor in animal skins who stirred a pot of mastodon stew, and he gravitates, as always, to the stove. "How long?" He doesn't have to explain the question; I already know what he's asking.

"They've been in there for fifteen minutes. Your timing's im-peccable." I turn off the stove and lift the pot cover, releasing a fragrant cloud of steam. Only that morning, I'd been aboard the *Lazy Girl* with Ben's lobsterman friend Captain Andy and watched these four crustaceans pulled green from the sea. Now they are a brilliant, mouthwatering red.

Simon reaches for one of the aprons hanging on the kitchen hook and swiftly ties it on. "Next step in the recipe?"

"You shell. I make the béchamel."

"You've turned into a poet!"

"And don't I know it."

We set to work, moving around the kitchen like longtime dance partners who know each other's moves. This is, after all, how we met years ago, as two college kids working summer jobs in a Cape Cod restaurant. I was promoted from dishwasher to salads; he went from salads to broiler—Simon was always one step ahead of me. He's ahead of me now too, cracking claws and extracting meat so efficiently that by the time I'm whisking sherry and egg yolks into the béchamel, he has already liberated a mound of succulent lobster meat from their shells.

I cloak the meat in the sauce and slide the lobster pie into the oven.

Simon uncorks a chilled bottle of sauvignon blanc and fills my wineglass. "Here's to teamwork," he says as we toast each other. "Is this recipe going into the book?"

"If you think it passes muster tonight. I scavenged it from a 1901 hotel cookbook. It was considered quite the gourmet dish in the Old Mermaid Hotel."

"So this is what you've been up to this past month."

"Testing old recipes. Writing. Immersing myself in the past." I look up at the antique tin ceiling. "This house puts me in the right frame of mind to immerse myself in that era."

"But did you really have to trek all the way up here just to write? And by the way, your book is now almost a year overdue."

"I know, I know."

"I really don't want to cancel your contract, but Theo's an annoying bean counter and he keeps asking when you'll deliver." He pauses, studies me. "You've never been this late for a deadline before. What's going on, Ava?"

To avoid answering his question, I finish off my glass of wine. "Writer's block," I finally answer. "But I think I've finally broken through. Since I moved into this house, I've been writing like crazy—and it's *good* stuff, Simon. The old creative juices are starting to flow again."

"Where did they go in the first place?"

I see him frowning as I refill my wineglass. How much have I had to drink this evening? I've lost count. I set the bottle back down and say quietly, "You know it's been tough for me these past few months. I've been depressed, ever since . . ."

"New Year's Eve."

I go very still and don't say a word.

"Stop blaming yourself, Ava. You threw a party, and he drank too much. What were you supposed to do, tie him up and keep him from getting in his car?"

"I didn't do enough to stop him."

"He wasn't your responsibility. Nick was an adult."

"I still blame myself. Even if Lucy doesn't."

"It sounds to me like you need to talk to someone about this. I know a very good therapist. I can give you her number."

"No." I pick up my glass and drain it in one gulp. "What I need right now is to eat dinner."

"Considering how much you've had to drink tonight, I'd say that's a good idea."

I deliberately ignore his remark and pour myself more wine. By the time the salad's been tossed and the lobster pie is on the table, I'm so irritated by what he said that I focus all my attention on the food, not on him. When did Simon become such a nanny?

He takes a bite of the lobster pie and sighs with pleasure. "Oh yes, this recipe *must* go in the book."

"I'm glad to hear that something I've done meets your approval."

"Oh for pity's sake, Ava. I wouldn't have signed you up for this book if I didn't think you'd deliver. Which begs the question again, when *will* you deliver?"

"And that's why you're really here."

"I didn't spend five hours sitting in traffic just to say hello. Of course that's why I'm here. And to check up on you, too. When your sister called me—"

"Lucy called you?"

"She hoped maybe I knew what was going on with you."

I stare down at my wine. "What did she tell you?"

"She says you two hardly talk anymore and she has no idea why. She worries it was something she said, something she did."

"No."

"Then what? I always thought you girls were joined at the hip."

I take a rebellious sip of wine to put off my answer. "It's this book. It's consuming me," I finally say. "I've been struggling for months, but now it's coming along. I've written six chapters since I got here. Living in this house has made all the difference."

"Why? It's just an old house."

"Don't you feel it, Simon? There's so much history in these walls. Think of the meals they cooked in that kitchen, the feasts they enjoyed in this dining room. I don't think I can write the book anyplace but in this house."

"And that's the only reason you left Boston? To look for inspiration?"

I manage to look him straight in the eye. "Yes."

"Well then, I'm glad you found it here."

"I did." *And I've found a great deal more.*

That night I lie awake, acutely aware of my houseguest sleeping just down the hall. I have not mentioned a word to Simon about my resident ghost because I know what he'd think. I saw his watchful glances at dinner as I kept refilling my wineglass with the elegant Chardonnay he'd brought from Boston. I know he thinks my drinking is the real reason I've been unable to finish my book. Booze and writers may be a cliché, but in my case, as in Hemingway's, it's true.

No wonder I see ghosts.

I hear the floor creak in the hall and the sound of water running in the guest bathroom. It's strange having someone else, someone real, in the house. Certainly ghosts don't flush the toilet or run the faucet. It's not a ghost who shuffles back to the guestroom and closes the door. I'm not used to living with human sounds now; it's people who seem alien to me, and I resent this invasion of my home, even if it's only for one night. This is the advantage of being a writer; I can go days without seeing another human being. The outside world is fraught with conflict and heartbreak; why should I leave my house when everything I want and need is within these walls?

Simon has upset the equilibrium and I feel the disturbance in the atmosphere, as if his presence has charged the air, which now moves in uneasy eddies through the house.

I am not the only one who feels it.

The next morning, when I come downstairs to the kitchen, I find Simon already awake and hunched at the table, gulping coffee. He's unshaven, his eyes are bloodshot, and for the first time since I've known him, he isn't wearing his trademark bow tie.

"You're up awfully early," I say as I go to the coffeepot and fill my own cup. "I was planning to be up first and make a nice frittata for breakfast."

He wipes a hand across his eyes and yawns. "I didn't sleep well. I thought I might as well get up and hit the road early."

"Already? But it's only seven."

"I've been up since three."

"Why?"

"Bad dreams." He shrugs. "Maybe this house is *too* quiet. I can't remember the last time I had nightmares like this."

Slowly I sit down at the table and study him. "What kind of nightmares?"

"There's nothing less interesting than someone else's dreams."

"I'm interested. Tell me."

He takes a deep breath, as if just the recounting of his nightmare requires the marshaling of nerves. "It's as if he was sitting on my chest. Trying to squeeze the breath out of me. I wondered if I was having a heart attack. I actually felt his hands around my throat."

He. His.

"I tried to fight him off, but I couldn't move. I was paralyzed, the way it always happens in dreams. And he kept choking me until I really thought . . ." He takes another breath. "Anyway, I couldn't go back to sleep after that. I just lay awake, listening for him. Half expecting him to come back."

"Why do you say *him?*"

"I don't know. I guess I could just as well say *it*. I only know it had me by the throat. And here's the weird thing, Ava. When I woke up, that feeling of being choked was so vivid, I was desperate for a glass of water. I went into the bathroom and saw myself in the mirror, and just for an instant I could have *sworn* there were marks on my neck." He gives a sheepish laugh. "Then I blinked and of course there was nothing. But that's how shaken up I was."

I stare at the exposed skin above his shirt collar but I see nothing unusual. No bruises, no marks left by phantom fingers.

He drains his coffee cup. "Anyway, I might as well hit the road early and beat the traffic back to Boston. I've already packed my bag."

I walk him outside to his car and stand shivering in the crisp sea air as he loads his bag into the trunk. Birds trill overhead and a monarch butterfly sketches colorful zigzags through a clump of milkweed. It is going to be a glorious day, but Simon seems desperate to escape.

He turns to give me a goodbye peck on the cheek, and I see him cast a nervous glance at the house, as if he doesn't dare turn his back on it. "Now finish the damn book, Ava."

"I will."

"And get back to Boston, where you belong."

I can't help but feel a sense of relief as I watch him drive away. The house is mine again, it's a beautiful summer morning, and the whole day lies ahead of me. I hear a noisy meow and look down to see Hannibal sitting at my feet, tail twitching, breakfast no doubt on his mind.

Food is on my mind, as well.

I turn back to the house. Only as I climb the stairs do I notice the FedEx package sitting on the porch swing. The driver must have left it yesterday afternoon, while I was busy inside preparing for Simon's arrival. I pick it up and recognize my own handwriting on the address label. It's the same FedEx package I sent to Charlotte Nielson last week and I stare at the reason it's been returned to me.

Three Delivery Attempts.

I stand on the porch, ignoring Hannibal's meows, as I consider this bounced-back package. Remembering what Donna Branca had told me: *Charlotte hasn't returned any of my emails and she hasn't been answering her phone.* I'm more than puzzled by this. I'm now thoroughly alarmed.

There is so much I need to ask Charlotte, so much I need to know about her stay in this house. About why she left so abruptly. Was it the ghost who drove her away?

Her address is on Commonwealth Avenue, not far from my own apartment in Boston. Surely there's someone in her building who can tell me where she has gone, and how I can reach her.

I glance at the kitchen clock: 7:47 A.M. If I leave now, I can be in Boston by one.

Nineteen

It's a beautiful day for a drive, but I scarcely pay attention to the views of glittering water and tidy seaside cottages; my mind is scrolling back through the odd details that have added up over the weeks since I arrived in Tucker Cove. I think about the cookbook and the bottles of whiskey in the kitchen cabinet, the lone flip-flop under the bed, and the silk scarf bunched up on the floor of the bedroom closet. When Charlotte Nielson abruptly packed up and left, she still had two months on her lease, a detail that now takes on troubling significance. What made her leave Brodie's Watch so abruptly?

I think I already know the answer: She left because of *him. What did Captain Brodie do to you, Charlotte? What finally sent you fleeing from the house? What should I be afraid of?*

Only last month I'd driven this same road north, fleeing Boston. Now I'm on my way back to ground zero where everything went wrong. I'm not coming to repair the damage, because it can never be repaired and I can never be absolved. No, this is a different mission entirely. I'm coming to meet the only other living woman who has lived in my house. If she too has seen him, then I'll know he's real. I'll know I'm not going insane.

But if she hasn't seen him . . .

One step at a time, Ava. First find Charlotte.

By the time I cross the border into New Hampshire, traffic has thickened and I join the usual stream of tourists heading home after a vacation of boating and hiking and feasting on lobster. Through windows I glimpse sunburned faces and backseats piled high with suitcases and coolers. In my car there is only me, carrying no luggage except for the emotional baggage that will weigh me down for the rest of my life.

I roll down my window and am startled by the heat that blows in. After a month in Tucker Cove, I'd forgotten how suffocatingly hot the city can be in early September, a concrete oven where tempers easily boil over. At a stoplight, when I pause just a millisecond too long after the traffic light turns green, the driver behind me leans on his horn. In Maine, almost no one honks, and I'm startled by the blare. *Thanks for the welcome back to Boston, asshole.*

As I drive down Commonwealth Avenue, a knot tightens in my stomach. This is the way to Lucy's apartment, the way to Christmas dinners and Thanksgiving turkey and Sunday brunches. The way to the person I love most, the person I never meant to hurt. The knot in my stomach turns to nausea as I drive past her building, past the apartment I helped her move into, past the olive-green drapes I helped her pick out. It's one P.M. on a Saturday, so she'd be home from making her usual rounds in the hospital, alone in that spacious apartment. What would she say if I knocked at her door now and blurted out what really happened New Year's Eve? But I don't have the courage. In fact, I'm terrified that she'll glance out the window, see me driving past, and wonder why I don't drop in to visit the way I always used to. Just as she wonders why I fled Boston for the summer, why I avoid her phone calls, why I have all but excised her from my life.

I'm too much of a fucking coward to tell her the truth, so I just keep driving, heading west toward the block where Charlotte Nielson lives.

By the time I pull up in front of her building, my hands are unsteady, my heart racing. I turn off the engine and sit still for a moment, taking deep breaths to calm myself. I notice two teenage boys loitering on the front steps of the building, watching me, no doubt wondering why I've been sitting so long in my car. I know they're probably harmless, but the sheer size of teenage boys, with their giant shoes and hulking shoulders, is intimidating, and I hesitate before I finally step out and walk past them to the building's entrance. I push the buzzer for Charlotte's apartment. Once, twice, three times. There's no response, and the front door is locked.

The boys are still watching me.

"Do either of you live here?" I ask them.

They give simultaneous shrugs, which mean . . . what? Don't they know where they live?

"I live here sometimes," says the bigger one. He has sun-bleached hair, and if he lived in California, he'd probably be hauling a surfboard. "Mostly in the summer, when I'm staying with my dad."

So it's one of those families.

"Do you know the other people who live in this building? Do you know Charlotte Nielson?"

"The lady in 314? Yeah." The boys exchange knowing smirks. "I'd sure like to know her better," he adds, and they both laugh.

"I really need to reach her. Can you give her this note? I'd like her to call me." I pull a notepad from my purse and jot down my phone number.

"She's not here. She's up in Maine."

"No, she's not," I tell him.

"Yeah, she is."

"She *was* in Maine, but she left a month ago. Didn't she come home?"

The boy shakes his head. "I haven't seen her since June. Just before she left for the summer."

I think about this for a moment, trying to reconcile it with what Donna Branca told me—that Charlotte left Brodie's Watch because of a family emergency. If she hadn't returned to Boston, where had she gone? Why wasn't she answering her emails and phone calls?

"So what's up with Charlotte?" the teenager asks.

"I don't know." I stare at the building. "Is your dad at home?"

"He went for a run."

"Can you give him my phone number? Ask him to call me back. I really need to reach Charlotte."

"Yeah. Okay." The boy stuffs the slip of paper with my phone number into the back pocket of his jeans, where I fear it will all too easily be forgotten, but there is nothing more I can do. My hunt for Charlotte all comes down to a teenage boy who will probably toss those jeans in the washing machine without ever remembering what's in his pocket.

I climb back into my car wondering if I should just spend the night in Boston rather than drive the four and a half hours back to Tucker Cove. My apartment has been sitting empty for weeks, and I should probably check on it anyway.

This time I avoid Commonwealth Avenue and instead take an alternate route, so I won't have to drive past Lucy's apartment. My no-go area is expanding. In the days after Nick's death, I forced myself to step through Lucy's front door only because she so desperately needed my comfort. Then I couldn't do it anymore. I couldn't tolerate her hugs, couldn't look her in the eye, so I just stopped going to see her. Stopped calling her, stopped returning her voicemails.

Now I can't even drive past her building.

My no-go areas keep expanding, like spreading blots of ink on the city map. The area around the hospital where Lucy works. Her favorite coffee shop and grocery store. All the places where I might run into her and be forced to explain the reason I've dropped out of her life. Just the thought of encountering her makes my heart pound, my hands sweat. I imagine those black blots enlarging, spreading on the map until the entire city of Boston is a no-go zone. Maybe I should move to Tucker Cove forever and lock myself away in Brodie's Watch. Grow old and die there, far from this city where I see my guilt reflected back at me everywhere I look, especially on this road to my own apartment.

This is the road where it happened. There is the intersection where the limousine slammed into Nick's Prius, spinning it around on the ice-slicked street. And that lamppost is where the crumpled Prius ended up.

Another black blot on the map. Another place to avoid. All the way to my apartment, I feel as if I'm driving an obstacle course where every corner, every street, is a bad memory, waiting like a bomb to explode.

And in my own apartment is the most devastating memory of all.

It doesn't hit me, not at first. When I step inside, all I register is the stale air of a home where no window has been opened in weeks. Everything is as I left it, my spare keys in the bowl near the door, the last few issues of *Bon Appétit* stacked on the coffee table. *Home sweet home* is what I should be feeling, but I'm still agitated by the drive, still unsure if I really want to spend the night here. I set down my purse, drop the keys in the bowl. I haven't eaten or drunk anything since this morning, so I walk into the kitchen for a glass of water.

That's where it hits me. New Year's Eve.

The memory is so vivid I can hear the pop of corks, can smell the rosemary and sizzling fat of the roasting porchetta. And I remember the happy, happy taste of champagne on my tongue. Too much champagne that night, but it was *my* party; I had spent all day in the kitchen shucking oysters and trimming artichokes and assembling mushroom tarts, and as my apartment filled up with my three dozen guests, I was ready to celebrate.

So I drank.

Everyone else did, too. Everyone except for Lucy, who had the bad luck of being on call for the hospital that night. She and Nick had driven separately, just in case Lucy had to leave the party for an emergency, and that night she sipped only sparkling water.

Of course she *was* called in, because it was New Year's Eve, the roads were icy, and there were bound to be accidents. I remember looking at her from across the room as she pulled on her coat to leave, and thinking: *There goes my perfectly sober sister, off to save another life, while here I am, finishing off my sixth glass of champagne.*

Or was it my seventh?

By the end of the evening, I had lost count, but what did it matter? I wasn't driving anywhere. And neither was Nick, who'd agreed to sleep in my guestroom because he was too wasted to get behind the wheel of a car.

I stare down at the kitchen floor and remember those cold, hard tiles against my back. I remember the nausea of all the champagne sloshing in my stomach. Suddenly the nausea is back, and I cannot stand being in this apartment a moment longer.

I flee the apartment and climb back in my car.

By this evening, I'll be home again, in Brodie's Watch. This is the first time I've actually thought of it as "home," but now it seems like the one place in the world where I can hide from the memories of that night. I reach for the ignition.

My cellphone rings. It's a Boston area code, but I don't recognize the number. I answer it anyway.

"My son told me to call you." It's a man's voice. "He says you came by my building a little while ago, asking about Charlotte."

"Yes, thank you for calling. I've been trying to reach her, but she hasn't responded to any emails and she doesn't answer her phone."

"Who are you, exactly?"

"My name is Ava Collette. I'm living in the house in Tucker Cove that Charlotte used to rent. I have a few things that she left behind, and I'd like to send them to her."

"Wait. Isn't she still staying there?"

"No. She left town over a month ago and I assumed she went home to Boston. I mailed her package there and it bounced back to me."

"Well, she hasn't been back in Boston. I haven't seen her since June. Not since she left for Maine."

We're both silent for a moment, pondering the mystery of where Charlotte Nielson might be.

"Do you have *any* idea where she is now?" I ask.

"When she left Boston, she gave me her forwarding address. It's a PO box."

"Where?"

"In Tucker Cove."

Twenty

Donna Branca isn't the least bit alarmed by what I've told her.

"The man you spoke to is just her neighbor, so he might not know where she's gone. Maybe she's out of state visiting relatives. Or she's traveling abroad. There's any number of reasons why she didn't go home to Boston." Her phone rings and she swivels around to answer it. "Branca Property Sales and Management."

I stare across the desk at her, waiting for her to finish the call and continue our conversation, but I can already see she's tuned me out and is fully focused instead on signing up a new rental property to manage: four bedrooms, view of the water, only a mile from the village. I'm just an annoying tenant, trying to play detective. This is Tucker Cove, not Cabot Cove, and only on *Murder, She Wrote* would a summer tourist investigate a woman's disappearance.

At last Donna hangs up and turns back to me with an expression of *why are you still here?* "Is there some reason you're worried about Charlotte? You've never even met her."

"She doesn't answer her cellphone. She hasn't responded to emails in weeks."

"In the letter she sent me, she said she'd be out of touch for a while."

"Do you still have that letter?"

With a sigh, Donna swivels around to a filing cabinet and pulls out the folder for Brodie's Watch.

"This is what she mailed me from Boston, after she vacated. As you can see, there's nothing alarming about it." She hands me a typed letter which is, indeed, matter-of-fact.

Donna, due to a family crisis, I had to leave Tucker Cove immediately. I won't be returning to Maine. I know there's still two months left on my lease, but I'm sure you'll have no problem finding a new tenant. I hope my deposit will be enough to cover the early departure. I left the house in good condition.

Cellphone coverage will be spotty where I'm going, so if you need to reach me, email is best.

Charlotte

I read the letter twice, my puzzlement deepening, and look at Donna. "Don't you think this is strange?"

"Her deposit covered everything. And she did leave the house in good shape."

"Why didn't she mention where she's going?"

"Somewhere out of cellphone range."

"Out of the country? Into the wilderness? Where?"

Donna shrugs. "All I know is, she was paid up."

"And now it's weeks later and she's still unreachable. Her neighbor in Boston has no idea where she is. He told me the number of her PO box in Tucker Cove is 137. For all we know, her mail is still sitting there, uncollected. Doesn't *any* of this bother you?"

For a moment she taps her fingers on the desk. At last she picks up the phone and dials. "Hello, Stuart? It's Donna Branca. Could you do me a big favor and check on a PO box for me? The number is 137. It belonged to one of my tenants, Charlotte Nielson. No, Stuart, I'm not asking you to reveal anything you shouldn't. It's just that Charlotte left town weeks ago and I want to know if her mail's being forwarded anywhere. Yes, I'll stay on the line." She glances at me. "He's bending the rules a little, but this is a small town and we all know each other."

"Can he give us her forwarding address?" I ask.

"I'm not going to push it, okay? He's nice enough just to be doing this for us." Her attention snaps back to the phone. "Yes, Stuart, I'm here. What?" She frowns. "It's all still there? And she never gave you a forwarding address?"

I lean forward, my gaze riveted to her face. Although I'm hearing only half the conversation, I know that something is very wrong and now even Donna is disturbed. Slowly she hangs up and looks at me.

"She hasn't picked up her mail in over a month. Her PO box is stuffed full and she never gave them a forwarding address." Donna shakes her head. "This is so strange."

"It's more than strange."

"Maybe she just forgot to fill out a change of address card."

"Or she couldn't fill it out."

We stare at each other for a moment and the same possibility suddenly rears up in both our minds. Charlotte Nielson has dropped off the face of the earth. She doesn't answer her phone or her emails and she has not picked up her mail in weeks.

"You know that body they found floating in the water?" I say. "It was a woman's. And she still hasn't been identified."

"Do you think . . ."

"I think we need to call the police."

Once again, the police are in my house, but this time they're not here about a minor break-in by a burglar who's tracked dirt across my kitchen floor. This time, they are Maine State Police detectives conducting a death investigation. Dental records have confirmed that the body found floating in the bay is indeed Charlotte Nielson, who has not collected the mail from her PO box in over a month. Whose last known communication was the typewritten letter sent to Donna Branca.

Who two months ago was living in Brodie's Watch and sleeping in my bed.

I sit in the kitchen as the police tramp through the bedrooms upstairs. I don't know what they think they'll find. I've long since finished the last bottle of her whiskey. The only traces of Charlotte left in the house are her Hermès scarf, her copy of *Joy of Cooking*, and the spare flip-flop that I found under the bed. There is also her handwritten list of local phone numbers, which is still tacked to the kitchen corkboard. Numbers for the plumber, the electrician, the doctor She had the precise penmanship you'd expect of an elementary school teacher, and if it's true you can judge a person by their handwriting, then Charlotte was a neat and careful woman who would not normally leave behind an expensive scarf or a well-thumbed cookbook. The fact she did makes me think she packed quickly, so anxious to flee this house that she didn't bother to look under the bed or reach into the deepest corner of the closet. I think of my first night here, when I'd found that bottle and poured myself a glass. A dead woman's whiskey.

I've already thrown away that empty bottle, but I should tell the police about it.

Outside, the weather's taken a turn for the worst. The storm that lashed the Carolinas a few days ago has now rolled up the

coast and raindrops splatter the kitchen window. I suddenly remember that I've left the east-facing windows open, so I leave the
kitchen and go into the sea room to close them. Through the rain-
streaked glass I see waves rolling in, gray and turbulent, and I hear
the wind-whipped branches of the lilac bush clawing the house.

"Ma'am?"

I turn to see the two detectives, Vaughan and Perry, which
sounds like a law firm. Unlike the local cops who came to investigate the break-in, these buttoned-down and humorless men deal
with serious crimes, and their demeanor reflects it. I have already
walked them through the upstairs rooms and pointed out where
I'd found Charlotte's scarf and flip-flop, yet they insisted on in-
specting the house on their own—looking for what, I wonder.
Since Charlotte's departure, the floors have been vacuumed, and
any traces she left of herself are now contaminated by my own.

"Have you finished upstairs?" I ask them.

"Yes. But we have a few more questions," says Detective Vaughn.
He has the air of command that makes me think he's seen military
service, and when he gestures to the sofa, I obediently sit down.
He settles into the brocade wing chair, which looks ridiculously
feminine for a man with his broad shoulders and Marine flattop.
His partner Detective Perry stands off to the side, arms crossed as
though trying to look casual, but not quite pulling it off. They are
both big men, imposing men, and I would not like to be in the
crosshairs of any investigation conducted by them.

"I knew something was wrong," I murmur. "But she thought I
was just being a busybody."

"Ms. Branca, you mean?"

"Yes. Charlotte wasn't answering her phone or emails, and
Donna wasn't the least bit curious. It's almost as if she refused to
believe anything was wrong."

"But you felt something was?"

"It bothered me that Charlotte never answered my emails."

"Why were you trying to reach her?"

"I had a few questions."

"About?" His eyes are too direct, too piercing.

I look away. "About this house. A few minor, um, issues."

"Couldn't Ms. Branca answer those questions?"

"You'd have to actually live here to understand." He remains silent and I feel compelled to keep talking. "There've been some odd noises at night. Things I can't explain. I wondered if Charlotte had heard them, too."

"You said you had a break-in here a few weeks ago. Do you think there's a connection to those noises you heard?"

"No. I don't think so."

"Because Ms. Nielson also reported an incident."

"Yes, I heard that from the local police. They thought it was probably some teenager who didn't realize the house was occupied. They said the same thing about my break-in."

He leans closer, his eyes laser-sharp. "Can you think of anyone who might have done this? Aside from some nameless teenager?"

"No. But if it also happened to Charlotte, could it be the same person?"

"We have to consider all the possibilities."

All the possibilities. I look back and forth at the two men, whose silence only makes me more agitated. "What *did* happen to Charlotte?" I ask. "I know she was found floating in the bay, but how did she die?"

"All we can tell you is this is a homicide investigation."

My cellphone rings, but I don't even bother to look at who's calling; I let it go to voicemail and stay focused on the detectives.

"Were there bruises?" I ask. "Did the killer leave any marks?"

Vaughn says, "Why are you asking, ma'am?"

"I'm just trying to understand why you're so certain it was murder. How do you know she didn't just fall off a boat and drown?"

"There was no seawater in her lungs. She was dead before her body entered the water."

"But it could still be an accident. Maybe she fell on the rocks. Hit her head and—"

"It was not an accident. She was strangled." He watches as I take in this information, no doubt wondering if these details are more than I can handle and he'll have a hysterical woman on his hands. But I sit perfectly still as I consider what he's just told me. There's so much more I want to know. Were there broken bones? Bruises left by real hands made of real flesh? Can mere ectoplasm kill a woman?

Could Captain Brodie?

I look down at my left wrist, remembering the bruise that has since faded. A bruise that I found the morning after my first encounter with the ghost. Had I caused that bruise myself while stumbling around in a drunken stupor, as I have on more than one occasion? Or was that bruise the evidence that he can inflict real harm on the living?

"Have there been other break-ins since the night you called the Tucker Cove police?" Detective Perry asks.

I shake my head. "No."

"Anyone calling you, harassing you?"

"No."

"We understand from Ms. Branca that there's been some carpentry work done here recently."

"Yes, up in the turret and the widow's walk. They've already finished the renovations."

"How well do you know the carpenters?"

"I saw Billy and Ned almost every day for weeks, so I'd say we're well acquainted."

"Did you spend much time talking to them?"

"I used them as my guinea pigs." At Vaughn's raised eyebrow, I give a laugh. "I'm a cookbook author. I'm writing a book about traditional New England foods and I've been testing recipes. Billy and Ned were always happy to sample the results."

"Did either one of them ever make you feel uncomfortable?"

"No. I trusted them enough to let them come and go even when I wasn't here."

"They had a key to the house?"

"They knew where to find it. I left the spare key for them on top of the doorjamb."

"So one of them could have made a copy of that key."

I shake my head in bewilderment. "Why are you asking about them?"

"They were also working in this house while Ms. Nielson lived here."

"Do you actually *know* Billy and Ned?"

"Do you, ma'am?"

That makes me pause. In truth, how can we truly know anyone? "They never gave me a reason *not* to trust them," I say. "And Billy, he's just a kid."

"He's twenty-three years old," says Perry.

How odd that they already know Billy's age. Now I do, as well. They don't need to point out the obvious: that twenty-three-year-old men are capable of violence. I think of the muffins and stews and cakes I prepared for them, and how Billy's eyes would light up whenever I appeared with new treats for them to sample. Was I feeding a monster?

"And the second carpenter? What do you know about Mr. Haskell?" His gaze offers no clue to what he's thinking, but his questions have veered into disturbing territory. Suddenly we're not talking about faceless intruders, but about people I know and like.

"I know he's a master carpenter. Just look around, at what he's done with this house. Ned told me he started working for the Sherbrooke family years ago. As a handyman for the owner's aunt."

"That would be the late Aurora Sherbrooke?"

"Yes. Why would he still be working for the Sherbrooke family if there'd been any problems? And he's more than just a carpenter. He's also a well-regarded artist. The gallery downtown sells his carvings of birds."

"So we hear," says Perry, sounding unimpressed.

"You should take a look at his work. His pieces are even sold in galleries in Boston." I look back and forth at the two detectives. "He's an *artist*," I repeat, as if that excludes him as a suspect. Artists create, they don't destroy. They don't kill.

"Did Mr. Haskell ever say or do anything that bothered you? Struck you as inappropriate or made you uneasy?"

Something has changed here. Both of these men have leaned ever so slightly forward, their eyes fixed on me. "Why are you asking about Ned?"

"These are routine questions."

"They don't sound routine."

"Please, just answer the question."

"All right, then. Ned Haskell never once made me uncomfortable. He never scared me. I *like* the man, and I trusted him enough to give him access to my house. Now tell me why you're focused on him."

"We follow every lead. It's our job."

"Has Ned done something wrong?"

"We can't comment," says Vaughn, an answer that tells me everything. He closes his notebook. "We'll be in touch if we have other questions. In the meantime, do you still keep your house key above the doorjamb?"

"It's there right now. I just haven't taken it down."

"I suggest you do that now. And while you're at home, use the dead bolt. I notice you have one."

The men head to the front door. I follow them, so many of my questions still unanswered. "What about Charlotte's car?" I ask. "She had a car, didn't she? Have you found it yet?"

"No."

"So the killer stole it."

"We don't know where it is. It could be out of state by now. Or it could be lying at the bottom of some lake."

"Then it could have been just a carjacking, couldn't it? Someone stole her car and threw her body into the bay." I hear the note of desperation in my voice. "It could have happened while she was driving out of town. Not here, not in this house."

Detective Vaughn pauses on the front porch and looks at me with those coolly enigmatic eyes. "Lock your door, Ms. Collette," is all he says.

That is the first thing I do after they drive away. I turn the dead bolt and walk around the house, checking that all the windows are latched. The storm clouds that have been darkening all afternoon suddenly rip open with a clap of thunder. In the sea room, I stand at the window watching rain sheet down the glass. The air itself feels charged and dangerous, and when I look at my arms, I see the hairs are standing up. Lightning streaks from the sky and the whole house shakes in the instantaneous thunderclap.

Any minute now, the power could go out.

I pick up the cellphone to check how much battery life is left, and whether it can last the night without charging. Only then do I see there's a voicemail, and I remember the phone call I ignored when I was talking to the detectives.

I play the message and am startled to hear the voice of Ned Haskell.

Ava, you'll probably be hearing things about me, things that aren't true. None of it is true. I want you to know I haven't done anything wrong. This isn't over yet, not by a long shot. Not if I can help it.

I stare at my phone, wondering if I should tell the police about his call. Wondering too, if that would be a violation of his trust. Of all people, why am I the one he reached out to?

A bolt of lightning spears the sea. I back away from the window and feel the clap of answering thunder deep in my bones, as if my chest is a roaring kettledrum. Ned's message unsettles me, and as the storm rages, I make one more round of the house, again checking windows and doors.

That night, I do not sleep well.

As lightning slashes the darkness and thunder rumbles, I lie awake in the same bed where a murdered woman slept. I think back to every interaction I ever had with Ned Haskell, and the memories play like a slideshow in my head. Ned on the widow's walk, his arm muscles bulging as he swings the hammer. Ned grinning at me over the bowl of beef stew I've ladled out for him. I think of what goes into the toolbox of a carpenter, all the blades and vises and screwdrivers, and how items meant for shaping wood can so easily be put to other purposes.

Then I think of the art gallery reception and how Ned had smiled so sheepishly as he stood beside his whimsical bird carvings. How can someone who creates such charming art grasp a woman's throat and squeeze the life out of her?

"Do not be afraid."

I glance up, startled by the voice in the darkness. A flash of distant lightning illuminates the room and every detail of his face is instantly seared into my memory. Black curls as unruly as storm-tossed waves. A face of rough-hewn granite. But tonight I glimpse something new, something I did not see in the portrait of Captain Brodie that hangs in the historical society. Now I see weariness in his eyes, the weather-beaten fatigue of a man who has sailed too many oceans and now seeks only a calm harbor.

I reach up and touch days-old stubble on his jaw. *So this was how Death found you,* I think. Exhausted by hours at the helm, your ship battered by the sea, your crew swept away by waves. How I long to be the safe harbor he seeks, but I am a century and a half too late.

"Sleep soundly, dear Ava. Tonight I will stand watch."

"I've missed you."

He presses a kiss to my head and his breath is warm in my hair. The breath of the living. "When you need me most, here I am.

Here I will always be." He settles beside me on the bed and the mattress sags under his weight. How can this man not be real when I can feel his arms around me, his coat against my cheek?

"You're different tonight," I whisper. "So kind. So gentle."

"I am whatever you need me to be."

"But who are *you*? Who is the real Captain Brodie?"

"Like all men, I am both good and bad. Cruel and kind." He cups my face in a weatherworn hand that tonight offers only comfort, but it's the same hand that has swung a whip and shackled my wrists.

"How will I know which man to expect?"

"Is that not what you desire, the unexpected?"

"Sometimes you scare me."

"Because I take you to dangerous places. I offer you a glimpse of the darkness. I dare you to take the first step, and the next." He strokes my face as gently as if he is stroking a child. "But not tonight."

"What happens tonight?"

"Tonight you sleep. Be unafraid," he whispers. "I will let no harm come to you."

And that night I do sleep, safe in the circle of his arms.

Twenty-One

I t's the talk of the town the next afternoon. I first hear about it when I'm buying groceries at the Village Food Mart, a shop so small you have to use a handbasket to collect your items because no shopping cart will make it down the narrow aisles. I stand at the vegetable section, perusing the pitiful choices of lettuce (iceberg or romaine), tomatoes (beefsteak or cherry), and parsley (curly or nothing). Tucker Cove may be a summer paradise but it's at the end of the grocery supply line, and since I missed shopping at yesterday's weekly farmer's market, I'm forced to take what I can get at the Food Mart. As I'm bending down to scavenge some red potatoes from the bin, I hear two women gossiping in the next aisle.

". . . and the police showed up at his house with a search warrant, can you believe it? Nancy saw three police cars parked out in front."

"Oh my god. You don't really think he killed her?"

"They haven't arrested him yet, but I think it's just a matter of time. After all, there was the thing that happened to that *other* girl. At the time, everyone thought it had to be him."

I crane my neck around the end of the display case to see two silver-haired women, their shopping baskets still empty, clearly more engaged in gossip than in groceries.

"Nothing was ever proved."

"But now it seems more likely, doesn't it? Since the police are taking such an interest in him. And there's that old woman he worked for years ago, up on the hill. I always wondered what she *really* died of . . ."

As they move away toward the paper goods, I can't help but trail after them, just to catch more of the conversation. I pause in front of the toilet tissue, pretending to mull over which brand to choose. There's a total of two options—how ever shall I decide?

"You just never know, do you?" one of the women says. "He always seemed so nice. And to think our minister hired him last year, to install the new pews. All those sharp tools he works with."

They are definitely talking about Ned Haskell.

I pay for the groceries and walk out to my car, disturbed by what I've just heard. Surely the police have their reasons to focus on Ned. The women in the store had talked about another girl. Was she too a murder victim?

Right down the street is Branca Property Sales and Management. If anyone has their finger on the pulse of a community, it's a Realtor. Donna will know.

As usual, she's sitting at her desk, the phone pressed to her ear. She glances up and quickly ducks her head, avoiding my gaze.

"No, of course I had no idea," she murmurs into the phone. "He's always been perfectly reliable. I've never had any complaints. Look, can I call you back? I have someone in the office." She hangs up and reluctantly turns to face me.

"Is it true?" I ask. "About Ned?"

"Who told you?"

"I heard two women talking about it at the grocery store. They said the police searched his house this morning."

Donna sighs. "There are too many damn gossips in this town."

"So it is true."

"He hasn't been arrested. It's not fair to assume he's guilty of anything."

"I'm not assuming anything, Donna. I *like* Ned. But I heard them say there was another girl. Before Charlotte."

"That was just a rumor."

"Who was the girl?"

"It was never proved."

I rock forward until I'm practically face-to-face with her. "You rented me the house. For weeks, he was working right above my bedroom. I deserve to know if he's dangerous. *Who was the girl?*"

Donna's lips tighten. Her friendly Realtor mask is gone and in its place is the worried face of a woman who withheld the vital detail that a killer might have been working inside my house.

"She was just a tourist," says Donna. As if that made the victim less worthy of consideration. "And it happened six, seven years ago. She was renting a cottage on Cinnamon Beach when she vanished."

"The way Charlotte vanished."

"Except they never found Laurel's body. Most of us assumed she went swimming and drowned, but there was always a question. Always these whispers."

"About Ned?"

She nods. "He was working in the cottage next door to hers, renovating a bathroom."

"That's hardly a reason to be considered a suspect."

"He had her house keys."

I stare at her. "What?"

"Ned claimed he found them on Cinnamon Beach, where he scavenges driftwood for his sculptures. Laurel's rental agent spotted the keys on the dashboard of Ned's truck, and she recognized her agency key ring. That's all the police had on him, just the missing woman's keys, and the fact he was working right next door to her cottage. They never found her body. There was no evidence of violence in the cottage. They weren't sure any crime at all was committed."

"Now there *has* been a murder. Charlotte's. And Ned was working right there, in her house. In *my* house."

"But I didn't hire him. Arthur Sherbrooke did. He insisted Ned had to do the renovations."

"Why Ned?"

"Because he knows the house better than anyone. Ned used to work for Mr. Sherbrooke's aunt, when she was still living there."

"That's the other gossip I heard today. Is there some question about how the aunt died?"

"Aurora Sherbrooke? None at all. She was old."

"These women seemed to think Ned had something to do with the aunt's death."

"Jesus. The goddamn gossip in this town never ends!" The starch suddenly seems to go out of Donna and she slumps back in her chair. "Ava, I've known Ned Haskell all my life. Yes, I've heard the rumors about him. I know there are people who simply refuse to hire him. But I never thought he was dangerous. And I *still* don't believe he is."

Neither do I, but as I leave Donna's office, I wonder how close I came to being another Charlotte, another Laurel. I think of him swinging a hammer in my turret, his clothes powdery with wood dust. He is powerful enough to strangle a woman, but could such a killer have also created those sweetly whimsical birds? Perhaps I missed something darker about them, some disturbing clue to a monster lurking inside the artist. Are there not monsters inside each and every one of us? I am all too well-acquainted with my own.

I climb into my car and have just buckled the seatbelt when my cellphone rings.

It's Maeve. "I need to see you," she says.

"Can we meet next week?"

"This afternoon. I'm on my way to Tucker Cove now."

"What is this all about?"

"It's about Brodie's Watch. You need to move out, Ava. As soon as possible."

Maeve hesitates on my front porch, as if summoning the courage to enter the house. Nervously she scans the foyer behind me and finally steps inside, but as we walk into the sea room she keeps glancing around like a frightened doe, on the alert for attacking teeth and claws. Even after she settles into a wingback chair, she still looks uneasy, a visitor in hostile territory.

From her shoulder bag she pulls out a thick folder and sets it on the coffee table. "This is what I've been able to track down so far. But there may be more."

"About Captain Brodie?"

"About the women who've lived in this house before you."

I open the folder. The top page is an obituary, photocopied from a newspaper dated January 3, 1901. *Miss Eugenia Hollander, age 58, dies at home after falling on stairs.*

"She died here. In this house," says Maeve.

"This article says it was an accident."

"That would be the logical conclusion, wouldn't it? It was a winter's night, cold. Dark. And those turret steps were probably only dimly lit."

That last detail makes me glance up. "It happened on the turret staircase?"

"Read the police report."

I turn to the next page and find a handwritten report by Officer Edward K. Billings of the Tucker Cove Police. His handwriting is exquisite, thanks to an era when schools demanded perfect penmanship. Despite the poor-quality photocopy, his report is readable.

The deceased is a fifty-eight-year-old lady, never married, who lived alone. Prior to this incident she was in excellent health, according to her niece Mrs. Helen Colcord. Mrs. Colcord last saw her aunt alive yesterday evening, when Miss Hollander seemed in good spirits and had eaten a hearty supper.

At approximately seven-fifteen the next morning, the housemaid Miss Jane Steuben arrived and was puzzled that Miss Hollander was not downstairs, as was her habit. Upon climbing to the second floor, Miss Steuben discovered the door to the turret stairs open, and she found the body of Miss Hollander crumpled at the foot of the staircase.

I pause, remembering the nights Captain Brodie led me up those same stairs by flickering candlelight. I think of how steep and narrow that stairway is, and how easily a headlong tumble can snap a neck. On the night Eugenia Hollander died, what was she doing on those stairs?

Had something—someone—lured her to the turret, just as I have been lured?

I focus once again on Officer Billings's precise handwriting. Of course, he would conclude her death was merely an accident. What else could it be? The deceased woman lived alone, nothing was stolen, and there were no signs of an intruder.

I look at Maeve. "There's nothing suspicious about this death. That's what the police believed. Why did you show me this?"

"I was looking for more information about the dead woman when I found a photo of her."

I turn to the next page in the folder. It's a black-and-white portrait of a pretty young woman with arching eyebrows and a cascade of dark hair.

"That photo was taken when she was nineteen years old. A beautiful girl, wasn't she?" says Maeve.

"Yes."

"Her name appears in a number of society columns published around then, in connection with a variety of eligible young men. At twenty-two years old, she became engaged to a wealthy merchant's son. As a wedding gift, her father gave her Brodie's Watch, where the young couple planned to live after their marriage. But that marriage never took place. The day before the wedding, Eugenia broke off the engagement. Instead she chose to remain a spinster, and she lived alone in this house. For the rest of her life."

Maeve waits for a response, but I don't know what to say. I can only stare at the photo of nineteen-year-old Eugenia, a beauty who chose never to marry. Who lived out her life alone in this house where I am now living.

"It's strange, don't you think?" Maeve says. "All those years, living alone here."

"Not every woman wants or needs to get married."

She studies me for a moment, but she is a ghost hunter, not a mind reader. She cannot possibly imagine what happens after dark in this house. In that turret.

She nods at the folder. "Now take a look at the next woman who lived in this house."

"There was another?"

"After Miss Hollander died on the stairs, Brodie's Watch passed to her brother. He tried to sell the house but couldn't find a buyer. There were rumors in town that the place was haunted and it had already fallen into disrepair. He had a niece, Violet Theriault, who'd been widowed at a young age. She was in some financial difficulty so he let her live here, rent-free. This was her home for thirty-seven years, until her death."

"Don't tell me she fell down the stairs, too."

"No. She died in bed, presumably of natural causes, at the age of sixty-nine."

"Is there a reason you're telling me about these women?"

"It's all part of a pattern, Ava. After Violet died, there was Margaret Gordon, a visitor from New York who rented Brodie's Watch for the summer. She never returned to New York. Instead she remained here until she died of a stroke, twenty-two years later. She was followed by Miss Aurora Sherbrooke, yet another tenant who came just for the summer, decided to buy the house, and lived here until her death thirty years later."

With every new name she reveals, I flip through the photos in the folder, seeing the faces of those who came before me. Eugenia and Violet, Margaret and Aurora. Now the pattern becomes apparent, a pattern that leaves me stunned. All the women who have lived and died in this house were dark-haired and beautiful. All the women bore a startling resemblance to . . .

"You," says Maeve. "They all look like *you*."

I stare at the final photo. Aurora Sherbrooke had lustrous black hair and a swan neck and arching eyebrows, and while I am not nearly as pretty as she was, the resemblance is unmistakable. It's as if I am a younger but plainer Sherbrooke sister.

My hands are icy as I turn the page to Aurora's obituary in the August 20, 1986, edition of the *Tucker Cove Weekly*.

AURORA SHERBROOKE, AGE 66

Ms. Aurora Sherbrooke passed away last week at her home in Tucker Cove. She was found by her nephew, Arthur Sherbrooke, who had not heard from her in days and drove from his home in Cape Elizabeth to check on her. The death is not considered suspicious. According to a housekeeper, Ms. Sherbrooke had recently been ill with the flu.

Originally from Newton, Massachusetts, Ms. Sherbrooke

first visited Tucker Cove thirty-one years ago. "She immediately fell in love with the town, and especially with the house she was renting," said her nephew, Arthur Sherbrooke. Ms. Sherbrooke purchased the house, known as Brodie's Watch, which remained her home until her death.

"Four women have died in this house," says Maeve.

"None of these deaths were suspicious."

"But doesn't it make you wonder? Why were they all women, and why did they all live and die here alone? I've gone through the Tucker Cove obituaries back to 1875, and I couldn't find any men who died in this house." She looks around the room, as if the answers might lie in the walls or the mantelpiece. Her gaze stops at the window, where our view of the sea has receded behind a curtain of mist. "It's as if this house is some sort of trap," she says softly. "Women walk in but they don't walk out. Somehow it charms them, seduces them. And in the end, it imprisons them."

My laugh is not entirely convincing. "That's why you think I should leave? Because I'll end up a prisoner?"

"You need to know the history of this house, Ava. You need to know what you're dealing with."

"Are you telling me these women were all killed by a ghost?"

"If it was *just* a ghost, I wouldn't be so concerned."

"What else would it be?"

She pauses to consider her next words. That hesitation only adds to my sense of foreboding. "A few weeks ago, I mentioned there are things other than ghosts that can attach themselves to a house. Entities that aren't exactly benign. Ghosts are simply spirits who haven't moved on because of unfinished business in this world, or who died so suddenly they don't realize they *are* dead. They linger between our world and the next. Even though they've passed on, they were once human, just like us, and they almost never cause harm to the living. But every so often I come across a house that harbors something else. Not a ghost, but . . ." Her voice wavers and she glances around the room. "Do you mind if we step outside?"

"Now?"

"Yes. Please."

I glance out the window at the thickening mist. I really don't feel like stepping out into that damp sea air, but I nod and rise to my feet. At the front door I pull on a rain jacket and we both walk outside onto the porch. But even there, Maeve is nervous, and she leads me down the steps and along the stone path that leads to the cliff's edge. There we stand cloaked in mist, the house looming behind us in the fog. For a moment the only sound is the crashing of waves far below.

"If he's not a ghost, what is he?" I ask.

"Interesting that you use the word 'he.'"

"Why wouldn't I? Captain Brodie was a man."

"How often does he appear to you, Ava? Do you see him every day?"

"It's not predictable. Sometimes I don't see him for days."

"And what time do you see him?"

"At night."

"Only at night?"

I think about the dark figure I saw standing on the widow's walk when I came back from the beach that first morning. "There've been times when I may have seen him during the day."

"And he always appears to be Captain Brodie?"

"This was his house. Who else would he appear to be?"

"It's not who, Ava. It's *what*." She glances back at the house, which has receded to only a vague silhouette in the fog, and she hugs herself to quell her trembling. Only yards from where we stand is the cliff's edge and far below, hidden in the mist, waves are pummeling the rocks. We are trapped between the sea and Brodie's Watch, and the fog seems thick enough to smother us.

"There are other entities, Ava," she says. "They may seem like ghosts, but they aren't."

"What entities?"

"Dangerous ones. Things that can cause harm."

I think of the women who lived in Brodie's Watch before me, women who died in this house. But doesn't every old house have such a history? Everyone dies, and we all have to die somewhere. Why not in your own home, where you've lived for decades?

"These entities aren't the spirits of dead people," says Maeve. "They may take on the appearance of people who once occupied a home, but that's to make us feel less afraid of them. We all think that ghosts can't hurt us, that they're just unfortunate souls trapped between spiritual planes."

"What have I been seeing, then?"

"Not the ghost of Captain Brodie but something that's assumed his form. Something that's been aware of you and watching you since the moment you stepped through the front door. It's learned your weaknesses, your needs, your desires. It knows what you want and what you're afraid of. It will use that knowledge to manipulate you, imprison you. Harm you."

"You mean *physically*?" I can't help but laugh at this.

"I know it's hard to believe, but you haven't encountered the things I have. You haven't looked into the eyes of . . ." She stops. Takes a deep breath and continues. "Years ago, I was called about a house just outside Bucksport. It was a mansion, really, built in 1910 by a wealthy merchant. A year after they moved into that house, his wife tied a rope around her neck and hanged herself from the upstairs banister. After her suicide, the place was said to be haunted, but it was such a beautiful home, high on a hill with views of the water, that it was never hard to find someone willing to buy the place. Again and again it changed hands. People would fall in love with the house, move in, and quickly move out again. One family lasted only three weeks."

"What made them leave?"

"The locals believed it was the ghost of the merchant's wife, Abigail, scaring them off. They talked about sightings of a woman with long red hair and a rope knotted around her throat. People *can* learn to live with ghosts, even develop affection for them and consider them part of their living family. But this haunting was far more frightening. It wasn't just the thumps at night or the doors slamming shut or the chairs rearranging themselves. No, this was something that made the family reach out to me in desperation.

"They had fled the house in the middle of the night, and were living in a motel when they called me. They were a family of four with two darling little girls, four and eight years old. They were from Chicago and they came to Maine with the idea of living in the country, where he'd write novels and she'd grow a vegetable garden and keep chickens in the yard. They saw the house, fell in love with it, and made an offer. It was June when they moved in, and for the first week, it was glorious."

"Only a week?"

"At first, no one talked about what they were all feeling. A sense of being watched. A sense that, even when they were alone, someone else was in the room. Then the older daughter told her mother about the thing that sat by her bed at night, staring at her. That's when the rest of the family began to talk about what they'd experienced. And they realized they'd all seen and felt a presence, but it took different forms. The father saw a red-haired woman. The wife saw a faceless shadow. Only the four-year-old saw what it truly was. Young children have no illusions; they detect the truth before we do. And what she saw was a thing with red eyes and claws. Not the ghost of Abigail, but something far older. Something ancient, that had attached itself to that house. To that hilltop."

Red eyes? Claws? I shake my head in disbelief at the turn this conversation is taking. "You sound like you're talking about a demon."

"That's exactly what I'm talking about," she says quietly.

I stare at her for a moment, hoping to see some glint of humor in her eyes, some sign that a punch line is coming, but her gaze is absolutely steady. "I don't believe in demons."

"Before you moved into Brodie's Watch, did you believe in ghosts?"

To that, I can muster no rebuttal. Although I am facing the sea, I feel the house looming behind me, watching me. I'm afraid to hear her answer, but I ask the question anyway. "What happened to the family?"

"They hadn't believed in ghosts before, but they realized *something* was in their home. Something they'd all seen and experienced. The husband searched newspaper archives and found an article about Abigail's suicide. He assumed it was her ghost haunting the house, and ghosts can't hurt you, right? Plus it made excellent dinner chitchat. *We have a ghost in our house! Isn't that cool?* But slowly it dawned on the family that what haunted their house was something different.

"The four-year-old began waking up every night, screaming in terror. She said something was choking her, and the mother actually saw marks on her neck."

My heart is suddenly pounding. "What sort of marks?"

"They looked like the imprint of fingers on her throat. Fingers that were too long to be a child's. Then the eight-year-old began waking up with nosebleeds. They took her to the doctor and he could find no reason for the bleeding. Even then they remained in the house, because they'd sunk so much of their savings into it. Then one night, something happened that changed everything. The husband heard a banging outside and he went out to investigate. The instant he stepped outside, the front door swung shut behind him, locking him out. He banged on the door, but his family couldn't hear him. Yet he could hear what was happening *inside* the house. His daughters screaming. His wife, falling down the stairs. He broke a window to get inside, and he found her lying dazed at the bottom of the stairs. She insisted that *something* had pushed her. *Something* wanted her dead.

"The family moved out that same night. And the next morning, I got the phone call."

"You've seen the house?"

"Yes. I drove there the very next day. It was a handsome building, with a wraparound porch and twelve-foot ceilings. Just the sort of home a wealthy merchant would build for his family. When I arrived, the husband was waiting in the front yard, but he refused to go inside. He just gave me the key and told me to look around for myself. I went in alone."

"And what did you find?"

"Nothing. At first." Once again she eyes Brodie's Watch, as if afraid to turn her back on it. "I walked through the kitchen, the living room. It all seemed perfectly normal. I climbed the stairs to the bedrooms and again, nothing struck me as out of the ordinary. But then I went downstairs to the kitchen and opened the door to the cellar. That was when I smelled it."

"What?"

"The stench of decay. Of death. I didn't want to go down those stairs, but I forced myself to take a few steps. Then I lifted my flashlight and saw the marks carved into the ceiling. Talon marks, Ava. As if a beast had clawed its way into the house from below. That was as far as I got. I backed out of the cellar, walked out the front door, and I never set foot in the house again. Because I already knew the family couldn't return. I knew what they were dealing with. It wasn't a ghost. It was something far more powerful, something that had probably been there for a long, long time. There are many words for what they are. Demons. Strigoi. Baital. But they all have this in common: They are evil. And they are dangerous."

"Is that what Captain Brodie is?"

"I don't know *what* he is, Ava. This could be just a haunting, a

spiritual echo of the man who once lived here. That's what I assumed at first, because you haven't experienced anything that's
scared you. But when I look at the history of Brodie's Watch, when
I know that four women have died here . . ."

"From natural causes. From an accident."

"True, but what *kept* those women here? Why did they turn
their backs on marriage and families to spend the rest of their
lives alone in this house?"

Because of him. Because of the pleasures of the turret.

I look up at the house, and the memory of what happened in
the turret makes my cheeks burn.

"What made them stay here? Grow old and die here?" Maeve
asks, studying me. "Do *you* know?"

"He . . . the captain . . ."

"What about him?"

"He understands me. He makes me feel I belong here."

"What else does he make you feel?"

I turn away, my face on fire. She doesn't press the question and
silence hangs between us for a painfully long time, long enough
for her to gather that my secret is too embarrassing to share with
anyone.

"Whatever he offers you, it comes with a price," she warns.

"I'm not afraid of him. And the women who lived here before
me, they must not have been afraid, either. They could have cho-
sen to leave, but they didn't. They stayed in this house."

"They also died in this house."

"Only after years of living here."

"Is that how you see your future? As a prisoner of Brodie's
Watch? Growing old here, dying here?"

"We all have to die somewhere."

She takes me by the shoulders and forces me to look her in the
eyes. "Ava, do you *hear* yourself?"

I'm so startled by her touch that for a moment I don't speak.

Only now do I process what I've just said. *We all have to die some-where.* Is that really what I want, to turn my back on the world of the living?

"I don't know what power this entity has over you," says Maeve, "but you need to step back and think about what happened to the women who came before you. Four of them *died* here."

"Five," I say softly.

"I'm not counting the woman who was found floating in the bay."

"I'm not counting Charlotte, either. There was also a girl, fifteen years old. I told you about her. A group of teenagers broke in on a Halloween night. One of the girls climbed up to the widow's walk, where she fell."

Maeve shakes her head. "I looked, but it didn't come up in my search of the newspaper archives."

"My carpenter told me about it. He grew up here, and he remembers it."

"Then we need to talk to him."

"I'm not sure we should."

"Why not?"

"He's a suspect. In the murder of Charlotte Nielson."

Maeve lets out a startled breath. She turns and stares at the house, which seems to be at the center of this maelstrom. Yet I myself feel no fear because I can still hear his words whispered in the darkness: *Under my roof, no harm will come to you.*

"If your carpenter remembers it," says Maeve, "other people in this town will remember it, too."

I nod. "I know just the person we should talk to."

Twenty-Two

It is just past five when Maeve and I arrive at the Tucker Cove Historical Society. The CLOSED sign is already hanging, but I knock anyway, hoping that Mrs. Dickens is still inside, tidying up. Through the smoked-glass door I see movement, and hear the thump of orthopedic shoes. Pale blue eyes, distorted by the thick lenses of spectacles, peer out the doorway.

"I'm sorry, but we're closed. The building will open at nine A.M. tomorrow."

"Mrs. Dickens, it's me. We spoke a few weeks ago, about Brodie's Watch, remember?"

"Oh hello. Ava, isn't it? It's nice to see you again, but the museum is still closed."

"We're not here to see the museum. We're here to speak with you. My friend Maeve and I are doing research on Brodie's Watch for my book, and we have questions you might be able to answer. Since you're the number one expert on the history of Tucker Cove."

That makes Mrs. Dickens stand a little straighter. On my last visit here, there'd been almost no other visitors. How frustrating it must be for her to be so knowledgeable about a subject that few people care about.

She smiles and opens the door wide. "I wouldn't call myself an *expert*, exactly, but I'd be happy to tell you whatever I know."

The house is even gloomier than I remembered, and the foyer smells of age and dust. The floor creaks as we follow Mrs. Dickens into the front parlor, where the logbook of *The Raven,* the ship formerly under the command of Captain Brodie, is displayed under glass.

"We keep many of our historical records in here." She pulls a key ring from her pocket and unlocks the door to a glass-fronted bookcase. On the shelves are volumes of leather-bound books, some of them so old they look ready to crumble. "We hope to digitize all of these records eventually, but you know how hard it is to find funds to do anything these days. No one cares about the past. They only care about the future and the next hip new thing." She scans the volumes. "Ah, here it is. The town records for 1861. That's the year Brodie's Watch was built."

"Actually Mrs. Dickens, our question is about something that happened far more recently."

"How recently?"

"It would be about twenty or so years ago, according to Ned Haskell."

"Ned?" Startled, she turns to frown at me. "Oh, dear."

"I guess you've heard the news about him."

"I've heard what people are saying. But I grew up in this town, so I've learned to ignore half of what I hear."

"Then you don't believe he—"

"I see no point in speculation." She slides the old book back on the shelf and claps dust from her hands. "If your question's about something that happened only twenty years ago, we wouldn't have that record here. You should try the *Tucker Cove Weekly.* They have archives going back at least fifty years, and I think much of that is digitized."

Maeve says, "I've already searched their archives for any articles mentioning Brodie's Watch. I never found anything about the accident."

"Accident?" Mrs. Dickens looks back and forth at us. "Something like that might not even make the news."

"But it should have. Since a fifteen-year-old girl died," I tell her.

Mrs. Dickens lifts her hand to her mouth. For a moment she doesn't speak, but just stares at me.

"Ned told me it happened on a Halloween night," I continue. "He said a group of teenagers broke into the empty house, and there may have been drinking involved. One of the girls went out onto the widow's walk, and somehow she fell. I don't recall her name, but I thought, if you remembered the incident, and which year it was, we might be able to track down the details."

"Jessie," Mrs. Dickens says softly.

"You remember her name?"

She nods. "Jessie Inman. She went to school with my niece. Such a pretty girl, but she had a wild streak." She takes a deep breath. "I think I'd like to sit down."

I'm alarmed by how pale she looks, and as Maeve takes her by the arm, I scurry across the room to fetch one of the antique chairs. Unsteady as she is, Mrs. Dickens hasn't forgotten her responsibilities as a docent and she looks down in dismay at the worn velvet seat. "Oh dear, this chair is off-limits. No one's supposed to sit in it."

"No one's here to complain, Mrs. Dickens," I say gently. "And we'll never tell."

She manages a faint smile as she settles into the chair. "I do try to follow the rules."

"I'm sure you do."

"So did Jessie's mother. That's why it was such a shock to her when she learned what Jessie had been up to that night. They weren't just trespassing. Those kids actually broke a window to get into the house. And probably do whatever kids with raging hormones do."

"You said she was a pretty girl. What did she look like?" Maeve asks her.

Mrs. Dickens shakes her head, baffled by the question. "Does it really matter?"

"What color was her hair?"

I fully expect her to tell us that the girl's hair was dark, and I'm surprised by her answer.

"She was fair-haired," says Mrs. Dickens. "Like her mother, Michelle."

And unlike me. Unlike all the other women who have died in Brodie's Watch.

"Did you know the mother very well?" I ask.

"Michelle attended my church. Volunteered at the school. She did everything a mother's supposed to do, yet she couldn't keep her daughter from making a *stupid* mistake. She died a few years after Jessie did. They said it was cancer, but I think what really killed her was losing her child."

Maeve looks at me. "I'm surprised an accident like that didn't make it into the local newspaper. I didn't find anything about a girl dying at Brodie's Watch."

"There were no articles," says Mrs. Dickens.

"Why not?"

"Because of who the other kids were. Six teenagers from the most prominent families in town. Do you think they wanted everyone to know their darling children smashed a window and broke into a house? Did lord-knows-what mischief in there? Jessie's death was a tragedy, but why compound it with shame? I think that's why the editor agreed not to publish the names or the details. I'm sure arrangements were made to repair any damage to the house, which satisfied the owner, Mr. Sherbrooke. The only thing that showed up in the newspaper was Jessie's obituary, and it said she

died from an accidental fall on Halloween night. Only a few people ever knew the truth."

"So that's why it didn't turn up in my search of the archives,"
says Maeve. "Which makes me wonder how many other women
have died in that house that we don't know about."

Mrs. Dickens frowns at her. "There were others?"

"I've found the names of at least four other women. And now
you've told us about Jessie."

"Which makes it five," Mrs. Dickens murmurs.

"Yes, five. All of them female."

"Why are you asking all these questions? Why are you interested?"

"It's for the book I'm writing," I explain. "Brodie's Watch plays
a big part in it and I want to include some history of the house."

"Is that the only reason?" Mrs. Dickens asks quietly.

For a moment I don't respond. She doesn't press me for an
answer, but just by the way she watches me, I know she's already
guessed the real reason for my questions.

"Things have happened in the house," I finally answer.

"What things?"

"They make me wonder if the house might be . . ." I give a
sheepish laugh. "Haunted."

"Captain Brodie," Mrs. Dickens murmurs. "You've seen him?"

Maeve and I glance at each other. "You've heard about the
ghost?" says Maeve.

"Everyone who grew up in this town knows the stories. How the
ghost of Jeremiah Brodie still lingers in that house. People claim
they've seen him standing on the widow's walk. Or staring out the
turret window. When I was a child, I loved hearing those stories,
but I never really believed them. I assumed it was something our
parents told us to make us stay away from that wreck of a place."
She gives me an apologetic look. "That was before you moved in,
of course, when it really *was* a wreck. Broken windows, a rotting
porch. Bats and mice and whatever other vermin lived inside."

"The mice are still there," I admit.

She gives a faint smile. "And they always will be."

Maeve says, "Since you grew up in this town, you must remember Aurora Sherbrooke. She used to live in Brodie's Watch."

"I knew who she was, but I didn't really know her. I don't think many people did. She'd come into town every so often to buy groceries, but that was the only time anyone saw her. Otherwise, she stayed up there on that hill, all alone."

With him. He was all she required for company. He gave her what she needed, just as he gives me what I need, whether it's the comfort of an embrace or the dark pleasures of the turret. Aurora Sherbrooke would not have shared that detail with anyone.

Neither will I.

"When she passed on, I don't remember any questions being raised about how she died," says Mrs. Dickens. "The one thing I do remember is that she'd been dead for a few days when her nephew found her." She grimaces. "That must have been an awful sight."

"Her nephew is Arthur Sherbrooke," I tell Maeve. "He still owns Brodie's Watch."

"And he hasn't been able to get rid of it," says Mrs. Dickens. "It's a beautiful piece of land, but the house has always had a bad reputation. The fact his aunt's body was lying there for days, decomposing. Then Jessie's accident. When his aunt died, the house itself was already falling apart. I'm sure he's hoping that after all these renovations, he'll finally find a buyer to take it off his hands."

"Maybe he should have just burned it down," says Maeve.

"Some people in town have suggested that, but Brodie's Watch has historical significance. It would be a shame to think of a house with such a pedigree going up in flames."

I imagine those grand rooms consumed by fire, the turret lit up like a torch as a hundred and fifty years of history are reduced to ashes. When a house is destroyed, what happens to the spirits who linger? What would happen to the captain?

"Brodie's Watch deserves to be loved," I say. "It deserves to be cared for. If I could afford it, I would buy it myself."

Maeve shakes her head. "You don't want to own that house, Ava. You don't know enough about its history."

"Then I'll ask someone who might know. The man who owns it, Arthur Sherbrooke."

Brodie's Watch stands dark and silent in the fading twilight. I step out of my car and pause in the driveway, looking up at windows that stare back at me like glassy black eyes. I think of the first time I saw Brodie's Watch and the chill I felt, as if the house was warning me away. I feel no such chill now. Instead I see my home, welcoming me back. I see the place that's sheltered and comforted me these past weeks. I know I should be disturbed by what happened to those who lived here before me. *The house of dead women,* Maeve calls it, and she advises me to pack up and leave. That's what Charlotte Nielson did, yet she ended up dead anyway, at the hands of a flesh-and-blood killer who squeezed the life from her and tossed her body into the sea.

Maybe if she'd stayed in Brodie's Watch, she'd still be alive.

I step inside and breathe in the familiar scents of home. "Captain Brodie?" I call out. I don't expect an answer, and I hear only silence, yet I feel his presence all around me, in the shadows, in the air I breathe. I think of the words he once whispered: *Under my roof, no harm will come to you.* Did he whisper those same words to Aurora Sherbrooke and Margaret Gordon, Violet Theriault and Eugenia Hollander?

In the kitchen, I feed Hannibal and take a pot of leftover fish chowder out of the refrigerator. As the chowder heats on the stove, I sit down to check my email. Along with a note from Simon, who *adores* the latest three chapters of *The Captain's Table* (hooray), there are emails from Amazon (*new titles you may be interested in*) and Williams Sonoma (*get cooking with our latest new kitchen-ware*). I scroll down and stop at an email that makes me go still.

It's from Lucy. I don't open it, but I can't avoid seeing what is written in the subject line: *I miss you. Call me.* Such innocuous words, but they are like a shout of accusation. I only have to close my eyes and once again I hear the pop of champagne corks. The shouts of *Happy New Year!* The screech of Nick's car pulling away from the curb.

And I remember the aftermath. The long days of sitting with Lucy in Nick's hospital room, watching his comatose body shrivel and fold into itself like a fetus. I remember the appalling sense of relief I felt on the day he died. I am the only one alive with the secret now, a secret that I keep caged and hidden, but it is always there, feeding on me like a cancer.

I close the laptop and shove it away. Just as I've pushed Lucy away, because I cannot bear to face her.

And so I sit alone in this house on the hill. If I were to collapse tonight, the way Aurora Sherbrooke did, who would find me? I look down at Hannibal, who's already cleaned his plate and is now licking his paws, and I wonder how long it would take before he'd start feasting on my flesh. Not that I would blame him. A cat's gotta do what a cat's gotta do, and eating is what Hannibal excels at.

The seafood stew is bubbling on the stove, but I've lost my appetite. I turn off the burner and reach for a bottle of Zinfandel. Tonight I need liquid comfort, this bottle is already uncorked, and I crave the bite of tannins and alcohol on my tongue. I pour a generous serving into a glass, and as I lift it to my lips, I catch sight of the recycling bin in the corner.

It is overflowing with empty wine bottles.

I set down my glass. My craving is still as powerful, but those bottles tell a sad story of a woman who lives alone with her cat, who buys wine by the case and drinks herself into oblivion every night, just to fall asleep. I have been trying to drown my guilt, but booze is just a temporary fix that destroys your liver and poisons your brain. It's made me question what is real and what is fantasy. Does my perfect lover really exist, or is he nothing more than a drunkard's delusion?

It's time for me to learn the truth.

I empty my wineglass into the sink and climb the stairs, fully sober, to bed.

Twenty-Three

By noon the next day I am in my car driving south toward Cape Elizabeth, where Arthur Sherbrooke lives. He is the late Aurora Sherbrooke's only living relative and the one person who probably knew her best—if, indeed, anyone really knew her. How many people, after all, really know *me*? Even my own sister, the person I love most, the person I'm closest to, does not know who I am or what I'm capable of. We keep our darkest secrets to ourselves. We keep them, most of all, from those we love.

I grip the steering wheel and stare ahead at the road, eager to focus on something else, anything else, besides Lucy. The history of Brodie's Watch has been a welcome distraction, a dive down a rabbit hole that keeps me digging ever deeper into the lives and deaths of people I have never met. Do their fates foreshadow my own? Like Eugenia and Violet, Margaret and Aurora, will I meet my death under Captain Brodie's roof?

I have visited Cape Elizabeth once before, when I spent the weekend at the home of a college classmate, and I remember handsome homes and manicured lawns sweeping to the sea, a neighborhood that made me think if I ever won the lottery, this was where I'd retire. A tree-lined road leads to a pair of stone pillars where Arthur Sherbrooke's address is mounted on a brass plaque. There is no gate barring my way so I drive down a road that winds toward a salt marsh, where a coldly modern concrete and glass house stands overlooking the reeds. The house looks more like an art museum than a residence, with stone steps leading through a Japanese garden to the front door. There a wooden sculpture of a fierce Indonesian demon stands guard—not the friendliest face to greet a guest.

I ring the bell.

Through the window, I spy movement, and the pebbled glass makes the approaching figure look like a spindly alien. The door opens and the man who stands there is indeed tall and lanky, with chilly gray eyes. Although Arthur Sherbrooke is in his early seventies, he looks as fit as a long-distance runner, and his focus is laser-sharp.

"Mr. Sherbrooke?"

"Professor Sherbrooke."

"Oh, sorry. *Professor* Sherbrooke. I'm Ava Collette. Thank you for seeing me."

"So you're writing a book about Brodie's Watch," he says as I step into the foyer.

"Yes, and I have a ton of questions about the house."

"Do you want to buy it?" he cuts in.

"I don't think I can afford it."

"If you know anyone who can, I'd like to get rid of the place." He pauses and adds, "But not at a loss."

I follow him down a black-tiled hallway to the living room, where floor-to-ceiling windows overlook the salt marsh. A telescope stands at the ready, and a pair of Leica binoculars sits on the coffee table. Through the window I spot a bald eagle soaring past, followed by three crows in hot pursuit.

"Fearless buggers, those crows," he says. "They'll chase away anything that invades their airspace. I've been studying that particular corvid family for ten generations, and they seem to get more clever every year."

"Are you a professor of ornithology?"

"No, I'm just a lifelong birdwatcher." He waves at the sofa, a haughty command for me to sit down. Like everything else in the room, the sofa is coldly minimalist, upholstered in stark gray leather that looks more forbidding than inviting. I sit facing a glass coffee table which is uncluttered by even a single magazine. The entire focus of the room is the window and the view of the salt marsh beyond.

He offers no coffee or tea but just drops down in an armchair and crosses his stork-like legs. "I taught economics, Bowdoin College," he says. "Retired three years ago, and ironically enough find myself busier than ever. Traveling, writing articles."

"About economics?"

"Corvids. Crows and ravens. My hobby's turned into something of a second career for me." He tilts his head, a movement that's unsettlingly birdlike. "You said you had questions about the house?"

"About its history, and the people who've lived in it over the years."

"I've done a bit of research on the subject, but I'm by no means an expert," he says with a modest shrug. "I can tell you the house was built in 1861 by Captain Jeremiah T. Brodie. He was lost at sea over a decade later. Subsequent ownership passed through several families until it came to me thirty-some years ago."

"I understand you inherited the house from your aunt Aurora."

"Yes. Tell me again how these questions are relevant to this book you're writing?"

"My book is called *The Captain's Table*. It's about traditional foods of New England, and the meals that might have been served in the homes of seafaring families. My editor thinks Brodie's Watch, and Captain Brodie himself, could serve as the focal point for the project. It would give the book an authentic sense of place and atmosphere."

Satisfied by my explanation, he settles more deeply into his chair. "Very well. Is there anything specific that you'd like to know?"

"Tell me about your aunt. About her experiences living there."

He sighs, as if this is one subject he'd rather avoid. "Aunt Aurora lived there for most of her life. In fact, she died in that house, which may be one of the reasons I can't seem to get rid of it. Nothing kills a house's resale value like a death. People and their stupid superstitions."

"You've been trying to sell it all these years?"

"I was her only heir, so I got stuck with that white elephant. After she died, I put it on the market for a few years, but the offers were insulting. Everyone seemed to find something wrong with the place. Too old, too cold, bad karma. If only I could've torn down the heap. With that ocean view, it would make a spectacular building site."

"Why didn't you just tear it down?"

"It was a condition of her will. The house had to remain standing or the trust fund would go to . . ." He pauses and looks away.

So there's a trust fund. Of course there had to be family money. How else could a mere university professor afford this multimillion-dollar property in Cape Elizabeth? Aurora Sherbrooke had left her nephew a fortune as well as a burden when she'd bequeathed him Brodie's Watch.

"She had enough money to live anywhere," he says. "Paris,

London, New York. But no, she chose to spend most of her life in that house. Every summer, starting when I was seventeen, I'd dutifully drive up to visit her, if only to remind her that she had a blood relative, but she never seemed to welcome my visits. It was almost as if I were invading her privacy. An intruder, disrupting her life."

Their lives. Hers and the captain's.

"And I never liked that house."

"Why not?" I ask.

"There's always a chill inside. Don't you feel it? Even on the hottest days in August, I could never get warm. I don't think I ever took off my sweater. I could spend the day sweltering on the beach, but when I stepped back into the house, it was like walking into a freezer."

Because he didn't want you there. I think of the first time I stepped into Brodie's Watch, and the initial chill I felt, like walking into a wintry fog. And then, in an instant, the chill had vanished, as if the house had decided I belonged there.

"I wanted to stop visiting her," he continued. "I pleaded with my mother not to make me return. Especially after the incident."

"What incident?"

"That damn house tried to kill me." At my startled expression, he gives a sheepish laugh. "Well, that's what it felt like at the time. You know the chandelier that's now hanging over the foyer? It's a replacement. The original chandelier was crystal, imported from France. If I'd been standing just two inches to my right, that thing would have crushed my skull."

I stare at him. "It fell?"

"Just as I walked in the door, the fixture gave way. It was only a freak accident, of course, but I remember what my aunt said after it happened: 'Maybe you shouldn't come anymore. Just to be safe.' What the hell did she mean by that?"

I know exactly what she meant, but I don't say a word.

"After I almost got killed there, I wanted to stay away, but my mother insisted I keep returning."

"Why?"

"To maintain family connections. My father was on the edge of bankruptcy. Aunt Aurora's husband left her with more money than she could ever spend in a lifetime. My mother was hoping . . ." His voice trails off.

So this is why the ghost didn't approve of Arthur Sherbrooke. From the moment this man stepped through the door, the captain would have known his true motives. It wasn't devotion to his aunt Aurora that brought Sherbrooke to Brodie's Watch every summer; it was greed.

"My aunt had no children of her own, and after her husband died, she never remarried. She certainly didn't need to."

"For love, maybe?"

"What I meant was, she didn't need any man's financial support. And there was always the danger that an opportunist would take advantage of her."

The way you tried to.

"Even without her money, I'm sure more than a few men must have been interested in her," I say. "Your aunt was a fine-looking woman."

"You've seen her photo?"

"During my research into the previous occupants, I came across your aunt's picture in a society column. Apparently she was quite the popular girl when she was young."

"Was she? I never thought of her as beautiful, but then I didn't know her when she was young. I just remember her as my oddball aunt Aurora, wandering that house at all hours of the night."

"Wandering? Why?"

"Who knows? I'd be in bed and I'd hear her creeping up the turret steps. I have no idea what would bring her upstairs because there was nothing up there, just an empty room. The widow's walk was already starting to rot and one of the windows leaked. Ned Haskell used to work as her handyman, fixing up the place, but she let all the help go. She didn't want anyone in her house." He pauses. "Which is why her body went undiscovered for days after she died."

"I heard you were the one who found her body."

He nods. "I drove up to Tucker Cove for my annual visit. Tried calling her before the trip but she didn't answer the phone. As soon as I stepped into the house, I could smell it. It was summertime, and the flies were . . ." He stops. "Sorry. It's a rather unpleasant memory."

"What do you think happened to her?"

"Some sort of stroke is my guess. Or a heart attack. The local doctor called it a natural death, that's all I know. Climbing those turret steps might have been too much for her."

"Why do you think she kept going up to the turret?"

"I have no idea. It was just an empty room with a leaky window."

"And a hidden alcove."

"Yes, I was quite surprised when Ned told me he'd found that alcove. I have no idea when it was walled up or why, but I'm sure my aunt didn't do it. After all, she didn't even bother keeping up the place. By the time I inherited, it was already in sorry shape. Then those kids broke in and *really* trashed the place."

"That was Halloween? The night the girl fell?"

He nods. "But even before that girl died, the house already had a reputation as haunted. My aunt used to scare me with stories of Captain Brodie's ghost. Probably to keep me from visiting so often."

I understand perfectly why his aunt might want to keep him away. I can't imagine a more irritating houseguest.

"Worst of all," he said, "she let it be known all over town that her house was haunted. Told the gardener and the cleaner that the ghost was watching, and if they stole anything, he'd know.

After that fool girl fell off the widow's walk, the damn place became unsellable. The terms of my aunt's will forbade me from tearing it down, so I could either let it slowly rot or I could fix it up as a rental." He eyes me. "Are you sure you can't afford to buy it? You seem like a happy enough tenant. Unlike the woman before you."

It takes me a moment to register the significance of what he's just said. "Are you talking about Charlotte Nielson? You've met her?"

"She came to see me, too. I thought maybe she wanted to buy the house but no, she asked about its history. Who lived there and what happened to them."

Gooseflesh suddenly ripples across my arms. I think of Charlotte, a woman I've never met, sitting in this room, probably on this same sofa, having this same conversation with Professor Sherbrooke. Not only do I live in the same house she did, I am following so closely in her footsteps that I might be Charlotte's ghost, reliving her last days on earth.

"She was unhappy living there?" I ask.

"She said the house made her uneasy. She felt like something was watching her, and she wanted to hang curtains in the bedroom. It's hard to believe a woman that high-strung would ever qualify as a schoolteacher."

"*Something* was watching her? That's the word she used?"

"Probably because she'd heard about the so-called ghost, so of course every creaky floorboard had to be *him*. I wasn't surprised when I heard she abruptly vacated."

"As it turns out, she had every reason to be uneasy. I assume you know about her murder."

He gives a maddeningly unconcerned shrug. "Yes. It was unfortunate."

"And you've heard who the prime suspect is? The man *you* hired to work on the house."

"I've known Ned for decades. Saw him every summer when I

visited my aunt, and I never saw any reason not to trust him. That's what I told Charlotte."

"She had concerns about him?"

"About everything, not just Ned. The isolation. The lack of curtains. Even the town. She didn't find it particularly open to strangers."

I think about my own experiences in Tucker Cove. I remember the gossipy ladies in the grocery store and coolly businesslike Donna Branca. I think about Jessie Inman and how the circumstances of her death were suppressed by the local newspaper. And I think of Charlotte, whose disappearance never raised an eyebrow until I started asking questions. To the casual visitor, Tucker Cove seems quaint and picturesque, but it's also a village that guards its secrets and protects its own.

"I hope none of this discourages you from staying," he says. "You *will* be staying, won't you?"

"I don't know."

"Well, for the rent you're paying, you won't be able to find anything like Brodie's Watch. It's a grand house, in a popular town."

It is also a house with secrets, in a town with secrets. But we all have secrets. And mine are buried deepest of all.

Twenty-Four

The waiting room is empty when I arrive at Ben's medical office late that afternoon. His receptionist, Viletta, smiles at me through the window and slides open the glass partition.

"Hello, Ava. How is your arm doing?" she asks.

"It's completely healed, thanks to Dr. Gordon."

"You know, cats carry a lot of diseases, which is why I stick with canaries." She squints down at her appointment book. "Was Dr. Gordon expecting you today? Because I don't see your name on the schedule."

"I don't have an appointment. I was hoping he'd have a spare minute to see me."

The door opens and Ben pokes his head into the waiting room. "I thought I heard your voice! Come on back to my office. I'm done for the day, and I'm just signing off on some lab reports."

I follow Ben down the hall, past the exam rooms and into his office. I've never been in his office before, and as he hangs up his white coat and sits down behind the oak desk, I survey the framed diplomas and the photos of his father and grandfather, the earlier generation of Dr. Gordons with their white coats and stethoscopes. One of Ben's oil paintings hangs there as well, unframed, as though it's only a temporary decoration being auditioned for the wall. I recognize the landscape, because I have seen that rocky jut of land in his other paintings.

"It's the same beach you've painted before, isn't it?"

He nods. "Very observant. Yes, I like that particular beach. It's quiet and private and there's no one around to bother me while I paint." He sets the stack of lab reports in his out-basket and turns his full attention to me. "So what can I do for you today? Has your ferocious cat attacked you again?"

"This isn't about me at all. It's about something that happened years ago. You grew up in this town, right?"

He smiles. "I was born here."

"So you'd know the town's history."

"Recent history, anyway." He laughs. "I'm not *that* old, Ava."

"But old enough to remember a woman named Aurora Sherbrooke?"

"Only vaguely. I was just a kid when she died. That had to be around . . ."

"Thirty-three years ago. When your dad was the town doctor. Was he *her* doctor?"

He studies me for a moment, frowning. "Why are you asking about Aurora Sherbrooke?"

"It's for this book I'm writing. Brodie's Watch is turning into a large part of it, and I want to know its history."

"But how does she come into it?"

"She lived in that house. She died in that house. She's part of its history."

"Is that really why you're asking about her?"

His question, spoken so softly, makes me go silent. I focus on the stacks of lab reports and patient charts on his desk. He's a man trained in science, a man who deals in facts, and I know how he'll react if I tell him the reason behind my questions.

"Never mind. It's not important." I stand up to leave.

"Ava, wait. Anything you have to say is important to me."

"Even if it's completely unscientific?" I turn to face him. "Even if it strikes you as superstition?"

"I'm sorry." He sighs. "Can we start this conversation again? You asked about Aurora Sherbrooke and whether my father was her doctor. And the answer is yes, he was."

"Does the office still have her medical records?"

"Not for a patient who's been dead this long."

"I knew it was a long shot, but I thought I would ask. Thank you." Once again, I turn to leave.

"This isn't about your book, is it?"

I pause in the doorway, wanting to blurt the truth, but afraid of how he'll react. "I've spoken with Arthur Sherbrooke. I went to see him about his aunt, and he told me she'd seen things in the house. Things that made her believe . . ."

"Believe what?"

"That Captain Brodie is still there."

Ben's expression doesn't change. "Are we talking about a ghost?" he asks calmly, a tone you'd use to soothe a mental patient.

"Yes."

"The ghost of Captain Brodie."

"Aurora Sherbrooke believed in him. That's what she told her nephew."

"Does he believe in this ghost, too?"

"No. But I do."

"Why?"

"Because I've seen him, Ben. I've seen Jeremiah Brodie."

His expression is still unreadable. Is this something they teach you in medical school, how to maintain a poker player's face so that patients can't read what you really think of them?

"My father saw him, too," Ben says quietly.

I stare at him. "When?"

"It was the day they found her. My father was called to the house to examine her body. It's the reason I remember her name. Because I heard him talk about it to my mother."

I glance up at the photo of Ben's father on the wall, so distinguished in his white coat. Not a man who looks prone to fantasies. "What did he say?"

"He said the woman was lying on the floor in the turret, dressed in her nightgown. He knew she'd been dead for some time because of the smell and the . . . flies." He pauses, realizing that some details are better left unsaid. "Her nephew and the police officers had gone downstairs, so my father was alone up there, examining the body. And out of the corner of his eye, he saw something move. On the widow's walk."

"That's where I first saw him," I murmur.

"My father turned and there he was. A tall man with dark hair and a black seaman's coat. An instant later, the man was gone. My father was certain of what he'd seen, but he never revealed it to anyone except my mother and me. He didn't want people to think their local doctor had gone insane. And to be honest, I never really believed it. I thought it was a trick of the light or a reflection in the window. Or maybe he was just bone-tired from too many late-night calls. I'd almost forgotten that story." Ben looks straight at me. "But now I find out you've seen him, too."

"It's not a trick of the light, Ben. I've seen the ghost more than once. I've *spoken* to him." At his startled look, I'm sorry I shared that detail. Certainly I'm not going to tell him everything else that has happened between Brodie and me. "I know it's hard for you to believe. It's hard for *me* to believe."

"But I want to, Ava. Who wouldn't want to believe there's an afterlife, that there's something beyond death? But where's the evidence? No one can prove there's a ghost in that house."

I pull out my cellphone. "Maybe there's someone who can."

Twenty-Five

Ben may be a skeptic, but he's curious enough to be at my house Saturday afternoon when Maeve arrives along with her ghost-hunting team.

"This is Todd and Evan, who'll handle the technical aspects tonight," she says, introducing the two burly young men who are unloading camera gear from a white van. They are brothers with identical red beards and they look so much alike that I can only tell them apart by their different T-shirts. Evan's is *Star Wars*, Todd's is *Alien*. I'm surprised that neither is wearing *Ghostbusters*.

A VW comes up the driveway and parks behind the white van. "And that'll be Kim, our team sensitive," says Maeve. Out of the VW emerges a stick-thin blonde with cheeks so hollow that I wonder if she has recently suffered an illness. She takes a few steps toward us and suddenly stops, staring up at the house. She stands motionless for so long that Ben finally asks, "What's going on with her?"

"She's fine," says Maeve. "She's probably just trying to get a feeling for the place and detect any vibrations."

"Before we unload everything, we're going to take a look around the house, film some baseline footage," says Todd. He's already filming and he slowly pans his camera across the porch, then steps into the foyer. Glancing up at the crown molding, he says, "This house looks pretty old. There's a good chance you've got *something* still lingering in here."

"Is it okay if I just wander around?" says Kim.

"Of course," I tell her. "The house is yours."

Kim heads down the hallway, followed by the two brothers who continue to film. When they're out of earshot, Maeve turns to Ben and me and confides: "I haven't told Kim any details about your house. She's coming in to this assignment blind, because I don't want to influence her reactions in any way."

"You called her your team *sensitive*," says Ben. "What does that mean, exactly? Is that like a psychic?"

"Kim has the ability to sense energies that still linger in a room, and she'll tell us which areas need special monitoring. She's been amazingly accurate."

"And how exactly does one judge accuracy?" This time, Ben can't keep the doubt out of his voice, but Maeve smiles, unruffled.

"Ava tells me you're a medical doctor, so I'm sure this sounds like a foreign language to you. But yes, we're able to confirm a great deal of what Kim tells us. Last month, she described a deceased child in very specific detail. Only later did we show her the child's photo, and we were blown away by how every detail matched what she'd described to us. Everything, right down to the lace collar on the little boy's shirt." She pauses, reading Ben's face. "You're doubtful."

"I'm trying to keep an open mind."

"What would it take to convince you, Dr. Gordon?"

"Maybe if I saw a ghost myself."

"Ah, but some people never do. They're simply not able to. So what can we do to change your mind, short of having the ghost materialize in front of you?"

"Does it really matter what I believe? I'm just curious about the process, and I wanted to observe."

Kim reappears in the foyer. "We'd like to go upstairs now."

"Have you sensed anything yet?" Ben asks.

Kim doesn't answer, but simply starts up the stairs with Todd and Evan trailing behind her, their cameras recording the ascent.

"How many of these investigations have you conducted?" Ben asks Maeve.

"We've visited around sixty or seventy locations, mostly in New England. When people experience disturbing phenomena, whether it's just creaky floorboards or full-body manifestations, they don't know where to turn. So they reach out to us."

"Excuse me?" Evan calls down from the upstairs landing. "There's a door at the end of the hall up here. Can we look inside?"

"Go right ahead," I answer.

"The door's locked. Can we have the key?"

"It can't be locked." I head up the stairs to the second floor, where Kim and her colleagues are standing outside the closed door to the turret.

"What's behind this?" asks Kim.

"It's just a staircase. It's never locked. I don't even know where the key is." I turn the knob and the door creaks open.

"Hey man, I *swear* it was locked," Todd insists. He turns to his brother. "You *saw* it. I couldn't get the thing open."

"It's the humidity," says Ben, providing a logical explanation as usual. He leans in to examine the doorjamb. "It's summertime, and wood tends to swell up. Doors get stuck."

"It's never been stuck before," I say.

"Well, if it *is* your ghost at work, why is he trying to keep us out of the turret?"

Everyone looks at me. I don't answer. I don't want to answer.

Kim is first through the doorway. She climbs only two steps and abruptly halts, her hand frozen on the banister.

"What's wrong?" says Maeve.

Kim stares up at the top of the stairs and says softly, "What's up there?"

"Just the turret," I tell her.

Kim takes a breath. And takes another step. It's clear she does not want to ascend, but she keeps climbing. As I follow the others, I think of the nights I so eagerly climbed these same stairs with the captain leading me by the hand. I remember silk skirts swishing at my legs and candlelight flickering above and my heart pounding in anticipation of what awaited me behind those velvet curtains. Ben touches my arm and I flinch in surprise.

"They're putting on quite a show," he whispers.

"I think she really does sense something."

"Or maybe they just know how to amp up the drama. What do you really know about these people, Ava? Do you actually believe them?"

"At this point, I'm ready to turn to anyone who can give me answers."

"Even if they're frauds?"

"We've come this far. Please, let's just hear them out."

We climb the last steps into the turret and watch as Kim paces to the center of the room, where she suddenly stops. Her head tilts up as if she's listening for whispers from beyond the curtain that divides the living from the dead. Todd's camera is still rolling and I can see the blinking *record* light.

Kim takes a deep breath, releases it. Slowly she turns toward the window and stares out at the widow's walk. "Something terrible happened here. In this room," she says softly.

"What do you see?" Maeve asks.

"It's not clear to me yet. It's just an echo. Like the outer ripples after you've cast a stone into water. It's the lingering trace of what she felt."

"She?" Maeve turns to me and I know we're both thinking of Aurora Sherbrooke, who died in this turret. How long did she lie here, still alive? Did she cry out for help, try to drag herself to the stairs? When you keep your friends and family at arm's length, when you cut yourself off from the world, this is your punishment: to die alone and unnoticed, your body left to decompose.

"I feel her fear," whispers Kim. "She knows what's about to happen, but no one can help her. No one can save her. She is all alone in this room. With him."

Captain Brodie?

Kim turns to us, her face alarmingly pale. "There's evil here. Something powerful, something dangerous. I can't stay in this house. I *can't*." She bolts for the stairway and we hear her footsteps thump down the stairs in a panicked tattoo.

Slowly Todd lowers the camera from his shoulder. "What the hell just happened, Maeve?"

Maeve shakes her head, bewildered. "I have no idea."

Maeve sits at my kitchen table, her hand trembling as she lifts a teacup to her mouth and takes a sip.

"I've worked with Kim for years and this is the first time she's ever walked away from an assignment. Whatever happened up there in the turret must have left powerful traces. Even if it's just a residual haunting, the emotions are still there, trapped in that space."

"What do you mean by a residual haunting?" Ben asks. Unlike everyone else, he appears unmoved by what we witnessed in the turret, and he stands apart from us, leaning against the kitchen counter. As always, the detached observer. "Is that the same thing as a ghost?"

"Not exactly," explains Maeve. "It's more like an echo left over from a terrible event. Powerful emotions triggered by that event get trapped in the place where it happened. Fear, anguish, grief—they can all linger in a house for years, even centuries, and sometimes the living can feel them, the way Kim did. Whatever happened upstairs left its mark inside that turret and the incident continues to play and replay, like an old video recording. Plus, I noticed the roof is slate."

"What does that have to do with anything?" Ben asks.

"Buildings with slate or iron or stone are more likely to retain those distant echoes." She looks up at the decorative tin ceiling in the kitchen. "This house almost seems designed to hold on to memories and strong emotions. They're still here, and people like Kim can feel them."

"What about people who aren't sensitive, like me?" says Ben. "I have to say, I've never experienced anything paranormal. Why don't I feel anything?"

"You're like most people, who live their lives unaware of the hidden energies all around us. Colorblind people never see the brilliant red of a cardinal. They don't know what they're missing, the way you don't know what you're missing."

"Maybe I'm better off that way," Ben concedes. "After seeing how Kim reacted, I'd rather *not* see any ghosts."

Maeve looks down at her teacup and says quietly: "A ghost, at least, would be harmless."

The thump of an aluminum case hitting the floor makes me snap straight in my chair. I turn to see Evan, who's just walked into the house with the last of their equipment.

"You want the A camera set up in the turret, right?" he asks Maeve.

"Definitely. Since that's where Kim had the strongest reaction."

He takes in a breath. "That room gives me the creeps, too."

"Which is why we need to focus there."

I stand up. "We can help you carry stuff upstairs."

"No," says Maeve. "I want you to let us handle everything. In fact, I prefer my clients to stay elsewhere for the night, so we can concentrate on our work." She glances at Hannibal, who's been slinking around the kitchen. "And your cat will definitely have to be confined, or his movements will confuse our instruments."

"But I want to stay and watch you work," says Ben. He glances at me. "We both do."

"I have to warn you, it can get pretty boring," says Maeve. "Mostly it's just sitting up all night watching the dials."

"What if we're perfectly quiet and stay out of your way?"

"You don't even believe in ghosts, Dr. Gordon. Why do you want to watch?" Maeve asks.

"Maybe this will change my mind about the whole thing," Ben says, but I know that's not the real answer. He wants to observe because he doesn't trust their gadgets or their methods or anything else about them.

Maeve frowns, tapping her pen on the papers. "It's not the way we normally do things. Ghosts are less likely to appear when there are too many people emitting bioelectric fields."

"This *is* Ava's house," Ben points out. "Shouldn't she decide what happens here?"

"Just understand there's a chance your presence may inhibit any manifestations. I *do* insist that you keep the cat locked away."

I nod. "I'll put him in his carrier."

Maeve glances at her watch and stands up. "It'll be dark in an hour. I'd better get to work."

As Maeve heads upstairs to join her team, Ben and I remain in the kitchen, waiting until she is out of earshot.

"I hope you aren't paying them," he says.

"They haven't asked me for a cent. They're doing it all for research."

"And that's the only reason?"

"What other reason would they have?"

He glances up at footsteps creaking along the second-floor hallway. "I just want you to be cautious about these people. They may sincerely believe in what they're doing, or . . ."

"Or?"

"You've given them complete access to your house. Why didn't they want us to stay and observe?"

"I think you're being a little paranoid."

"I know you want to believe, Ava, but psychics often swoop in just when people are at their most vulnerable. Yes, you've seen and heard things you can't explain, but you've just recovered from a bacterial infection. Cat scratch fever *could* account for what you've experienced."

"Are you telling me to call off the whole thing?"

"I'm just advising you to be careful. You've already agreed to this, so we'll let them do their thing. But don't leave them alone in your house. I'll stay, too."

"Thank you." I glance out the window, where dusk is rapidly fading to night. "Now let's see what happens."

Twenty-Six

I lure Hannibal into his crate with a bowl of food and he doesn't even notice when I latch his door shut; his face is too deeply buried in kitty chow. While Maeve and Todd and Evan set up their gear in various rooms around the house, I go to work doing what I do best: feeding people. I know that staying up late at night makes you ravenous, so I assemble ham sandwiches, hard-boil a dozen eggs, and brew a large pot of coffee to keep us all fueled through the night. By the time I've laid out the food on platters, night has fallen.

Ben pokes his head into the kitchen and announces: "They're going to turn off all the lights in a little bit. They said you should come upstairs now, if you want to take a look at their setup."

Carrying the platter of sandwiches, I follow him up the stairs. "Why do all the lights have to be turned off?"

"Who knows? Maybe it makes it easier to see ectoplasm?"

"Ben, a negative attitude is not going to help. You could sabotage the results."

"I don't see why. If the ghost wants to appear, he'll appear, whether I believe in him or not."

When we reach the turret, I'm startled to see how much equipment Maeve and her associates have hauled upstairs. I see cameras and tripods, a tape recorder, and half a dozen other instruments whose purpose is a mystery to me.

"All that's missing is a Geiger counter," Ben says drily.

"No, we've got one of those." Evan points to a meter on the floor. "We've also set up a camera in the downstairs hallway and another one in the master bedroom."

"Why the master bedroom?" asks Ben.

"Because the ghost's appeared there a few times. That's what we've been told."

Ben looks at me and I flush. "I've seen him there once or twice," I admit.

"But this turret seems to be ground zero for paranormal activity," says Maeve. "It's where Kim had the strongest reaction, so we're going to focus our attention on this room." She glances at her watch. "Okay, it's time to turn off all the lights. Settle in, everybody. This is going to be a very long night."

By two A.M., we've devoured all the ham sandwiches and boiled eggs, and I've refilled the thermoses with coffee four times. Ghost-hunting, I have discovered, is a thoroughly boring business. For hours we've been sitting in the semidarkness, waiting for something, anything, to happen. Maeve's team, at least, manages to stay busy monitoring their instruments, jotting notes, and repeatedly changing batteries.

The ghost has yet to make an appearance.

Maeve calls out, once again, to the darkness: "Hello, we want to speak to you! Who are you? Tell us your name."

The glowing red light on the tape recorder tells me it is continuously recording, but I can hear nothing. No ghostly voice answers Maeve's request, no ectoplasmic mist materializes. Here we are, with thousands of dollars' worth of electronic equipment, waiting for Captain Brodie to respond, and of course tonight is the night he does not cooperate.

Another hour passes, and I grow so sleepy I can barely keep my eyes open. As I nod off against Ben's shoulder, he whispers: "Hey, why don't you go to bed?"

"I don't want to miss anything."

"The only thing you're going to miss is a good night's sleep. I'll stay up and watch."

He helps me stand up and I'm so stiff from sitting on the floor, I can barely rise to my feet. Through bleary eyes I make out the silhouettes of Maeve and Todd and Evan huddled in the gloom. While they may be patient enough to wait up all night in the dark, I've had more than enough.

I feel my way down the turret staircase, to my bedroom. I don't even bother to undress. I just pull off my shoes, flop down on the bed, and sink into a deep and dreamless sleep.

I wake up to the *clack* of tripod legs snapping together. Sunlight shines in the window and through squinting eyes I see Todd crouched in the corner, stuffing a camera lens into an aluminum case. Ben stands in the doorway, a cup of coffee in hand.

"What time is it?" I ask them.

"It's after nine," Ben says. "They're about to leave." He sets a steaming mug on my nightstand. "I thought I'd bring you coffee before I take off, too."

I sit up, yawning, and watch as Todd sets the camera into his case. "I forgot there was a camera in my room."

Todd laughs. "We probably recorded six riveting hours of you sleeping in bed."

"What happened in the turret last night?"

"We still need to review the footage. Maeve will get back to you with a full report." Todd snaps his case shut and stands up to leave. "Something may turn up on video. We'll let you know."

Ben and I don't say a word as Todd heads downstairs. We hear the front door thump shut.

"Were you up with them all night?" I ask.

"I was. All night."

"And what happened?"

Ben shakes his head. "Absolutely nothing."

After Ben leaves, I haul myself out of bed and splash cold water on my face. What I really want to do is climb back into bed and sleep for the rest of the day, but I can hear Hannibal yowling downstairs, so I make my way down to the kitchen, where I find him glaring at me through the bars of his crate. The heaping mound of kitty chow I left for him last night is all gone, of course. It's too soon to feed him again, so I carry him to the front door and release him outside. Off he goes, a tiger-striped tub of lard waddling away into the garden.

"Get some exercise, why don't you?" I tell him and close the door.

Now that everyone has packed up and left, the house seems unnervingly quiet. And I feel more than a little embarrassed that I ever asked them to investigate Brodie's Watch. Just as Ben predicted, they found no evidence of a ghost. He would tell me such evidence doesn't exist, that believers like Maeve, with their cameras and elaborate equipment, are self-deluded people who think they hear patterns in random noise, who see dust particles floating past a camera lens and imagine supernatural orbs. He would say Brodie's Watch is just an old house with creaky floors and a notorious reputation and a tenant who drinks too much. I wonder what he thinks of me this morning.

No, I'd rather not know.

Seen in the harsh light of day, my obsession with Jeremiah Brodie looks utterly irrational. He has been dead for a century and a half, and I should leave him to rest in peace. It's time for me to get back to the real world. Back to work.

I brew a fresh pot of coffee, heat up the cast-iron pan, and fry diced bacon and potatoes until they're crisp, toss in chopped onions and green peppers, and pour in two scrambled eggs. It's my go-to one-skillet breakfast on mornings when I need to fuel up for a long day's writing.

I pour myself a third cup of coffee and sit down with my skillet-scrambled eggs. I'm fully awake now, feeling almost human, and also utterly famished. I devour my breakfast, glad to be eating alone so that no one sees me greedily shoveling eggs and potatoes into my mouth. I will devote the rest of this day to writing *The Captain's Table*. No distractions, no more ghost nonsense. The real Jeremiah Brodie is nothing more than scattered bones under the sea. I've been seduced by a legend, by my own desperate loneliness. If there are any demons in this house, then I myself have brought them, the same demons that have tormented me since New Year's Eve. All it takes is a few too many glasses of wine to summon them.

I set my dirty dishes in the sink and open my laptop to resume work on Chapter Nine of *The Captain's Table*, "Jewels from the Sea." Is there anything new to say about shellfish? I pull out my handwritten notes from my excursion aboard the lobster boat *Lazy Girl* last Saturday morning. I remember the smell of diesel and the gulls swarming overhead as our boat came abreast of the first lobster buoy. Captain Andy had winched up his trap from the water, and when it thumped down on his deck, there they were inside, green and glistening. With their glossy carapaces and insect legs, lobsters bear an unsavory resemblance to cockroaches. They are cannibals, he told me, and in confinement they'll eat one another. That bug-eat-bug savagery is why lobstermen band the claws. There is nothing delectable about a snapping live lobster, but boiling water will transform that green bug into tender, luscious meat. I think of all the ways I've feasted on it: Dripping with butter. Cloaked in mayonnaise and mounded on a toasted bun. Stir-fried Chinese style with garlic and black bean sauce. Stewed in cream and sherry.

I begin to type a paean to lobster. Not the food of sea captains, who would have considered it fit only for paupers, but the food of scullery maids and groundskeepers. I write about how the poor would have cooked it, simmered with corn and potatoes, or simply boiled in salted water and tossed into a lunch pail. Despite my hearty breakfast, I'm getting hungry again but I keep writing. When I finally stop to glance up at the clock, I'm startled to see it's already six in the evening.

Cocktail hour.

I save the new pages I've written and reward myself for a hard day's work by opening a nice bottle of Cabernet. Just one or two glasses, I promise myself. The cork gives a musical pop, and like Pavlov's dog I am already salivating, craving that first hit of alcohol. I take a sip and sigh with pleasure. Yes, it's a very nice wine, full-bodied and meaty. What shall I cook for dinner to go along with it?

My laptop chimes, announcing a new email in my in-box. I see the sender's name, and suddenly I'm not thinking at all about dinner or my work on *The Captain's Table*. My appetite has vanished; in its place is only a gnawing emptiness in my stomach.

The email is from Lucy.

It's the fourth email she's sent me this week, and my responses—when I respond at all—have been curt: *I'm fine, just busy.* Or: *I'll write more later.* This new message from her has a subject line that's only three words: *Remember this day?*

I don't want to open it, because I dread the tidal wave of guilt that always follows, but something compels me to reach for the mouse. My hand is numb as I click on the message. An image fills the screen.

It's an old photo of Lucy and me, taken when I was ten and she was twelve. We are both wearing bathing suits and our long, skinny arms are slung over each other's bare shoulders. We are tanned and smiling, and behind us, the lake shimmers, bright as silver. Yes, I remember that day very well. A hot and hazy afternoon at Grandma's lake cottage. A picnic of fried chicken and corn on the cob. That morning I had baked oatmeal cookies all by myself, at ten years old already comfortable in the kitchen. *Ava wants to feed everyone, Lucy wants to heal everyone* was the way our mother summed up her daughters. That day at the lake, I cut my foot on a rock and I remember how tenderly Lucy washed and bandaged my wound. While the other kids splashed in the water, Lucy had stayed by my side, keeping me company on the shore. Whenever I've needed her, whether I was sick or depressed or short of cash, she'd always be there for me.

And now she isn't, because I cannot bear to look her in the eyes and let her see who I really am. I cannot bear to be reminded of what I've done to her.

I sip Cabernet as I stare at that photo, haunted by the ghosts of who we once were. Sisters who adored each other. Sisters who would never hurt each other. My fingers hover over the keyboard, ready to tap a reply. A confession. The truth is like a boulder crushing me; what a relief it would be to throw off this burden and tell her about Nick. About New Year's Eve.

I refill my glass. I can no longer taste the wine, but I keep drinking it anyway.

I picture Lucy reading my confession as she sits at her desk, where photos of Nick smile at her. Nick, who will never grow old, who will forever be the man she adored, the man who adored her. She will read my confession and she will know the truth about him and about me.

And it will break her heart.

I close the laptop. No, I cannot do it, not to her. It's better to live with the guilt and die with the secret. Sometimes, silence is the one true way to prove your love.

As night falls, I finish off the bottle.

I don't know what time it is when I finally stagger upstairs and collapse onto the bed. Drunk as I am, I do not sleep. I lie awake in the darkness, thinking of the women before me who have died alone in Brodie's Watch. What secrets did they harbor, what past sins drove them to retreat to this house? Maeve had said that powerful emotions such as terror and grief will linger in a house years later. Can shame? A century from now, will someone sleeping in this room feel the same guilt that gnaws at me like a cancer? My anguish is almost physical, and I curl into a ball, as if I could squeeze away the pain.

The scent of the sea is suddenly so powerful, so vivid, that I taste the salt on my lips. My heart quickens. The hairs lift on my arms, as if the darkness is electrically charged. No, this is just my imagination. Captain Brodie does not exist. Maeve proved there is no ghost in this house.

"Whore."

I snap rigid at the sound of his voice. He stands over my bed, his face hidden, only his silhouette visible in the darkness.

"I know what you have done."

"You aren't real," I whisper. "You don't exist."

"I am what you seek. I am what you deserve." I cannot see his expression, but I hear the judgment in his voice and I know what lies in store for me tonight. *Here in my house, what you seek is what you will find,* he once told me. What I seek is penance, to wash away my sins. To make me clean again.

I gasp as he wrenches me to my feet. At his touch, the room whirls around me in a kaleidoscope of firelight and velvet. In an instant I am swept out of my own time, into his. A time when this is *his* house, *his* kingdom, and I am at his command. I look down and see that tonight I am not wearing a dress of silk or velvet, but merely a nightgown of cotton so sheer that I can see my own silhouette, shamefully exposed through the gossamer fabric. The whore, her sins revealed to all.

He leads me from the bedroom, into the hall. The wood floor

is warm beneath my bare feet. The door to the turret gives a warning creak as it swings open and we start up the staircase. In the doorway above, firelight glows a lurid red, as if hell awaits me above, not below, and I am ascending to my just punishment. My gown is whisper-thin, but I do not feel the night's chill. Instead my skin is feverishly hot, as if I am approaching the heat of brimstone. Two steps from the top I halt, suddenly fearful of stepping through the doorway. I have known both pain and pleasure in his turret. What punishment lies in store tonight?

"I'm afraid," I murmur.

"You have already agreed." His smile chills me. "Is it not why you have summoned me again?"

"I? Summoned you?"

His hand is crushing mine; I cannot resist, cannot fight him as he drags me up the last two steps into the turret. There, in the hellish firelight, I behold what has been awaiting me.

Captain Brodie has brought an audience.

He pushes me forward, into the circle of men. There is no place to retreat to, no place to hide. Twelve men surround me, staring from every direction as I stand pitifully exposed to their gazes. The room is warm but I am shaking. Like the captain, their faces are sunburned and their clothes are ripe with the scent of the sea, but these men are rough and unshaven, their shirts frayed and dirt-streaked.

His crew. A jury of twelve.

Brodie seizes me by the shoulders and slowly walks me around the circle, as if I am a prize calf for sale. "Gentlemen, witness the accused!" he announces. "It is up to you to pass judgment."

"No." In terror, I try to pull away but his grip is too firm. "No."

"Confess, Ava. Tell them your crime." He walks me around the circle again, forcing me to stare each man in the eyes. "Let them look deep into your soul and see what you are guilty of." He thrusts me toward one of the sailors, who stares at me with black and bottomless eyes.

"You said no harm would come to me!"

"Is this not what you seek? Punishment?" He pushes me forward and I stumble to my knees. As I cower there, in that circle of men, he paces around me. "Here you see the accused for what she truly is. You need feel no pity." He turns and points to me like a judge condemning a prisoner. "Confess, Ava."

"Confess!" one of the men calls out. The others join in, a chorus that grows ever louder until the chant is deafening. "Confess! Confess!"

Brodie drags me back to my feet. "Tell them what you did," he orders.

"Stop. Please."

"Tell them."

"Make them stop!"

"Tell them who you fucked!"

I sink back to my knees. "My sister's husband," I whisper.

In an instant, it all comes back. The clink of champagne glasses. The clatter of oyster shells. New Year's Eve. The last guest gone, Lucy off to the hospital to see a patient.

Nick and me, alone in my apartment.

I remember how unsteady we both were as we gathered up the dirty dishes and carried them to the sink. I remember the two of us standing in the kitchen, giggling as we emptied the last of the champagne into our flutes. Outside, snowflakes tumbled down and settled onto the windowsill as we clinked glasses. I remember thinking how blue his eyes were, and how much I'd always liked his smile, and why couldn't I be as fortunate as my sister, who is cleverer than I am, kinder than I am, and far, far luckier in love than I will ever be. Why couldn't I have what she had?

We didn't plan it. We never expected what happened next.

I was unsteady, and as I turned to the sink, I stumbled. In an instant he was beside me. That was Nick, always there to lend a hand, always quick to make me laugh. He pulled me to my feet, and in that wobbly, alcohol-drenched state, I tottered against him. Our bodies pressed together and the inevitable happened. I felt his arousal, and suddenly there it was between us, as explosive as a flame dipped in gasoline. I was just as frantic, just as guilty as he was, clawing at his shirt just as he was hiking up my dress. Then I was lying on the cold tiles beneath him, gasping with his every thrust. Loving it, needing it. I just wanted to be fucked and he was there, and that poisonous champagne had stripped away all our self-control. We were two mindless beasts rutting and grunting, heedless of the consequences.

But after we finished and we both lay half naked on the kitchen floor, the reality of what we'd just done made me so sick to my stomach that I stumbled into the bathroom and threw up, again and again, coughing and choking on sour wine and regret. There, hugging the toilet, I started to sob. *What's done cannot be undone.* Lady Macbeth's words came to me like a chant, a horrible truth that I wanted to erase, but the line just kept echoing in my head.

I heard Nick groan in the other room. "Oh my god. Oh my *god.*"

When I finally came out of the bathroom, I found him huddled on the floor, rocking back and forth and clutching his head in his hands. This broken Nick was a stranger I'd never seen before, and he frightened me.

"Jesus, what were we thinking?" he sobs.

"We can't let her find out."

"I can't believe this happened. What the fuck am I going to do?"

"I'll tell you what we're going to do. We are going to forget this, Nick." I kneel beside him, grab him by the shoulders, and give him a violent shake. "Promise me you'll never tell her. *Promise me.*"

"I need to get home." He shoves me away and lurches to his

feet. He's so intoxicated that he can barely button his shirt and buckle his belt.

"You've had too much to drink. You can't drive."

"I can't stay *here*." He staggers out of the kitchen and I follow, trying to talk sense into him as he pulls on his coat and heads down the stairway. He's too agitated to listen.

"Nick, don't leave!" I plead.

But I can't stop him. He's drunk, the roads are perilously slick with ice, and there's nothing I can do to change his mind. From the doorway I watch him stumble off into the night. Snow swirls down, fat, thick flakes that obscure my last glimpse of him. I hear his car door slam shut, and then the glow of his taillights fades into the darkness.

The next time I see Nick, he is lying comatose in a hospital bed and Lucy is slumped in a chair beside him. Her eyes are hollow with exhaustion and she keeps shaking her head, murmuring again and again, "I don't understand. He's always so careful. Why wasn't he wearing his seatbelt? Why was he driving drunk?"

I'm the only one who knows the answer, but I don't tell her. I will never tell her. Instead I bury the truth, guarding it like a powder keg that could explode and destroy us both. For weeks I manage to keep myself together, for Lucy's sake. I sit beside her in the hospital. I bring her doughnuts and coffee, soup and sandwiches. I play the loving younger sister, but guilt gnaws at me like a vicious rodent. I'm terrified that Nick will recover and tell her what happened between us. Even as Lucy was praying for Nick's recovery, I was hoping he would never wake up.

Five weeks after the accident, my wish was granted. I remember my overwhelming sense of relief when I heard the whine of the flatlining heart monitor. I remember holding Lucy as the nurse turned off the ventilator and Nick's chest at last fell still. While Lucy shook and sobbed in my arms, I was thinking, *Thank god it's over. Thank god he will never tell her the truth.*

Which makes me even more of a monster than I already was. I

wanted him dead and silent. I wanted the very thing that broke my sister's heart.

"Your own sister's husband," Brodie says. "Because of you, he is dead."

I bow my head, silent. The truth is too excruciating to admit.

"Say it, Ava. Tell the truth. *You wanted him to die.*"

"Yes," I sob. "I wanted him to die." My voice fades to a whisper. "And he did."

Captain Brodie turns to his men. "Tell me, gentlemen. For betraying those she loves, what does she deserve?"

"No mercy!" one man calls out.

Now another man joins him, and another, in a chant that will not stop.

"No mercy."

"No mercy."

I press my hands over my ears, trying to shut out the shouts, but two men grab my wrists and wrench them away from my head, forcing me to listen. Their hands are icy, not the warm flesh of the living, but the flesh of cold, dead men. I look wildly around at the closing circle and suddenly I do not see men. I see corpses, grim and hollow-eyed witnesses to the prisoner's execution.

Above them all towers Brodie, and his eyes are a cold, reptilian black. Why did I never see this before? This creature that has stalked my dreams, who aroused me, who punished me—why did I not recognize him for what he really is?

A demon. My demon.

I awaken with a shriek. Wildly I stare around the room and find that I am back in my bedroom, in my bed, and the sheets are twisted and soaked with sweat. Sunlight streams through the windows, as bright and harsh as daggers in my eyes.

Through the pounding of my heart I hear, faintly, the sound of my cellphone ringing. Last night I was so drunk I left it in the kitchen and I feel too drained to climb out of bed to answer it.

At last the ringing stops.

I squeeze my eyes shut and once again I see him, staring down at me with those black viper eyes. Eyes he's never revealed to me before. I see the circle of men, all with the same eyes, surrounding me, watching as their captain moved in to deliver his punishment.

I clutch my head, trying desperately to squeeze out the vision but I can't. It's seared into my memory. *Did it really happen?*

I look down at myself, searching my wrists for bruises. I see none, but the memory of those bony hands grasping my arms is so vivid I cannot believe there is not a single mark on me.

I stumble out of bed and examine my back in the mirror. No scratches. I stare at my own face and see a woman I scarcely recognize looking back, a woman with sunken eyes and wildly tangled hair. Who have I become? When did I transform into this wraith?

Downstairs my cellphone rings again, and this time I sense urgency in the sound. By the time I reach the kitchen, the ringing has again stopped, but I find two voicemails. Both are from Maeve.

Call me as soon as you can.

Then another: *Ava, where are you? This is important. Call me!*

I don't want to talk to her, or to anyone this morning. Not until I can clear my head and sound sane again. But her messages unsettle me, and after last night, I need answers more than ever.

She responds on the second ring. "Ava, I'm driving to your house right now. I'll be there in about half an hour."

"Why? What is this all about?"

"I need to show you something. It's on the video footage we recorded in your house."

"But I thought nothing happened that night. That's what Ben told me. He said none of your instruments recorded anything unusual."

"Not in the turret. But this morning, I finally finished reviewing the rest of the footage. Ava, something *does* show up. It was recorded on a different camera."

Suddenly my heart is thudding. "Which camera?" I ask, and the rush of blood through my ears is so loud that I barely hear her answer.

"In your bedroom."

Twenty-Seven

I am standing outside on the porch when Maeve pulls up at my house. She climbs out of her car carrying a laptop and her face is grim as she comes up the steps. "Are you all right?" she asks quietly.

"Why are you asking?"

"Because you look exhausted."

"To be honest, I feel awful."

"Because?"

"I had way too much to drink last night. And I had a terrible dream. About Captain Brodie."

"Are you sure that's all it was? A dream?"

I shove tangled hair off my face. I still haven't run a comb through it. I haven't even brushed my teeth. All I've managed to do is change into fresh clothes and gulp down a cup of coffee. "I'm not sure of anything anymore."

"I'm afraid this video may not provide the answers you need," she says, indicating her laptop. "But it might convince you to leave this place." Maeve steps inside and pauses, glancing around, as if sensing someone else is in the house. Someone who does not want her there.

"Let's go into the kitchen," I tell her. It's the one room where I have never felt the ghost's presence, never caught his premonitory scent. While Jeremiah Brodie was alive, the kitchen would have been a place only for servants, not for the master of the house, and only rarely would he have set foot here.

We sit down at the table and she opens her laptop. "We viewed the footage from all the cameras," she says. "Most of our instruments were set up in the turret, because that's where you've seen him before, and it's the room where Kim had the most violent reaction. We also know that's where Aurora Sherbrooke passed away, so we assumed that any paranormal activity would most likely occur there. In the turret."

"But you didn't record anything unusual in the turret?"

"No. I spent all day reviewing the turret recordings. I was disappointed, to say the least. And surprised, because Kim is usually spot-on. She can *feel* when something tragic has happened in a room, and I've never seen her react the way she did up there. It was genuine fear. Even Todd and Evan were spooked by her reaction."

"I was, too," I admit.

"It was quite a letdown when our instruments recorded no activity at all up there. I also viewed the footage from the hallway camera, and again, there was nothing. When I finally looked at the video from your bedroom, I wasn't expecting anything unusual. So I was shocked when I saw *this*." She taps a few keys and turns the laptop screen to face me.

It's a view of my bedroom. Moonlight glows in the window, and I can see myself in the semidarkness, lying on the bed. The video has a time stamp, which slowly ticks forward: 3:18 A.M. It's twenty minutes after I'd given up on the vigil in the turret and had climbed into bed. The time stamp advances to 3:19, 3:20. Except for that progression of time and the faint flutter of the curtains in the open window, nothing moves on-screen.

What I see next makes me jerk straight up in my chair. It is something black, something sinuous, and it slithers across the room, moving toward the bed. Toward me.

"What the hell is *that?*" I ask.

"Exactly what I said when I saw it. It's not bright, like an orb. It doesn't have the misty quality of ectoplasm. No, this is something different. Something we've never captured on camera before."

"Could it be just a shadow? Maybe from a cloud. A bird flying past."

"It's not a shadow."

"Did Todd or Evan come into my bedroom to readjust the camera?"

"No one did, Ava. At this specific time, both Evan and Todd were upstairs with me in the turret. So was Dr. Gordon. Take another look at this footage. I'll slow it down so you can see what this . . . *thing* does."

She rolls back the video to 3:19 and hits *play*. Now the time stamp moves much more slowly, the seconds crawling forward. In the frame I sleep soundly, unaware that something else is in the room. Something that comes from the direction of the door and approaches me. It swirls toward the bed, a tentacled shadow that slithers closer and drapes itself over me like a shroud. Suddenly I can feel that shroud choking me right now, wrapped so tightly around my throat that I can't breathe.

"Ava." Maeve shakes me. *"Ava!"*

I gasp in a breath. On the laptop screen, the thing has vanished. Moonlight glows on the sheets and there is no shadow, no strangling blackness. There is just me, sleeping peacefully in bed.

"This can't be real," I murmur.

"We can both see it. It's right there on video. It's drawn to you, Ava. It went straight for *you*."

"But what is it?" I hear the note of desperation in my own voice.

"I know what it's not. This is not a residual haunting. It's not a poltergeist. No, it's something intelligent, something that *wants* to interact with you."

"It's not a ghost?"

"No. This—this *thing*, whatever it is, moved straight to your bed. It's clearly drawn to you, Ava, and to no one else."

"Why me?"

"I don't know. Something about you attracts it. Maybe it wants to control you. Or possess you. Whatever this is, it's not benign." She leans forward and grasps my hand. "I don't say this to many clients, but I need to tell you now, for your own safety. *Get out of this house.*"

"It could be just a video artifact," says Ben as I scoop sweaters and T-shirts out of my dresser drawer and stuff them in my suitcase. "Maybe it's just a cloud passing across the moon, casting a weird shadow."

"As always, you have a logical explanation."

"Because there always *is* a logical explanation."

"What if you're wrong this time?"

"And it's a ghost on that video?" Ben can't help himself; he laughs. "Even if they do exist, ghosts can't hurt you, right?"

"Why are we even discussing this? You'll never believe any of it." I set another armload of clothes in the suitcase and cross back to the dresser for my bras and panties. I'm in too much of a rush to care that Ben's getting an eyeful of my underwear; I just want to pack up and leave this house before nightfall. It's already late afternoon and I haven't started boxing up my kitchenware. I cross to the closet and as I yank clothes from hangers, I suddenly think of Charlotte Nielson, whose scarf I found in this closet. Like me, she must have packed in a hurry. Did she too flee in panic? Had she felt the tentacles of that same shadow closing in around her?

I pull out a dress and the hanger falls to the floor with such a clatter that I flinch, my heart hammering.

"Hey." Gently Ben takes my arm and steadies me. "Ava, there's nothing to be afraid of."

"Says the man who doesn't believe in the supernatural."

"Says the man who won't let anything happen to you."

I turn to face him. "You don't even know what I'm dealing with, Ben."

"I know what Maeve and her friends *claim* it is. But all I saw on that video was a shadow. Nothing solid, nothing identifiable. It could have been—"

"Clouds passing across the moon. Yes, you've already said that."

"All right then, let's assume, for the sake of argument, that it *is* a ghost. Let's say ghosts are real. But they're not physical beings. How can they hurt you?"

"I'm not afraid of ghosts."

"Then what are you afraid of?"

"This is something different. Something *evil*."

"Or so Maeve says. And you believe her?"

"After last night, after what he did to me . . ." I stop, my cheeks suddenly burning at the memory.

Ben frowns. "He?"

Too ashamed to look at him, I stare down at the floor. Gently he tilts up my face and I can't avoid his gaze.

"Ava, tell me what's been happening to you in this house."

"I can't."

"Why not?"

I blink back tears and whisper: "Because I'm ashamed."

"What on earth do you have to be ashamed of?"

His gaze is too searching, too invasive. I pull away and go to the window. Outside the mist hangs as heavy as a curtain, hiding my view of the sea. "Captain Brodie is real, Ben. I've seen him, heard him. I've touched him."

"You touched a ghost?"

"When he appears to me, he's every bit as real as you are. He's even left bruises on my arms . . ." I close my eyes and I picture Captain Brodie standing before me. The memory is so vivid I can see his windblown hair, his unshaven face. I draw in a breath and inhale the scent of brine. Is he here? *Has he returned?* My eyes snap open and I frantically glance around the room, but all I see is Ben. *Where are you?*

Ben takes my shoulders. "Ava."

"He's here! I know he is."

"You said he's as real as I am. What does that mean?"

"I can touch him and he can touch me. Oh, I know what you're thinking. What you're imagining. And it's true, it's all true! Somehow he knows what I want, what I need. That's how he traps us here. Not just me, but the women before me. The women who spent their lives in this house, who died in this house. He gives us what no other man can give us."

Ben steps closer until we're face-to-face. "I'm real. I'm here. Give *me* a chance, Ava." He cradles my face and I close my eyes, but it's Captain Brodie I see, Captain Brodie I want. My master and my monster. I try to imagine Ben in my bed and what kind of lover he would be. It would be a plain vanilla fuck, like so many others I've known with men before him. But unlike Brodie, Ben is real. A man, not a shadow. Not a demon.

He leans close and presses his lips against mine in a warm and lingering kiss. I don't feel even the faintest tremor of excitement. He kisses me again. This time he cups my face and holds it captive, trapping my mouth against his, his teeth bruising my lips. I lose my balance, and suddenly I'm falling backward and my shoulders collide with the wall. I don't fight him as he presses against me. I want to feel something, *anything.* I want him to light the match and set me on fire, to prove that the living can satisfy me the way the dead do, but I feel no stirring of heat, no tingle of desire.

Make me want to fuck you, Ben!

He grabs my wrists and pins them to the wall. Through my

jeans I feel the hard evidence of his desire pressed against me. I close my eyes, ready to let this happen, ready to do whatever he wants, whatever he demands.

The deafening bang makes us jerk apart, startled.

We both stare at the bedroom door, which has just slammed shut. None of the bedroom windows are open. No breeze blows through the room. There is no reason at all for the door to have so violently swung shut.

"It's him," I say. "*He* did it."

Now I'm frantic to get out of the house and I waste no more time. I bolt to the closet and rake out the last of my clothes. This is why Charlotte left this house so abruptly. She too must have been frantic, terrified of staying a moment longer. I close and zip my suitcase.

"Ava, slow down."

"How does a door slam shut by itself? Explain *that,* Ben." I haul the suitcase off my bed. "It's easy for *you* to be calm about this. *You* don't have to sleep here."

"Neither do you. You can stay with me. Stay as long as you want to. As long as you need to."

I don't answer him, but simply head out of the room. Silently he takes my suitcase and carries it downstairs for me. In the kitchen, he's still silent as I pack up my precious chef's knives and tongs, my whisks and my copper pot, all the gear that a dedicated cook cannot live without. He is still waiting for me to respond to his offer, but I refuse to answer. I pack up two unopened bottles of wine (never let a good bottle of Cabernet go to waste) but leave the eggs and milk and cheese in the refrigerator. Let whoever cleans up after me take it; I just want to get the hell out of this house.

"Please don't leave," he says.

"I'm going home to Boston."

"Does it have to be tonight?"

"I should have left weeks ago."

"I don't want you to leave, Ava."

I touch his arm, and his skin is warm and alive and real. I know he cares about me, but that is not a good enough reason for me to stay.

"I'm sorry, Ben. I have to go home."

I pick up the empty cat carrier and carry it outside to the driveway. There I scan the yard, looking for Hannibal, but I don't see him.

I circle the house, calling his name. From the cliff's edge, I scan the path leading down to the beach. No Hannibal. I go back into the house and again call out his name.

"Don't do this to me, goddamn it!" I yell in frustration. "Not today! Not now!"

My cat is nowhere to be seen.

Twenty-Eight

Ben carries my suitcase up the stairs to his spare bedroom, where I find a braided green rug and a four-poster bed. Like Ben himself, it all looks like it came out of the L.L.Bean catalogue, and right on cue, Ben's golden retriever tip-taps into the room, tail wagging.

"What's your dog's name?" I ask.

"Henry."

"What a sweet boy." I crouch down to stroke the dog's head and he looks at me with soul-melting brown eyes. Hannibal would eat him alive for breakfast.

"I know you didn't plan on this," says Ben. "But I want you to know you're welcome to stay here as long as you need. As you can see, I've got this big house all to myself and I can use the company." He pauses. "I didn't mean it that way. You're far more to me than just someone to keep me company."

"Thank you," is all I can think of saying.

We stand in awkward silence for a moment. I know he is going to kiss me and I'm not sure how I feel about it. I stand perfectly still as he leans in and our lips touch. When he wraps his arms around me I don't resist. I'm hoping to feel the same heat I felt with the captain, the same delicious anticipation that kept luring me up those turret steps, but with Ben I feel no such excitement. Captain Brodie has ruined me for the touch of a real man, and even as I respond by mechanically looping my arms around Ben's neck, even as I submit to his embrace, I'm thinking of the climb up that staircase and the firelight glowing through the doorway above. I remember the hiss of silk skirts around my legs and the accelerating beat of my heart as the firelight grows brighter, as my punishment looms closer. My body responds to the memory. While these are not the captain's arms wrapped around me, I try to imagine they are. I long for Ben to take me as *he* did, to trap my wrists and push me against the wall, but he makes no such move. I am the one who wrenches him toward the bed and invites his assault. I don't want a gentleman; I want my demon lover.

As I pull Ben down on top of me, as I strip off his shirt and peel away my blouse, it's Jeremiah Brodie's face I picture. Ben may not be the one I want, but he will have to do because the lover I truly crave is the one I dare not return to, the one who both thrills me and terrifies me. I close my eyes and it's Captain Brodie who groans into my ear as he thrusts into me.

But when it's over and I open my eyes, Ben is the one I see smiling down at me. Ben, who is so predictable. So safe.

"I knew you were the one," he murmurs. "The woman I've been waiting for all my life."

I sigh. "You hardly know me."

"I know enough."

"No, you don't. You have no idea."

"What shocking secrets can you possibly be hiding?"

"Everyone has secrets."

"Then let me guess yours." He presses a playful kiss to my lips. "You sing opera off-key in the shower."

"Secrets are what you *don't* tell people."

"There's something worse? Lied about your age? Ran a red light?"

I turn my face to avoid looking at him. "Please. I don't want to talk about this."

I feel him staring at me, trying to penetrate the wall I've put up against him. I twist away and sit up on the side of the bed. Look down at my bare thighs, splayed apart like a hooker's. *Oh no, Ben, you do not want to know my secrets. You don't want to know all the sins I have committed.*

"Ava?" I flinch as he places his hand on my shoulder.

"I'm sorry, but this isn't going to work. You and me."

"Why are you saying this after we just made love?"

"We're too different."

"That's not really the problem, is it?" he says. His voice has changed, and I don't like the sound of it. "You're just trying to find a way to tell me I'm not good enough for you."

"That's not at all what I'm saying."

"But that's how it sounds to me. You're like the others. Like all the—" He stops, distracted by his ringing cellphone. He lurches to his feet to retrieve the phone from his trouser pocket. "Dr. Gordon," he answers curtly. Though he's turned away from me, I can see the muscles knotted in his bare back. He feels wounded, of course. He's fallen in love with me and I've rejected him. And at this most painful of moments, he's forced to deal with a crisis at the hospital.

"You've started the infusion? And how does her EKG look now?"

As he talks to the hospital, I gather up my clothes and quietly get dressed. Whatever desire I'd felt earlier has gone stone cold, and now I'm embarrassed to be seen naked. By the time he hangs up, I'm fully dressed and sitting primly on the bed, hoping we can both forget that anything ever happened between us.

"I'm sorry, but my patient's just had a heart attack," he says. "I have to go in to the hospital."

"Of course."

He pulls on his clothes and briskly buttons his shirt. "I don't know how long I'll be there. It could take a few hours, so if you get hungry, feel free to raid the refrigerator. There's half a roast chicken in there."

"I'll be fine, Ben. Thank you."

He pauses in the doorway and turns to look at me. "I'm sorry if I assumed too much, Ava. It's just that I thought you felt the same way I did."

"I don't know *what* I feel. I'm confused."

"Then we need to hash this out when I get home. We need to settle this."

But there is nothing to settle, I think as I hear him thump down the stairs and out of the house, and the front door bangs shut behind him. There is no fire between us, and above all, I need to feel fire. I look out the window and am relieved to see him drive away. I need this time alone to think about what I'll say when he comes back.

I'm about to turn from the window when another vehicle rumbles by. The gray pickup truck is startlingly familiar, because it used to be parked in my driveway every weekday. Is Ned Haskell working somewhere in this neighborhood? Ned's truck vanishes around the corner and I back away from the window, disturbed by my glimpse of him.

As I head downstairs, I'm glad that Henry is right at my heels, his claws tapping on wood. Why do I own a cat when I could have a dog like Henry, whose sole reason for existence is to protect and please his owner? Meanwhile, useless Hannibal is off prowling like the tomcat he is, once again complicating my life.

In the kitchen, I look in the refrigerator and confirm there is half a roasted chicken, but I have no appetite for food. What I really want is a glass of wine, and I find an already opened bottle with just enough Chardonnay left in it to get me started. I empty it into a glass and sip it as I wander into the living room with Henry still at my heels. There I admire the four oil paintings hanging on the walls. All of these are Ben's work, and once again I'm impressed by his skill. The same beach is the subject of all four paintings, but each has a different mood. The first captures a summer's day, the water reflecting bright shards of sunlight. Lying on the sand is a red-checked blanket, still bearing the rumpled indentations of the two people who had been lying there. Lovers, perhaps, who've gone off for a swim? I can almost feel the heat of the sun, taste the salt from the sea breeze.

I turn to look at the second painting. It's the same beach with the same jagged rock jutting up on the right, but autumn has tinted the vegetation in brilliant reds and golds. On the sand lies the same checked blanket, rumpled as before, with fallen leaves scattered across it. Where are the lovers? Why have they left behind their blanket?

In the third painting, winter has blown in, turning the water black and ominous. Snow covers the beach, but one small corner of the blanket has curled up from beneath that layer of snow, a startling red patch against white. The lovers are gone, their summer tryst long forgotten.

I turn to the fourth painting. Springtime has arrived. The trees are a bright green and a lone dandelion blooms in a scrubby patch of grass. I know this is meant to be the final painting in the series because once again there is the red-checked blanket on the sand. But the seasons have transformed it into a tattered symbol of abandonment. The fabric is dirt-streaked and littered with twigs and leaves. Any pleasures that were once enjoyed on that red-checked cloth are now long forgotten.

I imagine Ben setting up his easel on this beach, painting this same scene again and again as the seasons unfold. What kept drawing him back to this spot? The corner of a tag peeks out from behind the frame. I pull it out and read the label.

CINNAMON BEACH, SPRING, #4 IN A SERIES.

Why does that name sound so familiar? I know I've heard it before and I know it was a woman's voice that said the words. Then I remember. It was Donna Branca, explaining to me why suspicion had fallen on Ned Haskell. *There was a woman who went missing about five years ago. Ned had her house keys in his truck. He claimed he found them on Cinnamon Beach.*

The same beach that keeps reappearing in Ben's paintings. Surely it's just a coincidence. Others must have visited this cove, sunned themselves on this same sand.

The dog whines and I glance down, startled by the sound. My hands have gone cold.

Through the living room doorway, I spy an easel and canvas. As I move into the next room, I catch the scent of turpentine and linseed oil. Propped up before the window is Ben's current work in progress. So far it's just a sketch, the outline of a harbor scene waiting for the artist to breathe life and color into it. Leaning against the walls are dozens of paintings he's completed, waiting to be framed. I flip through them and see ships plowing through swells, a lighthouse lashed by storm-tossed waves. I move to the next stack of canvases and slowly flip through these, as well. Cinnamon Beach and the missing woman are still on my mind, still bothering me. Donna had said the woman was a tourist who'd rented a cottage near the beach. When she vanished, everyone assumed she'd simply gone for a swim and drowned, but when her house keys turned up on Ned's dashboard, suspicion had fallen on him. Just as it's fallen on Ned now, for the murder of Charlotte Nielson.

I flip to the last canvas in the stack and freeze, the hairs on my arms suddenly standing up as gooseflesh ripples across my skin. I am staring at a painting of my own house.

The painting is not finished yet; the background is dark blue and featureless and patches of bare canvas still show through, but there is no doubt this house is Brodie's Watch. Night swathes the building in shadow and the turret is but a black silhouette against the sky. Only one window is brightly lit: my bedroom window. A window where a woman stands silhouetted against the light.

I stare down at my fingers, which are tacky with dark blue paint. Fresh paint. Suddenly I remember the flickers of light I'd glimpsed at night from my bedroom window. Not fireflies, after all, but someone outside, standing on the cliff path, watching my window. While I lived at Brodie's Watch, while I slept in that bedroom, undressed in that bedroom, Ben has secretly been painting this portrait of my house. And me.

I cannot spend the night here.

I run upstairs and cast a nervous glance out the window, afraid I'll see Ben's car pull into the driveway. There is no sign of him. I haul my suitcase back down the steps, bump-bump-bump, and wheel it outside to my car. The dog has followed me and I drag him by the collar back into the house and shut him inside. I may be in a rush to leave, but I won't be responsible for an innocent dog getting hit by a car.

As I drive away, I keep glancing in the rearview mirror, but the street behind me is empty. I have no evidence against Ben, nothing but a glimpse of that painting in his studio and it's not enough, not nearly enough, to bring to the police. I'm just a summer visitor and Ben is a pillar of the community whose family has lived here for generations.

No, a painting is not enough to alarm the police, but it's enough to make me uneasy. To make me rethink everything I know about Ben Gordon.

I'm bent on getting out of town, but just as I'm about to turn onto the road heading south out of Tucker Cove, I remember Hannibal. I slap the steering wheel in frustration. *You jerk of a cat; of course you'd be the one to complicate everything.*

I make a sharp U-turn and drive toward Brodie's Watch.

It's early evening and in the deepening gloom, the fog seems thicker, almost solid enough to touch. I step out of the car and scan the front yard. Gray mist, gray cat. I wouldn't see him even if he were sitting a few yards away.

"Hannibal?" I circle around the outside of the house, calling his name, louder. "Where are you?"

Only then do I hear it, over the sound of breaking waves: a faint meow.

"Come here, you bad boy! Come on!"

Again, the meow. The mist makes it seem like the sound is everywhere at once. "I have dinner!" I yell.

He responds with a demanding yowl, and I realize the sound is coming from above. I look up and through the mist I see something move high overhead. It's a tail, flicking impatiently. Perched on the widow's walk, Hannibal peers down at me through the slats of the railing.

"How the hell did you get stuck up there?" I yell at him, but I already know how it happened. In my rush to pack up and leave, I didn't check the widow's walk before closing the door. Hannibal must have slipped outside where he was trapped.

I hesitate on the front porch, reluctant to enter the house again. Only hours ago, I had fled Brodie's Watch in fear, believing that I would never return. Now I have no choice but to step inside.

I unlock the door and flick on the light switch. Everything looks exactly the way it always has. The same umbrella stand, the same oak floor, the same chandelier. I take in a deep breath and detect no scent of the sea.

I start up the stairs, setting off the usual creaks on the steps. The landing is cast in gloom and I wonder if he waits in the shadows above, watching me. Upstairs I flick on another light switch and I see familiar cream walls and crown molding. All is silent. *Are you here?*

I pause to glance into my bedroom, which I'd left in such haste that the dresser drawers are open and the closet door is ajar. I move to the turret staircase. The door creaks as I open it. I think of the nights I stood at the base of these stairs, trembling with anticipation, wondering what pleasures and torments lay in store for me. I mount the steps, remembering the swish of silk at my ankles and the unyielding grip of his hand on mine. A hand whose touch could be both tender and cruel. My heart is thudding as I step into the turret room.

It is empty.

Standing alone in that room, I'm suddenly overwhelmed with such a sense of longing that I feel as if my chest has been hollowed out, my heart wrenched out of me. *I miss you. Whatever you are, ghost or demon, good or evil. If only I could see you one last time.*

But there is no swirl of ectoplasm, no rush of salt air. Captain Jeremiah Brodie has departed this house. He has abandoned me.

An insistent meow reminds me why I am here. Hannibal.

I open the door to the widow's walk and my cat saunters inside as if he's royalty. He plants himself at my feet and glares up with a look of *well, where's my dinner?*

"One of these days, I'm going to turn you into a fur collar," I mutter as I haul him into my arms. I haven't fed him since this morning, but he seems heavier than ever. Wrestling the armload of fur, I turn to the turret staircase and freeze.

Ben stands in the doorway.

The cat slips from my arms and thumps to the floor.

"You didn't tell me you were leaving," he says.

"I needed to . . ." I glance at the cat, who slinks away. "To find Hannibal."

"But you took your suitcase. You didn't even leave me a note."

I retreat a step. "It was getting late. I didn't want him to be out alone all night. And . . ."

"And what?"

I sigh. "I'm sorry, Ben. This isn't going to work out between us."

"When were you going to tell me?"

"I did try to tell you. There's so much about my life that's a disaster right now. I shouldn't be getting involved with anyone, not until I can straighten myself out. It's not you, Ben. It's me."

His laugh is bitter. "That's what they always say." He goes to the window and stands with shoulders slumped, staring out at the fog. He looks so defeated that I almost feel sorry for him. Then I think of the unfinished painting of Brodie's Watch and the woman's figure silhouetted in the bedroom window. *My* bedroom window. I take a step toward the stairway door, then another. If I'm quiet, I can be down those steps before he realizes it. Before he can stop me.

"I always liked the view from this turret," he says. "Even when the fog rolls in. Especially when the fog rolls in."

I take another step, trying desperately not to set off a creak and alert him.

"This house used to be nothing but rotted wood and broken glass. A place just waiting for someone to touch a match to it. It would have gone up in a flash."

I back away another step.

"And that widow's walk was ready to collapse. But the railing was sturdier than it looked."

I am almost at the doorway. I place one foot on the first step and my weight sets off a creak so loud it seems as if the whole house has groaned.

Ben turns from the window and stares at me. In that instant he sees my fear. My desperation to escape. "So you're leaving me."

"I need to go home to Boston."

"You're all the same, every one of you. You dangle yourselves in front of us. Make us believe. Give us hope."

"I never meant to."

"And then you break our hearts. You. Break. Our. *Hearts!*"

His shout is like a slap across the face and I flinch at the sound. But I do not move, just as he does not move. As we stare at each other, I suddenly register his words. I think of Charlotte Nielson, her decomposing body adrift on the sea. And I think of Jessie Inman, the teenage girl who fell to her death on a Halloween night two decades ago, when Ben would have been a teenager, like Jessie. I glance through the window at the widow's walk.

That railing was sturdier than it looked.

"You don't really want to leave me, Ava," he says quietly.

I swallow. "No. No, Ben, I don't."

"But you're going to anyway. Aren't you?"

"That's not true."

"Was it something I said? Something I did?"

Frantically I hunt for the words to soothe him. "It was nothing you did. You were always good to me."

"It was the painting, wasn't it? My painting of this house." I stiffen, a reaction I can't control, and he sees it. "I know you were in my studio. I know you looked at it, because you smeared the canvas." He points to my hand. "The paint is still on your fingers."

"Can't you understand why that painting spooked me? Knowing that you've been watching my house. Watching *me*."

"I'm an artist. It's what artists do."

"Spy on women? Slink around at night to watch their bedroom windows? You're the one who broke into my kitchen, aren't you? Who tried to break in while Charlotte was living here?" I'm finding my courage again. Preparing to counterattack. If I show fear, then he's already won. "That's not being an artist. That's being a stalker."

He seems stunned by my retort, which is just what I want him to be. I want him to know that I won't be a victim like Charlotte or Jessie or any other woman he's threatened.

"I've already called the police, Ben. I told them you've been watching my house. I told them they should take a good look at you, because I'm not the first woman you've stalked." Can he tell I'm bluffing? I don't know. I only know that now is the time to leave, while he's off-balance. I turn and head down the stairs, not at a rush, because I don't want to act like prey. I descend with the calm and measured pace of a woman in charge. A woman who's not afraid. I make it down to the second-floor hallway.

Still safe. Still no pursuit.

My heart is thudding so hard it feels ready to punch its way out of my chest. I walk down the hall toward the next staircase. I just have to get down those steps, out the front door, and climb into my car. Forget Hannibal; he'll have to fend for himself tonight. I'm getting the hell out of here and driving straight to the police.

Footsteps. Behind me.

I glance back and there he is. His face is twisted in rage. This is no longer the Ben I know; this is someone else, *something* else.

I bolt toward the last set of stairs. Just as I reach the top of the staircase he tackles me and the impact hurls me forward. I am falling, falling, a terrifying swan dive down the stairs that seems to happen in excruciatingly slow motion.

I don't remember the landing.

Twenty-Nine

Heavy breathing. Warm air huffing on my hair. And pain, great pounding waves of it, crashing in my head. I am being dragged up the stairs, my feet thumping over each step as I'm pulled higher and higher. I can make out only shadows and the faint glint of a wall sconce. It's the staircase to the turret. He is taking me to the turret.

He pulls me over the top step and drags me into the room. Leaves me sprawled on the floor as he pauses to catch his breath. Hauling a body up two flights of stairs is exhausting; why has he gone to the effort? Why bring me to this room?

Then I hear him open the door to the widow's walk. I feel the rush of cool air and the scent of the sea sweeps in. I try to rise but pain, sharp as the slice of a knife, shoots from my neck and down my left arm. I can't sit up. Just moving my arm is unbearable. Footsteps creak closer and he stares down at me.

"They'll know it was you," I tell him. "They'll find out."

"They never found out before. And that was twenty-two years ago."

Twenty-two years? He's talking about Jessie. The girl who fell from the widow's walk.

"She tried to leave me, too. Just like you are now." He glances toward the widow's walk, and I picture that cold and rainy Halloween night. A teenage boy and girl arguing while their friends are downstairs getting drunk and making out. He's trapped her here, where she cannot escape. Where murder requires only a shove over the widow's walk. Even twenty-two years later, the terror that girl felt still lingers in this room, powerful enough to be felt by those who are sensitive to echoes from the past.

It wasn't Aurora Sherbrooke's death that had shaken Kim so deeply on the day she visited this room with her ghost-hunting team. It was Jessie Inman's.

"That's life in a small town," says Ben. "Once they decide you're respectable, a pillar of the community, you can get away with everything. But you, Ava?" He shakes his head. "They'll see all the empty booze bottles in your trash bin. They'll hear about your hallucinations. Your so-called ghost. And worst of all, they know you're not from *here*. You're not one of *us*."

Just like Charlotte, whose disappearance raised no questions. One day she was here, and the next she was gone, and no one cared enough to investigate because she was an outsider. Not one of them. Not like the well-respected Dr. Ben Gordon whose roots run generations-deep in Tucker Cove. Whose father, also a doctor, had the power to keep his son's name out of the newspaper after the Halloween night tragedy. Jessie's fate was forgotten, and soon, so would Charlotte's.

Just as mine will be.

He bends down and grasps my ankles. Begins to drag me toward the open door.

I flail, try to break free, but the pain shooting down my arm is so agonizing that I'm reduced to kicking. Despite it he holds on, hauling me toward the widow's walk. This is how Jessie died. Now I know the terror Jessie felt as she struggled against him. As he lifted her up and over the railing. Did she hang on for a moment, her legs dangling over the abyss? Did she plead for her life?

I keep kicking, screaming.

He pulls my legs through the doorway and I reach out with my good arm to grab the doorframe. He yanks harder on my ankles but I hang on for dear life. I won't surrender. I will fight him till the end.

In fury he drops my ankles and brutally stamps his heel on my wrist. I feel bones snap and I shriek. My broken hand is useless and I cannot hold on.

He drags me out onto the widow's walk.

Night has fallen. All I see of Ben is his shadowy outline, wreathed in mist. Here is how it ends, tossed from the rooftop. A fatal plummet to the ground.

He grabs me under my arms and wrenches me toward the railing. The mist is as wet as tears on my face. I taste salt, inhale a final breath that smells like . . .

The sea.

Through the swirling fog, I see the figure looming in the darkness. Not mere mist but something real and solid, advancing toward us.

Ben sees it too and he freezes, staring. "What the fuck?"

Abruptly he releases me and I slam down onto the deck. A jolt of pain shoots from my neck, and it's so excruciating that for an instant everything goes dark. I don't see the blow, but I hear the fist thudding into flesh and Ben's grunt of pain. Then I make out the two shadows grappling in the fog, twisting and turning in a macabre dance of death. Suddenly they both lurch sideways, and I hear the crack of splintering wood.

And a shriek. Ben's shriek. For the rest of my life, that sound will echo through my nightmares.

A figure looms over me, broad-shouldered and cloaked in mist. "Thank you," I whisper.

Just before everything fades to black.

I cannot move my head. A cervical brace encases my neck and shoulders as I lie flat on my back in the ambulance, and I can only stare straight up, where I see the reflection of flashing blue lights on my IV pole. Police radios chatter outside and I hear yet another vehicle arrive, tires crackling over gravel.

A light shines in my left eye, then my right.

"Pupils are still equal and reactive," the paramedic says. "Ma'am, do you know what month it is?"

"September," I murmur.

"What day?"

"Monday. I think."

"Okay. Good." He reaches up to adjust the bag of saline that's hanging over my head. "You're doing great. Let me just tape down that IV line more securely."

"Did you see him?" I ask.

"See who?"

"Captain Brodie."

"I don't know who that is."

"When you came up to get me, he was there, on the widow's walk. He saved my life."

"I'm sorry, ma'am. The only person I saw up there with you was Mr. Haskell. He's the one who called the ambulance."

"Ned was there?"

"He's still right outside." The paramedic sticks his head out the back of the ambulance and calls out: "Hey, Ned, she's asking about you!"

A moment later, I see Ned's face looking down at me. "How're you feeling, Ava?"

"You saw him, didn't you?" I ask.

"She's asking about someone named Brodie," the paramedic explains. "Says he was up there on the widow's walk."

Ned shakes his head. "The only people I saw up there were you and Ben."

"He tried to kill me," I say softly.

"I wasn't sure about him, Ava. All these years, I wondered how Jessie really died. And when Charlotte . . ."

"The police thought you killed her."

"So did everyone else. When you got involved with Ben, I worried it was happening all over again."

"That's why you followed him here?"

"I heard you screaming up on the roof, and I knew. I think I always knew it was him. But no one listened to me, and why would they? He was the doctor and I'm just . . ."

"The man who tells the truth." If my wrist wasn't encased in bandages, if it didn't hurt just to move, I would have grasped his hand. There's so much I want to say to him, but the paramedics have already started the engine and now it's time to leave.

Ned climbs out and swings the door shut.

I'm trapped, stiff as a mummy in my neck brace, so I can't look out the rear window at the morgue van that's waiting to transport the body of Ben Gordon. Nor can I catch a final glimpse of the house where I would have met my death, were it not for Ned Haskell.

Or was it the ghost who saved me?

As the ambulance bounces down the driveway, I close my eyes and once again I see Jeremiah Brodie standing on the widow's walk, keeping watch as he always has.

As he always will.

Thirty

A white curtain hangs beside my bed, cutting off my view of the doorway. My hospital room is a double, and the patient in the other bed is a popular woman who has a steady stream of visitors bearing flowers. I can smell the scent of roses, and through the curtain I hear greetings of: "Hi, Grandma!" and "How ya feeling, honey?" and "We can't wait for you to come home!" The voices of people who love her.

On my side of the curtain there is silence. My only visitors have been Ned Haskell, who stopped by yesterday to assure me that he is looking after my cat, and the two Maine State Police detectives who came to see me this morning, to ask many of the same questions they asked me yesterday. They have searched Ben's house and they found the painting I described. They found his laptop, which contained photos of me as well as Charlotte, taken with a telephoto lens through our bedroom window. Perhaps what happened to me is also how it happened to Charlotte: a flirtation between the town doctor and the pretty new tenant of Brodie's

Watch. Had she sensed a disturbing undercurrent in his pursuit and tried to break it off? Faced with rejection, had he reacted with violence, just as he had with fifteen-year-old Jessie Inman two decades ago?

When you own a boat, it's easy to dispose of a body; what's difficult is hiding the fact your victim has gone missing. He'd packed up Charlotte's belongings and made it appear to everyone that she had left town on her own, but details had eventually tripped him up: the PO box overflowing with her mail. The decomposing body that unexpectedly surfaced in the bay. And her car, a five-year-old Toyota packed with her belongings, which only yesterday was found abandoned fifty miles from Tucker Cove. Had it not been for those details—and for all the questions I kept asking—no one would have known that Charlotte Nielson never made it alive out of the state of Maine.

My murder too, could just as easily have been overlooked. I'm the crazy tenant who saw ghosts in her house, who had a bin full of empty wine bottles in her kitchen. A woman who just might stagger up to the widow's walk one night and tumble over the railing. The townsfolk would shake their collective heads about the unfortunate death of a boozy outsider. The curse of Captain Brodie strikes again, they'd think.

I hear more visitors spill into the room and there's a fresh round of "Hi, darlin'!" and "You look so much better today!" But I lie alone on my side of the curtain, staring out the window, where raindrops tip-tap on the glass. The doctors say that I can leave the hospital tomorrow, but where will I go?

I only know I will not return to Brodie's Watch, because there *is* something in that house, something that both terrifies me and also draws me in. Something that was captured on camera the night the ghost hunters were there, something that moved in to engulf me as I slept. But now I wonder about the shadow that slithered toward me across my bedroom. Perhaps it was there not to attack me, but to protect me from the real monster in my house:

not a ghost, not a demon, but a live man who had already killed one girl in the turret.

The door whooshes open and shut again, admitting yet more visitors for my popular roommate. I watch the rain spatter the window and think about what happens next. Home to Boston. Finish the manuscript. Stop drinking.

And Lucy. What do I do about Lucy?

"Ava?"

The voice is so soft I almost don't hear her through the chatter of my roommate's visitors. Even as I register the voice, I can't believe it's real. She is just another ghost, someone I've conjured up, as I once conjured up the ghost of Captain Brodie.

But when I turn to look, there is my sister stepping past the bed curtain. In the gray light through the window, her face is sallow, her eyes sunken with fatigue. Her blouse is wrinkled and her long hair, which is usually swept back into a tidy ponytail, tumbles windblown and tangled to her shoulders. Yet she is beautiful. My sister will always be beautiful.

"You're here," I murmur in wonder. "You're really here."

"Of course I am."

"But why—how did you know?"

"I got a call this morning from some man named Ned Haskell. He said he's a friend of yours. When he told me what happened to you, I jumped right in the car and just kept driving."

Of course it would be Ned who called her. During his visit yesterday, he'd asked me where my family was, and I'd told him about Lucy. My cleverer, kinder older sister. "Don't you think she should be here?" he'd asked.

"Why the hell didn't you tell me you were in the hospital?" Lucy demands. "Why did I have to hear about it from a complete stranger?"

I have no good answer. She sits down on my bed and takes my uninjured hand and I squeeze it so hard that my knuckles turn white. I'm afraid to let go, afraid that she will dissolve like Brodie, but her hand remains as solid as ever. It's the same hand that held mine on my first day of school, the hand that braided my hair and brushed away my tears and high-fived me when I landed my first job. The hand of the person I love most in the world.

"You have to let me help you, Ava. Please let me help you. Whatever the problem is, whatever's bothering you, you can tell me."

I blink away tears. "I know."

"Be honest with me. Tell me what's wrong. Tell me what I did to turn you away from me."

"What *you* did?" I look at her tired, perplexed face and I think: *Here is yet another way I've harmed her. Not only did she lose Nick, she thinks she lost me, as well.*

"Tell me the truth," she pleads. "What did I do wrong? What did I say?"

I think of how the truth would destroy her. Confession might help *me* heal, might relieve *me* of this overwhelming burden of guilt, but it must be my burden alone. When you love someone as much as I love her, the ultimate gift I can bestow is ignorance. Captain Brodie has forced me to face my guilt, to atone for my sins. Now it's time for me to forgive myself.

"The truth, Lucy, is that . . ."

"Yes?"

"It's my fault, not yours. I've been trying to hide it from you, because I'm ashamed." I wipe my face but I can't keep up with the tears that keep trickling down and soaking my hospital gown. "I've been drinking too much. And I've ruined *everything*," I sob. The answer is both honest and incomplete, but there is enough truth in it to make her nod in recognition.

"Oh, Ava. I've known about it for a long, long time." She wraps her arms around me and I inhale the familiar Lucy scents of Dove soap and kindness. "But we can do something about it, now that you're ready to let me help. We're going to work on this together, the way we always do. And we're going to get through this." She pulls back to look at me, and for the first time since Nick died, I can look her in the eye. I can hold her gaze and also hide the truth, because that is what you sometimes have to do when you love someone.

She brushes a strand of hair off my face and smiles. "Tomorrow, I'll get you out of here. And we'll go home."

"Tomorrow?"

"Unless you have a good reason to stay in Tucker Cove?"

I shake my head. "I have no reason at all to stay," I tell her. "And I am never, ever coming back."

Thirty-One

One year later

Awidow and her two children now live in Brodie's Watch. Rebecca Ellis bought the house in March, and already she has put in a vegetable garden and built a stone patio that faces the ocean. All this I learned from Donna Branca when I called her three weeks ago, to find out if the house is available to be photographed. My new book *The Captain's Table* is scheduled for publication next July, and because the book is as much about the place as it is about the food, Simon wants to include photos of me at Brodie's Watch. I told him I didn't want to return, but he insisted these photos are necessary.

Which is why I now find myself riding in a white van with a photographer and a stylist, headed back to the house I fled a year ago.

Donna told me that the family's been happy living in their new home, and Rebecca Ellis has had no complaints whatsoever. Perhaps the captain's ghost has finally departed. Or perhaps he was never there in the first place, except as a figment of my imagination, conjured up by shame and guilt and far too many bottles of booze. I have not had a drink since I left Tucker Cove, and the nightmares are less and less frequent, but I am still nervous about returning to Brodie's Watch.

Our van climbs the driveway and all at once, there it is looming above us, the house that still casts a long shadow over my dreams.

"Wow, what a gorgeous place," says Mark the photographer. "We'll get some great shots here."

"And look at those huge sunflowers in the garden!" pipes up our stylist Nicole from the backseat. "Should we ask the new owner if I can cut a few for the photos? What do you think, Ava?"

"I've never met the new owner," I tell her. "She bought the house months after I left. But we can always ask."

The three of us climb out of the van, stretching away the kinks that have settled in during the long drive from Boston. Unlike the misty afternoon when I first beheld Brodie's Watch, today is bright and summery, and in the garden, bees buzz and a hummingbird swoops past on its way to a mound of sweet pink phlox. Rebecca has transformed what was once a front yard of weedy shrubs into floral drifts of yellow and pink and lavender. This is not the forbidding Brodie's Watch that I remember; this house beckons us to step inside.

A smiling brunette emerges from the house to greet us. Dressed in blue jeans and a T-shirt emblazoned with MAINE ORGANIC FARMERS, she looks like just the sort of back-to-earth woman who'd plant exuberant gardens and happily dig in the peat and manure all by herself.

"Hello, glad you all made it!" she calls out, coming down the porch steps to greet us. "I'm Rebecca. Are you Ava?" she asks, looking at me.

"I am." I shake her hand and introduce Nicole and Mark. "Thank you so much for letting us invade your house."

"I'm pretty excited about this, actually! Donna Branca told me these photos will be in your new book. I think that's pretty cool, having my house featured." She waves us toward the front door. "My kids are spending the day at a friend's house, so you won't have them underfoot. The house is all yours."

"Before I bring in the gear, I'd like to walk through it first," says Mark. "Take a look at the light."

"Oh, of course. It's always about the light for you photographers, isn't it?"

Mark and Nicole follow the owner through the front door, but I pause for a moment on the porch, not yet ready to enter. As their voices fade away into the house, I listen to tree branches rattling in the wind and the distant whoosh of waves on the rocks, sounds that instantly bring back last summer, when I lived here. Only now do I realize how much I have missed those sounds. I miss waking up to the crash of the waves. I miss my picnics on the beach and the scent of roses on the cliff path. When I wake up in my Boston apartment, I hear traffic and I smell exhaust, and when I step outside, instead of moss, I see concrete. I look at the open front door and think: *Perhaps I should never have left you.*

At last I step inside and take a deep breath. Rebecca has been baking and the air smells like fresh bread and cinnamon. Following the voices, I head down the hall to the sea room, where Mark and Nicole stand at the windows, transfixed by the view.

"Why on earth did you ever leave this place, Ava?" Nicole asks. "If this were my house, I think I'd spend every day right here, looking at the sea."

"It's nice, isn't it?" says Rebecca. "But wait till you see the turret. Now *there's* a view." She turns to me. "I heard it was in pretty rough shape when you moved in."

I nod. "For the first few weeks, I had two carpenters hammering upstairs." I smile, thinking about Ned Haskell, whose wooden carving of a sparrow wearing spectacles and a chef's hat now adorns my desk in Boston. Of all the people I met in Tucker Cove, he is the only one who regularly writes to me, and whom I now consider a friend. *People are complicated, Ava. What you see isn't always what you get,* he'd once said. Words that were never truer than about Ned himself.

"They'd have to drag me kicking and screaming out of this house," says Nicole, still entranced by the view. "You never thought about buying it, Ava?"

"It was out of my price range. And there were things about the house that . . ." My voice fades. Quietly I say, "It was just time for me to move on."

"Can you show us the rest of the house?" Mark asks Rebecca.

As they troop up the stairs, I don't follow them, but remain at the window, gazing out to sea. I think of the lonely nights when I'd stumble up those same stairs to my bedroom, drunk on wine and regret. The nights when the scent of the sea would herald Captain Brodie's arrival. When I needed him most, there he was. Even now, when I close my eyes, I can feel his breath in my hair and the weight of his body on mine.

"I heard what happened to you, Ava."

With a start, I turn to see Rebecca has returned and is standing behind me. Mark and Nicole have gone outside to unload their gear and Rebecca and I are alone in the room. I don't know what to say. I'm uncertain what she means by *I know what happened to you.* She can't possibly know about the ghost.

Unless she too has seen him.

"Donna told me about it," Rebecca says quietly. She moves closer, as if to share a secret. "When I inquired about buying the house, she had to disclose its history. She told me about Dr. Gordon. About how he attacked you, up on the widow's walk."

I don't say anything. I want to know what else she's heard. What else she knows.

"She told me there were other victims. The tenant who lived here just before you moved in. And a fifteen-year-old girl."

"You knew all that, yet you still bought the house?"

"Dr. Gordon's dead. He can't hurt anyone now."

"But after all the things that happened here . . ."

"Bad things happen everywhere, and the world moves on. The only reason I could afford a house this beautiful is *because* it comes with a flawed history. Other buyers were scared off, but when I walked through the front door, I instantly felt as if this place was welcoming me. As if it *wanted* me to be here."

As it once wanted me.

"And then I came into this room and I smelled the sea, and I was certain this is where I belong." She turns to the window and stares out at the water. Mark and Nicole noisily chatter in the kitchen as they set up lights and tripods and cameras, but Rebecca and I are silent, both of us mesmerized by the view. Both of us know what it's like to be seduced by Brodie's Watch. I think of the women who grew old and died here, who were equally seduced by this house. All of them were dark-haired and slender, like me.

Like Rebecca.

Nicole steps into the room. "Mark's almost ready to start shooting. Time for hair and makeup, Ava."

And then there's no other chance to speak in private with Rebecca. First I must sit in the makeup chair to get brushed and fluffed, and then it's time to smile for the camera in the kitchen, where I pose with heirloom tomatoes and the copper pots and pans that we've brought up from my Boston kitchen. We move outside, where I pose among the sunflowers, and then it's on to the stone patio for photos overlooking the sea.

Mark gives a thumbs-up. "That's it for the exteriors. Now we need just one more location."

"Where do we go next?" I ask.

"The turret. The light's gorgeous up there and I want to get at least one shot of you in that room." He picks up the camera and tripod. "Since your book's called *The Captain's Table*, let's have you pose looking out to sea. Just like the captain in your title."

They all head upstairs, but I pause at the bottom of the steps, reluctant to follow them. I don't want to see the turret again. I don't want to revisit the place where so many ghosts still linger. Then Mark calls down: "Ava, are you coming?" and I have no choice.

When I reach the second floor, I glance into the bedrooms of Rebecca's children and see scattered tennis shoes and Stars Wars posters, lavender curtains and a menagerie of stuffed animals. A boy and a girl. Ahead is my old bedroom, its door closed.

I turn instead to the turret staircase. One last time, I mount the steps.

The others don't even glance at me when I enter. They are too busy staging lights and reflectors and tripods. Silently I survey all the changes that Rebecca has made to the room. A pair of wicker chairs is tucked into the alcove, inviting visitors to an intimate chat. A white sofa sits warming in the sunshine, and on the end table is a stack of gardening magazines and a nearly empty mug with a few last sips of cold coffee. A crystal dangles at the window, casting rainbows of light on the walls. This is a different room, a different house than I remember, and I am both relieved and sorrowful about the changes. Brodie's Watch has moved on without me, to be claimed by a woman who has made the home her own.

"Ready for you, Ava," says Mark.

As he snaps the final photos, I assume the role everyone expects of me, the cheerful food writer in the captain's house. For the book's introduction, I wrote that Brodie's Watch was where I found inspiration, and it's true. Here is where I tested and perfected my recipes, where I learned there is no finer condiment than the scent of sea air. It's where I learned that wine does not cure grief, and when you dine with guilt, even the most tenderly prepared meal is tasteless.

This is the house where I should have died, but instead learned to live again.

After the last photo is snapped, and the gear is packed up and carried downstairs, I linger alone in the turret, waiting for one last ghostly whisper, one last whiff of the sea. I hear no ghostly voice. I see no dark-haired sea captain. Whatever once bound me to this house has since vanished.

In the driveway, we say our goodbyes to Rebecca, and I promise her an autographed copy of *The Captain's Table*. "Thank you for opening your house to us," I tell her. "I'm so glad Brodie's Watch has finally found someone to love it."

"We do love it." She squeezes my hand. "And it loves us, too."

For a moment we stand looking at each other, and I remember Jeremiah Brodie's words, spoken so softly to me in the darkness.

Here in my house, what you seek is what you will find.

As we drive away, Rebecca waves goodbye to us from her front porch. I lean out the window to wave back and suddenly I glimpse something up on the widow's walk high above, something that, just for an instant, looks like a figure in a long black coat.

But when I blink, he is gone. Perhaps he was never there. All I see now is sunlight gleaming on slate and one solitary gull, soaring across the cloudless summer sky.

Acknowledgments

Writing a book is a lonely journey, but the road to publication is not, and I'm grateful for the superb team that guides me every step of the way. My literary agent Meg Ruley of the Jane Rotrosen Agency has been my fiercest advocate, the kind of agent every writer dreams of finding. Thank you, Meg, for over two decades of being my advisor, my champion, and my friend. A huge thanks to my Ballantine (US) team: Kara Cesare, Kim Hovey, and Sharon Propson, and to my Transworld (UK) team: Sarah Adams, Larry Finlay, and Alison Barrow.

Most of all, thanks to the one person who's been with me on this adventure from the very beginning: my husband, Jacob.

ABOUT THE AUTHOR

Bestselling author **Tess Gerritsen** is also a physician. Her thrillers starring homicide detective Jane Rizzoli and medical examiner Maura Isles inspired the hit TV series *Rizzoli & Isles*.

But Tess's interests span far more than medicine and crime. As an anthropology student at Stanford University, she catalogued centuries-old human remains, and she continues to travel the world, driven by her fascination with ancient cultures and bizarre natural phenomena.

She lives with her husband in Maine.

For more information about Tess Gerritsen and her novels, visit her website: www.tessgerritsen.com

HAVE YOU READ THEM ALL?
Tess Gerritsen's other gripping
stand-alone thrillers are:

GIRL MISSING
Her stunning first thriller
The first body is a mystery. The next body
is a warning. The final body might be hers . . .

'Gerritsen is a better writer than such founders of the
school as Kathy Reichs and Patricia Cornwell'
Observer

HARVEST
How far would you go to save a life? A young surgical
resident is drawn into the deadly world of organ smuggling.

'Suspense as sharp as a scalpel's edge'
Tami Hoag

LIFE SUPPORT
A terrifying and deadly epidemic is about to be unleashed.

'If you like your crime medicine strong,
this will keep you gripped'
Mail on Sunday

THE BONE GARDEN
Boston 1830: A notorious serial killer preys on his victims,
flitting from graveyards and into maternity wards.
But no one knows who he is . . .

'Fascinating . . . gory . . .'
Mail on Sunday

PLAYING WITH FIRE
What if your child wanted you dead?

'I defy you to read the first chapter and not singe your
fingers reading all the rest'
David Baldacci

The thrillers featuring Jane Rizzoli and Maura Isles are:

THE SURGEON

Introducing Detective Jane Rizzoli of the Boston Homicide Unit . . .
In Boston, there's a killer on the loose. A killer who
targets lone women and performs ritualistic acts of
torture before finishing them off . . .

'Baby, you are going to be up all night'
Stephen King

THE APPRENTICE

The surgeon has been locked up for a year, but his
chilling legacy still haunts the city, and especially Boston
homicide detective Jane Rizzoli . . .

'Gerritsen has enough in her locker to seriously worry Michael
Connelly, Harlan Coben and even the great Dennis Lehane. Brilliant'
Crime Time

THE SINNER

Long-buried secrets are revealed as Dr Maura Isles
and Detective Jane Rizzoli find themselves part of an
investigation that leads to the awful truth.

'Gutsy, energetic and shocking'
Manchester Evening News

BODY DOUBLE

Dr Maura Isles has seen more than her share of corpses.
But never has the body on the autopsy table been her own . . .

'This is crime writing at its unputdownable, nerve-tingling best'
Harlan Coben

VANISH

When medical examiner Maura Isles looks down at the body
of a beautiful woman she gets the fright of her life.
The corpse opens its eyes . . .

'A horrifying tangle of rape, murder and blackmail'
Guardian

THE MEPHISTO CLUB

Can you really see evil when you look into someone's eyes?
Dr Maura Isles and Detective Jane Rizzoli
encounter evil in its purest form.

'Gruesome, seductive and creepily credible'
The Times

KEEPING THE DEAD

A mummified corpse is brought before Dr Maura Isles for scanning.
She's been dead for centuries, or so the academics believe –
until the image of a very modern bullet is revealed . . .

'A seamless blend of good writing and pulse-racing tension'
Independent

THE KILLING PLACE

Dr Maura Isles has vanished, seemingly into thin air.
Detective Jane Rizzoli's search leads her to the snowbound
village of Kingdom Come, where the person who was watching
Maura now lies waiting for her.

'Bone chilling. Gerritsen plays on our fears'
Daily Mail

THE SILENT GIRL

A severed hand is found in a Chinatown alley in downtown Boston, reopening a horrifying murder-suicide case from nineteen years before. Detective Jane Rizzoli and Dr Maura Isles must track down and defeat an old evil, before it kills again . . .

'Suspense doesn't get smarter than this. Not just recommended but mandatory'
Lee Child

LAST TO DIE

Three children, orphaned by seemingly motiveless and extreme acts of violence, are placed in a boarding school for traumatized children. But Detective Jane Rizzoli and Dr Maura Isles soon discover that even this place of safety cannot shut out a gathering threat . . .

'Intelligent and unrelentingly realistic'
Sunday Express

DIE AGAIN

Six years ago a group of travellers set off on an African safari – but only one woman returned. Now it seems the 'safari killer' has resurfaced in Boston. Detective Jane Rizzoli has to go and visit the sole survivor in Africa, and see if she can convince her to face death once again . . .

'Gerritsen proves she is still at the top of her game . . . fantastically gripping'
Karin Slaughter

I KNOW A SECRET

A mysterious figure watches from the sidelines as Rizzoli and Isles race to find a killer. She has the answers they're looking for – but she has to stay quiet, if she wants to stay alive . . .

'Expect a white-knuckle ride to very dark places'
Paula Hawkins